THE PRINCESS AND THE FOOL

by Paul Neafcy

© 2015 Paul Neafcy

Contents

Part One: The Fallen and the Falling

Part Two: The Finders and the Keepers

Part Three: The Hope and the Fury

Part Four: The Learned and the Learning

Part Five: The Found and the Lost

Part Six: The Dead and the Living

Part Seven: The End and the Beginning

Part One:
The Fallen and the Falling.

The Letter

As far back as my memory serves we have always been at war.

Elderhaime and Fairford.

The Sibling lands.

Two countries, seemingly with nothing but a border in common.

It is known that my father was a warlike man. A man who believed battle to be the province of heroes rather than fools and puppets, but my father is gone now - succumbed to the terrible affliction which sullies our lands - and with him dies any desire for violence in this once noble family.

I inherit the task of healing the rift which yawns between us.

I would have the sun rise tomorrow over a land of peace, freedom and, above all, hope.

It is in this spirit of fellowship that I humbly implore the Princess Katherine, on this her eighteenth birthday, to consider all our futures as I ask for her hand in marriage.

I believe that if we cast aside our people's, nay, our families' differences, we can take the first step towards uniting our lands and ending countless years of pain and mistrust.

"What love did hew shall same renew."

Please be my Queen, Katherine.
With all my hope,

King Warwick of Fairford.

The Princess

"I'm not marrying that bollocks!"

Her words hung in the air like a stench, the courtiers wrinkling their noses accordingly.

She looked around the hall, searching the throngs of overdressed guests for a face wearing anything but shock, disdain or abject panic.

The silence was overwhelming. Moments ago, before the messenger read the letter aloud, the hall had roared with laughter and song. Now even the Fool stood quiet.

Happy Birthday to me.

She turned to her father. "I'm not."

"Kathy, don't be hasty."

She looked at him on his throne. All greying beard and gilded robes under the ancient crown. King Duncan of Elderhaime. The Wyrmslayer. The Wanderer. The Lone King. The Royal Widower, and whatever other nicknames his loyal subjects bestowed on him. She just called him Dad, though he'd hardly earned that title either.

She wondered if all Dads thought they could tell everyone what to do, or just the ones that were Kings.

He never looked comfortable on that throne.

"Hasty?" she laughed. Did he think pausing for thought would make the proposal of a complete stranger - a Tyrantson, no less - any more appealing? "I will not be used as a bargaining chip! As a proviso on some peace treaty!"

"We should discuss this in private." He leaned forward in his throne, fixing her with his best Kingly glare.

She didn't care about the widening eyes around them. The people of the court could tell as many tales of her disobedience as they liked. It was about time someone stood up to the old man, and if it had to be her, then so be it.

"What is there to discuss? He's never even met me! If he's that bothered about peace, he should've come to the bloody negotiations!"

She remembered long nights of heated discussion behind closed doors. Her father and the Tyrant locked in verbal battle for the future of both their lands. She remembered the arguments kept her awake and the Tyrant left with nothing changed.

She had watched from her balcony as the Royal procession, decked in the purple livery of Fairford, snaked away along the road. She had asked the Fool what the point was. He told her Kings get bored if they're not arguing or fighting about something. Nobody likes knocking around a big old castle with nothing to do.

She understood that part.

The old man shook his head. "King Warwick is not his father's son. He will make a fine husband."

She knew then that her fate was sealed. The accord was already struck.

It wasn't supposed to be like this.

"What love did hew shall same renew," said her dad.

She had read that tale.

"Love?" she said. "I've never even met the man, how can he love me?"

"Sometimes love must make way for duty."

At that, something twisted inside her. "Well, you'd know all about that," she sneered.

She knew she'd hurt him before the words had left her mouth, but he hurt her first and worse.

She thought she heard a gasp from the crowd, but it could've just been her own breath coming short. She wasn't going to start crying in front of everyone, but it's a hell of a surprise to be given away to a stranger as your own birthday present.

She blinked back the tears and hoisted her now ridiculous skirts to try and run. She felt stupid. She was supposed to have become a woman today and yet here she was, running sobbing to her room like a little girl. How can you become a woman if nobody treats you like one? She was an item of property to be traded for political favour, nothing more. Her dad didn't care for her feelings. He didn't even know her anymore.

She stumbled from the hall, leaving behind the lavish frocks, the satins and silks and the golden bowls and silver chalices and dancing fools and staring eyes and gaping mouths.

What did she care? It was a room full of people she didn't know.

It was a world full of people she didn't know.

She kicked her stupid, high shoes off and bunched her skirts up tighter. She ran through cold, ancient corridors that had once seemed like home.

Her home was her prison. She was of age now, and ready to be palmed off on the nearest male of so-called "noble" bearing. She had been farmed like cattle.

She took the stairs two at a time, nearly toppling on the last one. She fell through the door to her room, tearing at the absurd green dress that had seemed so beautiful and brilliant but hours ago.

She wasn't going to cry.

She wasn't sad, she was angry.

Rosalind was skulking in the doorway, but she waved her away. She could undress herself, tonight of all nights.

She felt frustration coursing through her as if her heart were pumping fire. She burned.

There were too many bloody clasps and threads on this stupid dress.

She wasn't going to cry.

Stupid, bloody, stupid dress.

She ripped it.

And she was free.

She stepped out of the all-encompassing volume of its emerald folds and stamped across the room to the balcony door.

She stepped out into the night air, feeling the breeze whip at her underskirts.

From up here she could see out over the castle walls, over the town of Elderhaime that huddled around them, across the fields of the Reeceland and out to the valley beyond. There, on the horizon, were the distant black shapes of the Eastrod mountains and, somewhere in the darkness at their feet, the castle of Fairford. The home of the enemy. The home of her betrothed.

"What love did hew shall same renew." Her Dad was willing to cast her aside because of a line from a tale.

If this were indeed a tale, King Warwick would be looking out on his balcony at this very moment and their hearts would sing to each other in perfect harmony or some such putrid nonsense.

She wanted to be sick.

But she would not cry. She squeezed her fists tight and pushed her knuckles onto the granite wall of the balcony.

She would not cry over this.

She was nobody's Queen.

The Fool

Follow that.

The birthday girl proclaiming her royal suitor a "bollocks" and stropping off in a huff is fair certain to banjax any festivities, mirthful though it was.

There was that belting moment of silence as the door slammed behind the Princess. Nobody knowing what to say.

Except him.

The Fool eyed the King. Duncan looked tired and alone. Well, he didn't really look alone, seeing as how he was in a room packed with all kinds of noble folk, but the Fool thought he probably felt it.

Hard graft being a King.

Especially with your only heir giving you gyp in front of your assembled toadies.

It was Mister Punch who piped up first.

"Well!" the puppet exclaimed, drawing all eyes to his carved mush. Eyes that, if un-distracted, would've seen the King put his head in his hands.

"Insolent, impudent, uncontrollable?" Punch looked around at the lords and ladies. "She's definitely a woman now!"

They laughed.

The Fool looked disapprovingly at Punch. "Punchy!"

The men loudly agreed with the puppet, the ladies tutted and slapped their blokes playfully.

If anyone but him or his wooden companion had spoken so disrespectfully of the Princess, they would've been in the stocks before they could blink, but this was his job: to amuse. To distract. To jingle the bells on his red and green hat 'til nobody knew what to think. And Punch played his part.

He raised the Puppet again. "Someone get after her before she escapes!"

More laughs.

"She'll be marching on Fairford herself by this time tomorrow!"

The Fool cartwheeled to the centre of the court, confident that all eyes were on him.

Rhymes.
Think.

He started clapping a rhythm. They joined in.
He sang the lines as they came to him:

There lived in Castle Elderhaime,
A Princess, Katherine was her name,
The Fairford King she was to Wed,
But she went storming off to bed,

He kept the song going as the King raised his head again. He nodded along, obviously not listening.

She didn't get angry and start to greet,
The letter just swept her off her feet,
She's overjoyed to share Warwick's rule,
If it isn't so, then I must be a Fool!

He capered and sang and eventually the minstrels joined in and then took over. The gathered nobles had come for revelry and to send them away disappointed would be to scatter seeds of ill will.

Politics. How did he end up here? Dancing for the amusement of the rich and powerful like a -

Well…

When the music was a-jigging and the guests were a-reeling, he thought he would head back to the throne, to the King's side, but as he bounced and caroused his way through the dresses and tunics and jewellery, a fat hand grabbed his arm.

It was one of the landlords. What was his name?

"Excellent joshing, Spillend!" said the man. His round face was red with booze.

He shook the Fool's hand vigorously, pressing a coin into his palm.

"A silf for the show, my friend!" he roared. The Fool didn't trust people who roared. People should roar in battle, not conversation. Lions and bears and unmen and boga roar. Animals and monsters.

"Thank you, my lord!" the Fool bowed his head, but the man did not let him go.

He could smell the applewine on his breath. That stuff was like Baelicblood. Sour and reeking and vicious and sure to turn any who taste it to dim deeds.

The man pulled him close, spoke into his ear. "How do you do it?" he whisper-bellowed over the music.

The Fool was looking at the various stains down the front of the Lord's tunic. Applewine, sauce from the feast boar… Blood? No, not blood. Not yet.

How many pints filled this inflamed pustule of a man's skin-sack body? How long would it take to trickle out?

He could see the crimson pool spreading over the dance floor, licking at the hems of the ladies' dresses -

He had to stop thinking like that.

He looked at the man's hairy, bloated face.

The man owned a few farms down by Solsted, at the bottom of the Lip. His name was Hortha.

He was harmless.

No blood.

"How do I do what?" asked the Fool.

"The Puppet! How does it talk?"

Punch was hanging from the Fool's belt and Lord Hortha's stubby fingers reached for him.

Without thinking, the Fool grabbed his wrist and stepped back, twisting the man's arm away from himself.

He knew he'd cocked up straight away.

Hortha's jowly jaw dropped. "You dare lay your hand on me?"

Knackers.

To touch a nobleman unbidden could mean death for a lowborn no-mark like him.

Better play it down.

The Fool let him go. "Apologies, my Lord," he bowed his head. "Just protecting trade secrets."

He shouldn't have let this booze-balloon stop him.

He saw the blow coming and let it land.

Hortha slapped his hat off. "Impudent peasant! You'll learn your place!"

The Fool sighed and wondered how long it would be before this ox tired himself out.

"Apologies, my Lord," he said again. He bent down to pick up his hat and Hortha put a boot on his shoulder and pushed.

The Fool had taken more committed beatings. This was just so the big man could reassert himself in front of his friends and neighbours. Most of whom were now dancing around the Fool as if they didn't even see him.

Seeing a nobleman thump a peasant was like seeing the sun follow the moon.

The Fool sat on the tiled floor, looking up at the hulking form above him. Hortha's face was even redder now he was cross. The Fool wondered how strong his heart was. If a noble pops his clogs while thrashing a serf, is the serf at fault? It would no doubt be an interesting legal conundrum.

"Give me that thing!" said Hortha, reaching for Punch once more.

The Fool was thinking about broken bones and blood stains again when the King grabbed Hortha's wrist in much the same manner he had.

A King can touch a nobleman any way he wants, he thought. And he nearly laughed because it sounded rude.

"Lord Hortha," said the King. "Why do you beat my Jester? Does his bunglery not amuse?"

"The little bugger grabbed my wrist, sire!" Hortha was still indignant, but already shrinking like a chided child.

"Did he?" the King looked at the Fool with a raised eyebrow.

"It bloody hurt! The cheek of it! Laying hands on his superiors in such a manner!"

"My Lord," said the King. "I can only apologise. We keep our dogs on a long leash around here, and some of them tend to stray."

The Fool pulled his hat back on. So he was a dog, now? Maybe he should start cocking his leg at every corner of the castle.

The King glared down at the Fool. "I'll take care of him myself."

And with that, he grabbed the Fool by the scruff of the neck and dragged him, sliding along the wooden floor, out of the hall.

Were the nobles applauding as he went? It was such a performance after all.

If only they knew.

He could only think of how well polished his backside was making the floor.

A single line of shine from this tiny arse of mine.

They stepped out into the empty corridor and, as soon as the door closed behind them, Duncan let go of his collar, took his hand and pulled him to his feet.

"Don't do that," the King said. "We need them to be friendly."

"He was trying to steal Punch."

Duncan laughed a little at the thought. "That would've gone well."

A draught blew down the corridor, flickering the torches. The smile fell from Duncan's face. "You're breaking your promise."

Duncan's eyes were shiny and sad in the torchlight, but the Fool smiled as wide as he could. "Never."

He set off down the corridor.

Before he rounded the corner, the King called after him.

"She'll be all right, won't she?"

The Fool looked at the King. He shrugged.

Probably not, he thought.

I know she's there.
I reach for her, but she can't touch me
She's leaving.
I'm in bed and I cannot move.
A shadow in the doorway. A breath on the breeze.
She's here and then she is gone.
Is that blood?
She's leaving us all alone.
I cannot see her face.
I can never see her face.

The Princess

She was drooling on herself.

The carriage jolted her from the same old dream and she was immediately dazzled by the view before her.

They were on the Elderfarway heading east along the Lip, the very edge of which was only a couple of hundred feet away. A short walk and a sheer drop. Beyond the precipice, the Siblands spread out like a carpet of green before her, the glittering line of the Thurwund snaking like a silver seam across her vision from north to south.

From up here she felt like she could see the whole world.

"It's beautiful, isn't it?" said her Dad. "I hoped you would wake before we entered the wood."

He was sitting in the opposite corner of the carriage. As far away from her as was possible in this tiny wooden box.

He looked almost as tired as she felt.

"I've seen it before, Dad," she sighed. "I go riding out here all the time with Rosalind and the guards."

"Of course."

That was the end of that conversation.

She wiped the dribble from the shoulder of her dress and pulled her silken travel-train tighter around herself. She looked around. Her Dad must've meant the Fothwood. Had they come that far already?

The sun sat low in the sky. She realised they had been travelling almost the whole day.

They had left Elderhaime early, just as the sun rose, and all the townspeople had come out to wave them off. They lined the streets and threw acorns. She read in a book once that this was a blessing for the soon-to-be-wed, but she was pretty sure they were trying to put one of her eyes out. A hail of acorns is no kind of blessing.

Once they were out of Elderhaime town, there was less hurling of blessed nuts, but nigh on every farmstead they passed on the Reeceland had a Gleaming Pole outside and some grotesque chubby children dancing around it, tying themselves in knots with pink ribbons.

It was as if everyone was overjoyed about her wedding but her.

In the few days since her birthday, she had been washed and measured and weighed and bathed and scrubbed and doused in sand and it seemed every chambermaid in the castle had poked or prodded her with a needle or a flannel at some point or another.

She felt like they were preparing her for market.

You're a child; you're property of your father. You become a woman; you become property of some other man.

A woman is never her own.

Her life was over before it had even begun. The carriage might as well have been rolling towards the gallows.

She leaned out of the window and looked back towards home. There were six carriages in all. A small preliminary group of nobles and advisers, to be followed by the full quota of unnecessary wedding guests in the coming days. Unnecessary guests for an unnecessary wedding.

Each carriage was surrounded by four Royal Guards in the red and gold of Elderhaime. She looked at the Golden crown emblazoned on their chests and wondered if the guards were there to protect the caravan, or to stop her from running. There were about thirty of them with the Royal carriage at the head of the column, where she sat.

Thirty men to keep one girl in check.

Wouldn't want the Folqueen of Sibland to hurt herself, would we? No. That wouldn't do at all.

She slumped back down in her chair and watched the Fothwood creep by the window. The forest was sparse enough on the south side of the road for her to still see out over the Lip. Soon they would turn north and the road would decline as the cliff sloped down to the Bergstall, and then there was only the Holtland between her and Fairford.

Between her and her husband.

But before the turn, as the Lip itself arced northward, it rose to form a buttress of limestone jutting out from the cliff side. The Longing Cliff.

The stories told that this was a favourite place for young, lovelorn girls to leap to their deaths. Their longing for their loves, lost in battle or somewhere, led them over the edge.

They should've called it Idiot's Drop. Or Stupid Jumping Place.

Still, she wondered.

She waited.

She waited 'til she felt the carriage turn the corner.

Then she opened the carriage door and ran.

Into the trees.

Straight for the cliff.

The Fool

He turned cartwheels alongside the caravan. Larking for the amusement of whoever was watching.

The Princess gazed glumly out of the royal carriage, as she had the whole journey, but she didn't seem to see the green of the forest nor the blue of the sky. Not to her was this a beautiful summer's day of shine and warmth and glory, she would bear no witness to the natural wonders that abounded around her.

She was having a right old sulk.

Six years, it had been, by his reckoning. Six years since Duncan had introduced him to her.

"Kathy, I've got you a Fool. He'll be your friend. Have fun. Goodbye!"

That wasn't quite how it had gone, but looking back on it, it wasn't far off.

Six long years of bungling and pleganning. All that time it had been his job to make her laugh. A job which had become increasingly difficult of late.

She'd been glum at first - who wouldn't be? - but it's easier to cheer up a twelve year old lass with daft games and liesaying. A young woman of eighteen was a different matter.

He thought of how much she had changed. It used to break his heart to see her weep over a torn dress or a lost doll, but what did he feel now? It wasn't like he could just give her a cuddle and wipe her tears away anymore.

That'd be weird.

Wouldn't it?

But not too weird? She was only about four years younger than him.

It would help if he actually knew when his birthday was.

It must be hard growing up with one parent gone and one only present in body.

He never had parents, so he wouldn't know. Of course, he must've had them at some point, but not that he could call to mind. Not much of a family tree sprung in his garden, and no mistake. More of a family stump. Maybe a fallen family branch or twig. A family splinter.

He couldn't blame the Princess for having a sour mug now, it's not every day your towardness is signed away to a fella you never met. On your birthday, verily. That was some bitter ale to swill.

The King sat in the carriage with the Princess, and the tension sat between them like another passenger. He doubted if either had uttered a word since they left the castle. He had tried a couple of times to raise a smile, chattering and mocking their silence, throwing a few acorns, but he had been dismissed. So now he was gambolling along beside the procession, singing and gaming for some of the lads in the guard.

The Princess had been a shadow of herself since the letter arrived.

The King had replied in the affirmative and the date had been set for the Stilnesday after next. Ten days time. He never understood why weddings had to be on Stilnesday. It was supposed to be the day of peace, and there was nothing peaceful about a wedding.

It could be up to a four-day ride through the Holtlands and over the Folds to Fairford Keep, but for the Princess, he thought, it must seem like the rest of her life.

Maybe it was this thought that made her leg it.

They were just rounding the crest of the Lip when the shout went up.

"Princess!"

She had bolted from the carriage and run headlong into the trees.

The King ordered the Guards to hold their positions. "I will not have my daughter hunted like a boar." He looked to the Fool with a warning in his eyes. "The cliff."

The Fool understood.

He could feel the derision and confusion around him. Why would the King trust such a mission to a dunnelheaded Jester?

It was a good question.

He broke for the trees.

It didn't take long to pick up her trail. She had snagged her massive, silky train on the branches and left it hanging.

And people laughed at *his* clothing.

Punch said a muffled something about the Princess catching her death of cold, but the Fool shushed him and ran on.

He didn't much care for wandering in the woods. He rarely left the castle these days and being under the green shadow of the trees was stirring unwanted memories.

Green Shadows.

He didn't have time for that now.

He found the Princess sitting at the edge of The Longing Cliff, her feet dangling over the brink. For a yawning moment he feared the worst, but shook the notion from his head.

She was far too stubborn to do that.

Wasn't she?

The Princess gazed out over the green valley, watching the sunlight sparkling on the Thurwund. The wind whipped at her hair, all done up in some extravagant new style.

She looked so -

So -

He shouldn't think that. He couldn't.

He perched next to her on the edge. The wind nearly took his hat, but he held it down and tied the chinstrap.

The wind wasn't satisfied with that and continued pulling at them both. He noticed the Princess was a little under-dressed in her silk gown.

He shouldn't notice that.

He tried to think of something to say.

Her skirts flapped around her legs like they were trying to escape. A lecherous draught from below tried to lift them. She held them down with both hands.

He looked away.

It was a fair way down. Two, three hundred feet? He could see the Underfarway below them, no more than a thin line of grey in the green.

"Must you always follow me, Fool?" she shouted finally. "Will I never see any peace?"

Another good question. "Not for yourself, I fear."

The wind snatched their words away and he imagined them being heard by some farmhand back on the Reece.

And still they sat.

Even with the roaring in his ears, the silence between them ached.

He wasn't sure what to say, and that didn't happen very often. It dawned on him that he and his puppet were the closest thing this girl had to friends.

And he felt like he was betraying her.

Everyone was trying to convince her that doing what she least wanted to do was the very thing she should be doing.

The silence dragged on.

He had just the thing for moments like this.

He yanked Mister Punch out of his rucksack and brandished him at the Princess. She glared at his carved features.

"Ey up, Princess!" said Punch.

She looked away, back out over the Lip. "The mood for frivolities escapes me, Fool."

"Aw, come on, Princess! Give a puppet a chance!" Punch continued.

"That's not even a puppet. It's just a wooden head on a stick." She wasn't talking to Punch.

"That still counts."

"Spare me."

She wasn't having it.

He lowered the puppet. He knew Punchy's feelings would be hurt, but he'd have to wait 'til eftward.

"Sorry, Princess," said the Fool. "There was a time you would take counsel with Mister Punch and no other…"

"I am a child no more."

That much was true. The girl he had known was long gone. Lost somewhere in the corridors of Elderhaime castle. Perhaps she still ran through the gardens of an afternoon, giggling to herself. We are all haunted by the ghasts of the people we used to be.

He had his fair share of ghasts.

He tucked Punch back into his rucksack.

He wondered how this would work. Would she ever see her Father's side? Could she?

He wanted to reassure her. She mattered. She could change their world. She was an author of eardlore. A sculptor of history.

But it all just sounded like lies to get her back on the carriage.

Jesters were often called Liesayers, but he thought he had lied to her more than enough up to this point.

He stood up.

He held out a hand.

She looked at it, then up at his eyes.

He shrugged.

The Princess looked back out at the valley and let out another sigh. "I could jump."

He smiled.

"He could've come after me," she said.

"And run you down like a fox with all the guard crashing through yon woods?" he raised an eyebrow. "And you dressed so immodestly."

"I lost my train."

"We'll pick it up," he waved his hand. "On the way back."

She stared into the distance a moment longer, and he watched as the rebellion drained from her.

He thought perhaps there would forever be a ghost of this Princess, sitting here on the edge of the cliff, never to become Queen.

She grabbed his hand and pulled herself to her feet.

"Thanks for coming after me, Fool."

She turned away without looking at him.

On the way back to the cavalcade, with the trees sheltering them from the wind, he started larking again. Cartwheels and songs mostly, just trying to lighten the mood. Distracting, as usual.

She walked a little behind, watching with a grudging amusement. "I envy you, Fool".

"Many do. I think it's the hat. Everyone covets the hat." He shook his head, swinging the three dangling points in a green and red blur.

"Your life is as simple as your mind. All you must concern yourself with is when to sing, when to dance and when to fall down."

"Those can be difficult choices."

"You know not the meaning of hardship."

There were a great many possible responses to this accusation, but the Fool made none of them.

He stopped dead, one hand extended to stop Katherine.

She had heard it too.

Ahead of them, someone was screaming.

The Father

Do you know how it feels to be stabbed?
I do.
I was run through a couple of times in the old days, but Althea was always on hand to patch me up like a tapestry.
That doesn't mean I was ready this time.
How could I be so stupid? How could I let this happen?
They're all dead. All of them slaughtered.
The Fool was not long gone when Afol of the Guard informed me of a rash of Rotters approaching on the road side.
He knows I've always taken pity on the afflicted.
They came holding their lantern and bell on a staff before them, a warning to fellow travellers. It is not an uncommon sight to behold on the road, as they are so often moved on from villages and towns. Nobody welcomes you once the rot sets in, and your very presence feels a threat to those close by.
There must have been at least a dozen. Swathed in grey linens, they shuffled toward us. I had Afol give them a pouch of silfrings and my best wishes. I watched from the carriage as the leader took the bag and said something to the guard.
And Afol fell.
An arrow through his heart.
He lay on his back in the mud.
The leader of the Rotters cast off his shroud, revealing a mask of bandages underneath.
The afflicted drew weapons, crossbows and swords. They were so fast and everyone was off guard.
Under their cloaks, not a one of them bore the burn.
They were not afflicted.
How could I be so stupid?
I was out of the carriage. A blade in my hand for the first time in years, the familiar warmth of another's blood on my

hands and face. I killed two before they knew what was happening. But it wasn't enough.

More came out of the trees. They overpowered us. I saw Egesung kill four of them before they took his legs from under him, and it took three men to put down Langmon.

The new lad, a brave wee dreng, took down a man twice his size. What was his name? Fresh-faced thing. I didn't see them kill him, but he was laid low when the battle was over.

They were good men. They fought to the last.

The cowards beat me down with clubs. They wanted me alive, at least for now. Two of them held my arms.

I told them to take the money and go. The leader said they wanted a little more than our silver.

He asked where Katherine was. No one answered, but he kept asking.

When the guards were all dead, he slit the throats of the nobles. Lord Gregory wept for the life of his son, but they bled him too.

I killed them all. I brought them out here on this fool's errand. For all I know, this was Warwick's plan all along. Lure an old man into the wilderness with the promise of peace and slaughter him and his people like pigs in the mud.

And he seemed such a nice boy.

I thought of Katherine. I hoped the Fool heard the sounds of battle and hid her away. He would keep her safe, I knew, if anyone could.

I thought of how long it had been since we shared a civil word, my daughter and I.

I let myself think of Amanda then. Might I ever have seen her again?

The leader of the fake afflicted was a showboater. I'd met his type many times before, gloating over their cowardly victories, taking untold pleasure in the suffering of others. He didn't know about the dagger. If I kept him talking, maybe I could find the right moment to drive it into his eye.

He asked me again.

Where is the Princess?

I asked him what they wanted with her.

The truth is, King Duncan, that we want nothing of her. Or more precisely, we want to MAKE nothing of her.

He loved hearing himself talk.

I made my move, but these bones have grown old and weary. The dagger was taken from me before I got anywhere near the bandaged bastard. In my day I would've carved half of them up before they put me down. Now I couldn't even manage one.

He picked up my knife. I would have spat in his face, but my mouth was dry. Facing death can give you a hell of a thirst.

I called him a coward. His eyes raged through the cloth mask.

No. I'm making a brave new world. You and your daughter are going to help me usher in a new age. An age of chaos. You get to be first.

The first thing I thought was at least I don't have to listen to him blathering on anymore. Then I thought about breathing. Funny how getting stabbed knocks the wind out of you, like falling in cold water. You feel yourself deflate like an old pig's bladder you kicked too hard.

I slid to the floor.

I thought I heard Kathy shout me.

I'm here, child.

I didn't feel any blows after the first, though many more came. The man in bandages was very angry, but merciful numbness was upon me as he did his worst.

I saw the blades of grass rising from the mud. I saw through the leaves above as the sky got brighter and brighter.

I wondered if I would see Amanda soon.

I thought again about Kathy.

Run, Kathy. Don't ever let them catch you.

I wanted to tell her I was sorry. I wanted to tell her I loved her.

But it's too late.
The sky turns white and I am gone.

The Princess

Dad.

She didn't know if she shouted it, whispered it or thought it. They turned to look at her though. All except the one with the bandaged head. He was too busy.
She had to save him. She had to run at them. She had to take that dagger off the one with the bandages and kill them all. She had to save her Dad.
But she couldn't move.
He was lying down now. The King, lying in the mud. She knew they were coming, but she couldn't move.
There was a green and red arm around her waist. It lifted her off the ground.
The bandaged man was still hurting her Dad. She watched the dagger rise and fall again and again.
We have to go.
But I have to save him.
Princess.
I can't lose them both.
"Princess, RUN!"
She heard the Fool this time, and the world came rushing back to her. The men were coming. No, not men. Cowards. Brigands. Animals.
Something whistled past her head and she ran. She ran faster than she had ever run before. Her ears ringing with their jeers and howls.
She stole a backward glance. The Fool had snatched her train from the branch where she snagged it. He was lagging behind as she ran.
"Fool!"
She could see them coming. Green and brown tunics through the trees. The Fool was fumbling with the train, apparently tying knots in the sleeves.

"Don't wait for me," he said.

"Fool, leave it!"

He looked at her then, and his eyes bore a threat she had never seen before. "I said run."

She ran. She ran and ran until her heart began to punch her ribcage from within.

She was running through the trees. The Fool not far behind. As if they were children again, chasing through the gardens. She could hear Mister Punch the Mad Puppet calling out to her as she ran. They wouldn't catch her, she'd be safe in her Mother's arms before the Fool and his wooden friend could get her.

But her Mother was gone.

And now her Father was too.

She burst through the trees. The view across the valley was beautiful. Her eyes could follow the Thurwund river all the way to the Dunmoors from here.

She stepped out to the precipice, the wind catching her skirts again. It was a long way down.

The Longing Cliff.

It was a fine view.

She heard the sounds of the chase approaching and wondered if anyone would ever find her. Who would come looking from the castle, she wondered? Would the people of Elderhaime gather to mourn the end of their Royal family's line?

They were almost on her now. She wondered what they did to The Fool. She dangled her foot over the edge and felt the wind rise to meet her.

I'll see you soon, Daddy.

"Princess, don't!"

She didn't turn around. The Fool had caught her after all.

"Wait for me," he said.

She could hear them, so close now. Shouting and clattering armour and weapons. Soon there would be crossbows.

He pulled her to him, his arm around her waist once more. It felt strange.

Strange that her last moments should be in an embrace with her court Jester.

What would people think?

But he was all she had now.

She would have to make do with the moment of comfort as she turned her body into his, nestling her face into his neck, clinging on.

"Don't let go," he said. "Whatever happens, don't let go."

She tried to see his eyes, but he was looking beyond her, back to the trees.

"What are we going to do?" she asked.

"Something very foolish."

She held on to him.

And they flew away.

The Brigand

    We all heard it. As soon as the boss put that blade to the King.
    I saw her. Pretty as a picture, she was. Long, blond hair, sweet little figure, wearing one of them silky dresses the nobles wear indoors. Suppose she wasn't planning on being out in the woods.
    She was stunned, which you would be, watching your dad get shanked. To be honest, I was a wee bit stunned by her. It's not often you see a pretty thing like that out here in the holt and no mistake.
    Before we even really clocked what was going on, she was gone.
    We heard someone telling her to run and the boss told us to get after her. He was trying on the King's crown. It didn't have too much blood on it.
    Chasing through the woods is more or less what we're best at, but these two were fair nippy.
    Dermot Bottlebottom led the way, roaring and loping through the branches. He was silly with wine as usual.
    We saw the bloke in a clearing up ahead. He looked like he was trying on some clothes or summat, carrying this huge jacket. Was probably worth a shiny gob or two, I reckoned. I'd have to see if the boss would let me have it after.
    Maybe he'd let us have her, n'all.
    I couldn't help but laugh when I saw the fella. He was dressed like a jester. All green and red and with the silly tri-prong hat. Bells n'all. He legged it when he saw us, and Dermot was right after him.
    Almost made me feel sorry for the girl. All the world after her, and only one Jangler for protection.
    It was a bad joke.
    I raced past Dermot, lying in the bracken. He must've fallen down drunk again.

I whipped past a few more trees and was out.
There they were.
They stood at the top of the cliff, the Princess and the Fool, looking for all the world like a couple of sweethearts in a cuddle. The massive coat was draped around them.
I could hear the others coming.
I thought the boss'd be well pleased if I nipped it in the bud before he got there. Not kill them, he likes to do that. And I was thinking we keep her alive, if only for a while. But if I got them on their knees ready or summat, he'd be made up. Might even let me have the girl first.
I took a step forward, forming my first threat in my mind.
The Jester said something to the Princess and stepped off the cliff.
They were gone.
They jumped.
The Boss was going to be so pissed off.
I swallowed my shock and hopped it over to the edge.
The rest of the lads were arriving now.
I peered down. For a moment I saw nothing.
The lads joined me at the edge. The boss too.
I told them they jumped. They must be dead.
The boss repeated what I said. I don't think he believed me. Then he pointed out why.
Following his finger, you could just see the massive coat floating down to the bottom of the valley floor. It billowed up like a dome, two knots in the sleeves and the Princess and the Fool dangling underneath, safe as houses. They landed gently on the ground hundreds of feet below us.
I had never seen the like.
I said that the Jester must've been a Wizard or summat.
The boss asked if I was sure it was a Jester.
I said it could've been a Wizard dressed as a Jester. Couldn't be sure.
He told me to take a closer look and pushed me over the edge.

My tunic wasn't big enough to catch the wind.
Someone once told me you die before you hit the ground.
I died after.

The Princess

She was staring into the fire when she realised she hadn't spoken for a while.

Or moved.

Or anything.

The Fool had sat her down and constructed a makeshift camp around her while she just looked.

Darkness came on.

He jammed branches into the ground in a circle around where she sat. He draped her train over them to keep the wind out.

She just sat in silence. Her dad was dead. She watched him die.

The Fool chopped wood and pulled branches from trees.

Her Dad died in the road and she just ran away.

The Fool fashioned a small bow from a bent stick and threads of bark.

She ran from the Bandaged Brigand. Her Father's murderer was still out there.

The Fool sawed with the bow until smoke began to rise and a spark took.

She ran to the edge of the world and jumped off. And the Fool carried her through the air like a babe in arms.

The Fool built the fire around the ember, and she stared through the rising flames.

She looked up at the ridiculously over-sized cloak covering the makeshift tent. She remembered insisting it was too big when her Dad presented it to her. He said it was instead of a blanket, for the road. Turned out it was also for making magic wings and shelter from the elements.

For the smallest fraction of a moment, she thought she would have to thank her Dad when she got home.

Only for a moment.

What were they even doing? All of them. Out there on the road.

They were escorting her.

It was her fault.

If it wasn't for her running -

No, if it wasn't for that stupid wedding proposal.

Wait.

"It was a trap."

The Fool looked up from his fresh fire. It was the first thing she'd said since they landed in a ditch at the foot of the cliff.

"What?"

"This whole thing was a trap. The proposal, all of it."

He frowned at her.

"Think about it! What better way to get us all out in the Holtlands, unsuspecting? Warwick wants to end the war, sure enough, by murdering me and my Dad."

"Warwick's not a murderer."

"How can you know?" The Fool offered no answer, but she didn't wait for one. "It all makes sense. Well if he thinks he can best us so easily, he's another thing coming."

She was on her feet, striding towards the darkness.

"Princess!"

She stopped. The title echoed in her heart.

"It's not Princess anymore, Fool." She stared at the blackness before her. The firelight cowered at the edge of the trees. "I rose this morn as Princess but I shall sleep this night as Queen."

"Your Majesty," He couldn't bring himself to call her it. "Where are you going?"

"Where do you think I'm going?"

"A tavern? I could murder a pint."

She looked at him then. She wanted to hit him. She wanted to beat him until he never jested again.

He must've seen it. He couldn't hold her gaze.

"Sorry, poor choice of words."

She breathed. "I'm going home." She turned away again.

"Home?"

"Where there are gates and locks and an army waiting to be amassed."

"You're gonna get there on your own?"

"I am a Prin-" She caught herself. "A Queen. I don't need your help. I have just witnessed a craven act of war by agents of Fairford. Agents who are no doubt abroad at this very moment hoping to find us before we can raise the alarm."

I sound like Dad.

"And here we sit, next to a beacon." She pointed at the fire.

"I made sure we put some distance between us and them. While you were sleep walking. Unless they climbed down after us, we'll be fine." He had the audacity to wink. "I'll look after you."

The gall of it. "Like you just looked after me by throwing me off the Lip?"

"That was a successful escape. An ingenious one, I might add."

"You could've warned me."

"Wasn't time. I was improvising. S'what Fools do." Did he just pick his nose?

She studied him for a moment. She had thought she knew this man. What was he, four years her senior? The boy she had played with, always growing older slightly ahead of her, now a man. An irresponsible, slovenly man at that.

"Well, from now on, you do as I say. Escort me home."

The Fool stood up. "As you command, Your Majesty." He bowed low. He was mocking her. "But we cannot set out in the darkness. Please humour a young fool and wait 'til first light." He held something out to her. "I'll give you a biscuit."

She couldn't help but smile.

She sat in the dark. Back in the makeshift tent, eating the biscuits from the Fool's pack. She watched him placing branches on the fire.

She thought about their embrace on the cliff top. It had felt like going home. Hardly becoming of a maiden Queen, but she had thought she was about to leap to her death.

That kind of thing wouldn't happen again. The leaping or the embracing. As the long day ended, the Fool was still a dunderhead. Even if she couldn't quite fathom how he was skilled enough to conjure fire in minutes, or fashion a flying contraption from a royal train.

She looked up again at the silken canopy over her head. "Who knew you had such a talent for making useless objects with dress clothes?" she said.

"Hey!" He pretended to be hurt. "I can make useless objects out of other stuff too."

He ambled back towards her and perched at a respectful distance, cross-legged on the ground.

He pulled the Punch Puppet out of his pack and she smiled again. He was good at throwing his voice. She had watched him closely since she was a child and never once saw his mouth move whilst Punch was talking, nor his throat vibrate. She had sometimes heard him practising behind closed doors. Talking to himself about things she couldn't make out. Alternating between Punch's voice and his own, long into the night.

She looked at the crudely carved puppet. Nothing more than a leering wooden face on the end of a thick oaken shaft. With a tiny copy of The Fool's hat perched on top, of course, bells and all.

"Speaking of useless objects…" she said.

"Oi!" Fake upset again. Making fun of him seemed the only way to keep the encroaching darkness at bay.

He stroked the Puppet like a pet. "Forfend the rudeness towards Mister Punch, please. He happens to be a Fool's best friend."

"He doesn't have much competition, does he?"

"Not lately." The Fool looked so hurt for a moment that she regretted her words, but apologising would spoil the game. It dawned on her that her Dad was the Fool's friend. She wasn't the only one who needed cheering up.

Before she could say a word, the Fool raised Punch, its wooden features grinning at her.

"Useless object, am I?"

The voice always impressed her, so different from The Fool's. Deeper, broader, with an accent she couldn't place.

The puppet turned to the Fool. "She cuts me to the quick, boss. She knows nothing of my many purposes. The time the leg came off the table and you used me to prop it up…"

She smiled a little.

"Or when you needed the midden in the night, but were wanting for a torch so you set my hat on fire…"

The Fool patted Punch's hat, jingling the bells.

"And all those times when you get lonely at night, and you take me to your chamber-"

"That's enough, Punchy, you're labouring the point a bit."

Katherine laughed for the sake of laughing. She laughed because she could. She laughed to be alive.

She caught the Fool smiling at her.

"See," he said. "You're better off with me than on your own."

Her laugh became a sigh. "I don't know. You get used to being on your own."

She tried to rest that night, but sleep slipped through her grasp. She sat side-by-side in silence with the Fool and watched the fire die at the end of the worst day of her life.

So far.

Part Two:
The Finders and the Keepers.

The Sundering of the Siblands

Extract from
"The Enemy of Truth: A Historical Study of the Legends of Firgenland"
by Dimman Notoric

King Njal came to Firgenland from the South, sailing from the Calanlands for warmer climes. His people prospered and in their prosperity built the great city of Haime and its magnificent keep.

King Njal and his subjects lived in peace for many years and Njal raised two strong sons named Arnhult and Asmund. When the great Otenwar came and the giants marched down from the Eastrod Mountains, it was Asmund and Arnhult who beat them back. They had Gunnar the Mason build the strongholds of Fairford and Firgensted and the outposts of the Otenward Spire and the Hogahold to keep watch should the Oten ever return.

When Asmund and Arnhult returned to Haime, they were heralded as heroes by their ailing father and given their pick of the fairest women in the land to take as brides.

It is here that the threads of history and myth are woven so tightly as to be indivisible.

What is known is that both Asmund and Arnhult each chose the same maiden to be their bride. She was a young beauty by the name of Kari. Some say she was the daughter of the blacksmith of Haime castle, while others maintain she was a chambermaid. The lyrics to the popular song "As We Went Along the Way" suggest that the brothers stumbled across the object of their desire on a hunting trip through the Holtlands and strongly imply that Kari was an Elf, Fearie or Witch of some sort ("…Eyes more green than any we'd seen…")and that she placed some gramword enchantment ("…She spoke in our heads and stole our souls…")on the Princes in the name of mischief ("…As if the very daughter of Ryneweard himself…").

The next event all accounts agree upon is the escape from Haime of Arnhult and Kari. The tale most often told in Fairford claims that Arnhult rescued his true love from the clutches of Asmund, who had been driven mad with jealousy upon discovering that Kari favoured his brother. Of course, the most popular telling in Elderhaime speaks of Arnhult stealing away Asmund's true love against her will.

Whichever is true, Arnhult took Kari to the Otenwar stronghold of Fairford and declared everything east of the Thurwund river to now be the sovereignty of his new Kingdom.

Asmund turned the full might of Haime against his brother, but Arnhult called the seasoned armies of the Eastrod to him. Some say that the battle burned the Holtlands and the Thurgan ran red with blood. The armies fought to a standstill and Asmund eventually returned home without his prize.

There began a feud which some scholars claim has lasted over two hundred winters. A more substantial estimate was made by Freemung Lerner in his tome "The Royals of Elderhaime" using evidence discovered in his studies of the Elderhaime family tree. He deduced that the conflict may have begun as far back as three hundred and forty years before Seyrul Sterbehilder even introduced the modern calender.

Over the indeterminate years, Haime became known as Elderhaime, but the conflict still went on.

There have been periods of truce and times of battle, many have attempted negotiations and many have failed (most notably Gordon the Trusting of Elderhaime, who took his entire council to a moot with Quelland the Long Knife of Fairford. It didn't end well).

It is a commonly held belief that the only way to heal the Sundering is with a marriage between members of the two royal families. This belief can be traced to a well-known nursery rhyme sung to children by peasants and nobles alike:

Arnhult and Asmund broke their hearts in two,
Fol-doe-dee-roe-doe, what are we to do?
They fought for love and that's enough,
To cleave a kingdom through.

Old Lord Ryneweard doubled up with laughter,
Fol-doe-dee-roe-doe, he is not our master,
What love did hew shall same renew,
In glory ever after.

What love did hew shall same renew,
In glory ever after.

The Monster

His bandages itched.

There were times when he just wanted to tear them off. He wanted to scratch the scorched flesh underneath until his fingernails clawed bone. But that would only make it worse.

No, he was resigned to what could be a lifetime of burning pain, cooling ointments and irritating linens, safe in the certainty that nothing could ever hurt as much as his head being set on fire.

He cursed the one who did this to him.

And yet, this matted mask of bandages didn't half make him look scary.

Children cried, women screamed, men quivered at the sight of his countenance. With his old face, and his old name, he had hardly appeared formidable. He had become accustomed to ridicule, dismissal and even the bullying of those who deemed themselves his superiors. But now, with his demonic visage and new, much more apt title, they would not deride him so easily.

He needed to change his bandages. Re-apply the ointment. But that would have to wait. The Bitch Princess was lost in the woods and that was not part of the plan. The idiot who let her get away had spoken of a Jester, which made his heart race, pumping boiling blood until he felt his head was too small and his eyes must surely leap from their sockets in red, seething gouts.

But he had to be calm.

He didn't like killing more than one of his men in a day. One was good for morale. Kept everyone scared, made everyone work that little bit harder. Any more than that and maybe people would think it safer to work against him than for him.

Brigands could be so fickle.

He rode into the clearing where they had made camp. A small gathering of tents and a couple of cagecarts.

He dismounted by his tent - the largest and most impressive, of course. He was still disappointed to see no banners flying, but the seamstress in Littleton could only work so fast on his designs, even with the threat of murder and rape hanging over her.

He imagined the fear that would clasp poor, innocent hearts upon sight of a banner bearing a white, bandaged skull emblazoned on a pitch-black background. He liked the thought of that.

They would know his name.

First things first, though.

"Bowman!"

Bowman scuttled forward. It was pathetic really. Bowman only existed to serve.

"Ready the Finders."

"Yes, Sir. They are restless and in need of sport."

"They shall have it".

Bowman scraped away.

He could feel drool on his chin. That tended to happen when he talked. Or maybe it was his burns weeping. He pressed his bandages to his chin to soak up the damp, wincing at the pain of contact.

He had enjoyed killing the King. Everyone had heard the tales of Duncan the Wanderer, a true hero. An actual legend, broken and defeated, crumpled at his feet with that stupid look on his face. That look that they all get when they die, that cross between surprise and confusion at their own mortality, as if they expected to live forever. Nobody lived forever.

Not yet, anyway.

That joy was short-lived. Now, knowing that the Princess was at large, out there in the woods, possibly with that idiot helping her…

He realised he was grinding his teeth. Had to stop that.

Wherever the Princess and her accomplice were, they were at least three days hike from Elderhaime, even further from Fairford, alone and on foot and with presumably minimal provisions.

He knew where they would go.

So why not go? Face him.

It wasn't that he was afraid, of course.

Definitely not.

Better to have his prey brought before him, show them how well he was doing. He didn't go to them, they came to him. Safer too, here in the midst of his men.

Not that he was scared.

He made his way through the camp, eyeing anyone who didn't tip a respectful nod in his direction.

The carts had been rigged with huge cages on the back, thick bars of wood bolted together and gated. The Keepers slept, manacled each to one cart. There were four Finders in each cage.

He thought of the rhyme as he placed a hand on the cage.

"Hiders and seekers..."

One of the Finders moved towards him. Spidering forward out of the shadows in the cage.

"Finders and Keepers..."

He reached through the bars and it sniffed him cautiously.

"Losers be weepers."

It licked his hand with its fat, forked tongue.

"You'll have your sport."

He couldn't remember the last time anything other than these fell beasts showed him affection.

As it should be.

Better to instill fear than love.

Better to feel rage than joy.

His name was Fury, and he was very, very angry.

The King

The throne was uncomfortable.

He thought some great wit or philosopher might have something thought provoking to say about that.

He had watched his father sit in this throne and drive his country into the ground.

He had sworn things would be different under his rule and, with his father's death, he had taken steps.

The Tyrant King.

Warwick's Father was named Pintel Anlafson, but he had made sure everyone forgot that.

Most men were given their names - first by parents, then by peers - but The Tyrant had forged his own, in blood and steel, until there was no other word for him but the one he chose.

Tyrant.

And once this name was wrought, it became an heirloom, handed down to Warwick and his brother Felix.

Tyrantson.

The name was a brand.

A badge of honour.

A brand. Seared into his skin for all to see.

The only way anyone would remember him as anything other than the son of a tyrant was to make his own name.

What would they call him then?

After so many years on the brink of open war, could a wedding really pull the Sibling Lands back from the precipice?

He had to believe it.

He looked across the throne room at Gunnar's Window, waiting for the sun.

The tales said that Gunnar the Mason laboured for eleven years on the depiction of the coronation of Arnhult, the first King of Fairford. Wrought in stained glass, thirty feet high, the window covered the entire south wall of the wide throne room.

At that moment, the window looked dull and worn, the reds and yellows appearing mere browns and greys.

The true beauty of the window only became apparent during the summer, at dawn.

The window was not visible from outside the hall but, high in the wall behind it, Gunnar had placed a lens which caught the light when the sun was in a certain spot in the sky. Supposedly, it was the position the sun was in at the exact moment of the coronation. Every morning for about three moons a year, the sun peered over the Eastrod mountains and shone down upon Fairford Castle and the Great Hall was lit with wonder.

So much work, so much sacrifice, for a few fleeting moments of beauty.

A waste of time.

It was a grand gesture.

And grand gestures endured.

King Warwick of Fairford waited for the sun.

"You seem troubled, brother."

Felix was eight years his junior, but almost a man now. His moustache was almost visible in the growing light. He wore the long, purple tunic of a royal adviser, a position Warwick had granted him out of little but a sense of guilt for his own first-born right to the throne.

It wasn't that he didn't trust Felix's counsel, simply that he thought his brother was not ready for the struggles of rule.

Felix had wept when Warwick told him of their Father's death. Warwick understood. Before they knew him as a Tyrant, he was just Father. Perhaps it was easier to remember one with the other gone.

He's weak. He was always weak.

He smiled at his brother. "Just the worries of a husband-to-be, Felix."

"There is no cause for worry, I am sure. We have lived in darkling times for long enough."

Warwick looked sidelong at him. He always knew what to say. "You no longer think me a fool to believe marriage to a Princess of Elderhaime will salve our countries' ailments?"

Felix smiled. "I have always thought you a fool, brother, you know that."

Warwick laughed. Maybe that's what they would call him. The Fool King.

The sun crept across Gunnar's Window, bathing the throne room in warmth, and old Arnhult was crowned in light once more.

Extract from Lord Felix Tyrantson's Diary:
Seven Years of Age

First Rynesday, Third Moon of Spring, 203
Lord Ashfall says I must make a diary to help my writing. Here it is. My name is Felix and I live in a castle. The castle is called Fairford castle and is big and made of stone. I live with my Mum and Dad and my big brother Warwick. My Dad is the king which means everyone else has to do what he says. Me and my brother are princes which means everyone has to do what we say too. Except Mum and Dad. We have to do what they say. My bedroom is in the tower and I can see out over the whole country to the mountains. I like playing in the gardens with my cat. Her name is Belinda. She is ginger. She likes milk and meat and sometimes chases mice. In the gardens I play swords with my brother or the guards. I win usually. Today I had to stay in because it was raining and I did my studies with Lord Ashfall and started writing this diary. He showed me how to carve a soldier out of wood. I will show Dad when he comes home. I hope the sun comes out tomorrow.

First Dracaday, Third Moon of Spring, 203
The sun did come out today after all. I played in the garden with Warwick. I killed him a lot. Dad was away, so we had dinner with just Mum. It was a big pig with an apple in its mouth. After dinner I read some stories with Warwick. One was about a man called Njal who sailed a ship here from far away and had adventures. It was my favourite.

Second Stilnesday, Third Moon of Spring, 203
Dad came back today. There were lots of men who were hurt and he was very angry. I heard him shouting at Mum after dinner. He didn't have a nice time while he was away. I

showed him my wooden soldier and he broke it. Not on purpose. He just knocked it out of my hand by accident. I wasn't holding it tight enough. I should have left him alone because he was busy. And he was in a bad mood because lots of people got killed by people from Elderhaime. I hate those people from Elderhaime. They really are awful.

Third Rynesday, Third Moon of Spring, 203
Belinda died today. Dad kicked her down the stairs. I think she was annoying him. I was sad and Warwick got angry when he saw what Dad had done. He told him it was cruel. Dad said he didn't know what cruel meant, but I think he does. Warwick is very clever about words. Warwick and Me buried Belinda in the garden and Mum came and some of the guards and maids and kitchen girls came too. They said they liked Belinda because she kept the rats away. They said they need another cat. Mum said one thing is for sure it won't be Belinda. Mum told me about the place where cats go when they die. It's warm and sunny and there's lots of mice and milk and big beds and stuff. She said I couldn't go there, but Belinda might visit me when I die. I hope so. Mum makes me feel better.

Fourth Sunday, Third Moon of Spring, 203
Dad's gone away again. He says he has to go and fight Duncan, but I don't think my Dad ever does any fighting. He just tells people to fight and they do because he is the king. I wonder if there is anything a person wouldn't do for the king. Warwick wanted to go with him, but Dad said he is too young. Warwick told me that he only wanted to go to stop Dad doing anything bad. Maybe he meant like hurting any more cats.

The Princess

Mud.

She was wearing slippers and the mud was never less than ankle deep. She hadn't expected to be hiking her way through woodland when she dressed the previous morning. The filth was creeping up the increasingly ragged hem of her dress.

They had spent the night in the Dunholt, the dense forest at the foot of the Lip. The Fool said it was probably best to keep to the trees rather than follow the Underfarway. That road led west from Crossford to Underton, and any number of traders and travellers and worse could pass by.

She knew from the sun and her memories of map-books that they were heading east. Towards Crossford. Away from Elderhaime.

Away from home.

When she had complained at this, the Fool had listed their choices. Either they follow the Lip east to where it sloped down to level ground, or they try and climb the sheer cliff-face itself. Having no supplies, food, rope or weapons, he suggested that the nearest settlement might be a worthwhile stop on either journey.

So they were going to Crossford.

The Fool led the way with a spring in his step, singing and dancing and behaving in the manner his profession suggested.

She was beginning to wonder about him.

They reached the village after walking all morning.

The Fool raised a hand. They stood, hidden in the trees by the road.

The road crossed the Thurwund over a stone bridge, before passing by the tall gate of Crossford town and heading on through the trees towards Fairford. Towards the enemy.

"This is halfway," said the Fool.

"What?" They were whispering, though no one could be seen.

"This bridge. It's supposedly dead twixt Elderhaime and Fairford. The heart of the Siblands."

She looked again.

Crossford was but a scattering of thatched roofs sitting on stone walls around a courtyard of mud, all surrounded by a wooden fence. The river glided past, a few short piers dipping their toes into the water here and there. Behind the village, the Holtlands rose up. Hills, thick with trees. A wilderness containing untold boga and unmen, according to the tales.

She didn't believe the tales.

"Well," she said. "Are we going to stand here all day?"

She stepped forward, but the Fool had hold of her arm.

The impudence.

She looked at his hand.

It was his left hand. The one without the glove.

For a strange moment there was only the sensation of his skin on hers.

"We need a story," he said.

She shook him off. "What do you mean?"

"You're the Princess."

"Queen."

"Yeah, that."

"So I shall announce my presence to my subjects and demand their assistance." Of course, because her loyal subjects had shown so much respect when they stabbed her Dad.

The Fool could tell she didn't believe it. "There are no heralds here, your Majesty. They wouldn't believe you, and if they did, that could be even worse."

She understood. "A Queen would be a valuable hostage."

"For either side. They could sell you back to Elderhaime, to Fairford or even to… whoever that was with the bandages back there."

She thought about this.

If she hadn't been scared before, she was now. She was suddenly aware of the wilderness around her, her thin dress of the finest Setlan silk, her soft little slippers now covered in filth.

She didn't belong out here amongst these people.

"You'll have to go in alone," she said. "They'll know I'm not one of them."

"No." He shook his head. The bells on his hat jangled. "I have a better idea."

He knelt down. Picked something up. Stood and held it out to her. "Mud."

"Mud?"

"Mud."

He didn't mean… "What do you want me to do with that?"

"Put it on."

"Put it on? It's not a bonnet, Fool, it's a handful of slutch."

"Yeah, wear it." He smeared some on his face. "It's a disguise. I know it's not the height of fashion for ladies at court, but these people spend their lives caked in this shite. You wanna pass for one of them, you're gonna have to slap a bit on."

She couldn't believe this. As if she hadn't suffered enough degradation in the past days.

He flicked mud at her.

He flicked mud in her face.

Right.

She scooped a hand full of filth from the floor and hauled her arm around to slap him in the face with it.

He was quick. He ducked her arm and flicked more mud on her.

"Fool, stop it!" she threw her handful at him, and caught him full in the face.

She laughed.

He laughed back at her.

Then he held up his filthy hands.

"No!" she was still laughing.

He ran at her, reaching for her face.

They were kids again and he was pretending to wipe a bogey on her cheek.

She grabbed his wrists, warm skin in one hand, cold leather in the other, and grappled with him.

They ended on the ground, of course.

Covered in shite.

She was pinned beneath him as he pushed his mucky hands into her hair.

"Get off!"

He stopped, surveying his handiwork. She was suddenly aware of those brown eyes scouring her face. His brow furrowed like a scholar at study.

She wasn't laughing any more.

"That'll do," he said.

She slapped his face. It wasn't playful.

"Let me up, Fool," she said.

He was shocked by the slap. Good. He should be.

He got off her and stood up, offering her a hand.

She didn't take it.

"You presume too much," she said, pulling herself to her feet.

He was looking at the floor. "Sorry."

"I am your Queen, not some child for you to ridicule."

He nodded.

She felt something then which she did not expect. Longing. Longing for a simpler time.

But you can't ever go back. Only forwards. Things change, things fall apart no matter how you try to cling and scrabble and hold them together.

They stood for a moment, heads bowed, as if in mourning.

She sniffed. "And you made me roll in something smelly."

He looked up. And smiled. "I'm sorry."

She shrugged. "How do I look?"

"Ready."

The Fool checked the road for anyone approaching, and they stepped out from under the trees.

The sun was shining.

What a day to be out and about, covered head to toe in muck.

The fence around the village was about eight feet high, but because the land sloped away from it up to the woods, it didn't offer much in the way of privacy. It was as if the village was determined to see over the fence in case it missed anything exciting passing on the road or the river.

The village gate bore the hand-carved legend "Crossford". There was a sentry up in a small shack that overlooked the fence. He gave them a nod as they passed.

He barely looked at them.

She was used to servants averting their gaze when she entered a room, but this was different. The sentry actively looked, decided these people held no interest whatsoever, and turned his head.

Through the gate, chickens, ducks and geese roamed loose, but she didn't see many people.

"It's so quiet," she said.

"Not much to sing about out here," said the Fool.

There were graves.

At the side of the path were a line of freshly dug burial mounds. Twelve altogether.

"Fool," she knew she should have stayed in the woods.

"Yep." He didn't seem bothered, but he wasn't singing and capering any more.

"Those are graves. New graves."

"Yep."

"Was there a brigand attack?"

"Maybe. But this is the Heart of the Siblands. Anyone travelling anywhere within the Four Corners is going to pass through Crossford at one point or another. And there's a lot of bad blood out there as you know. A lot of spirits that don't mix."

They walked on.

A sad faced little girl peered out of a window as they passed. Katherine thought about waving to her, but she was already gone.

The few people they did see either scowled at them or made themselves scarce.

It wasn't the most welcoming place.

They stopped under a painted sign above a grey stone doorway. It named the building as "The Brown Trousers", and featured an appropriately inappropriate illustration.

It was an ale house.

"How earthy," said Katherine.

Before the Fool had chance to respond, the door to The Brown Trousers was flung open.

"We don't serve Rotters in 'ere!"

A tattered old man was hurled to the ground at their feet. A burly man stood in the doorway. "Go an' mither someone else, you scabby bleeder!"

The door slammed shut.

"I only wanted a pint!" The old man cried out, looking like a sad pile of rags. "I got money!"

"Looks like your money's no good here, chief." The Fool was already reaching out his un-gloved left hand to pull the old man to his feet. Katherine grabbed his arm.

"Wait," She could see the red and yellow stains on the old man's bandages, the familiar signature of the affliction. "Don't touch him!"

She had heard many stories of the affliction spreading through sneezes and spit, but the surest way to welcome the curse was to simply touch someone already suffering its effects. "You'll catch it!"

The Fool frowned at her. Then he offered the man his gloved hand instead.

He surely wouldn't actually place a bare hand on someone covered with Rot?

The old man took his hand.

The Fool pulled him to his feet.

"Fates bless you, son!" The old man slapped the Fool on the back. "It's a rare man indeed will offer a hand to one filled with rot."

The Princess cringed, trying to remember the medicine books. Could you catch the sickness through your clothes? She didn't think so, that was why Rotters wrapped themselves in cloaks and bandages, wasn't it? She stepped back a little from the old man all the same and tried to cover her mouth and nose without being rude.

He was ranting. "The bloody nerve of it! My flesh may be on the turn, but I didn't cross the Haunted Dunmoors and the Brigand-Infested Forests to be broomed out by a bastard barkeep!"

"Your eloquence is wasted, my friend," said the Fool. "They think your coins are diseased too." He seemed to think for a moment, before grinning at Katherine. "Why don't you sit yourself down here and let me bring a pint out to you?" he said.

Now they were supplying ale to beggars. This was indeed a worthy first day as Queen. Starting from the bottom and all that.

"If you please, sir!" The old man beamed. "That would be right noble of you!"

Katherine thought the Fool was about as far from nobility as it was possible to get. "A tavern? Fool…"

But he was already through the door.

The Fool

The pub hadn't changed much, though it had been a few winters since he was last within its walls.

Two exits. The one they walked through and another door at the far side, presumably leading out to a back yard.

He doubted anyone would peg him as the annoying lad from all those years ago. No, he was a fully grown annoying bloke now.

No obvious threats. Only about four punters and one fella behind the bar. As quiet as the rest of the town. It hadn't even been this quiet back when the war was raging.

The barkeep was the one who had tossed the Old Rotter into the gutter. He thought about teeth being knocked out by tankards, but this wasn't the only establishment that turned away the afflicted and this wasn't the time to start a crusade.

The bastard could keep his skull intact for now.

Everyone in there had either come straight in from a morning in the fields or been there all night. The air was thick with pipe smoke and piss stink.

He felt right at home.

He strode through the musty room and slammed a couple of gobbets on the bar. "Ale! Ale me up, good sir! And a couple of rounds of bread and cheese, if you have it to spare."

The barkeep was a grumpy old sod with barely a word to say, but the regulars at the bar had a few japes about his foolish getup. "Is the Carny rolled in?" "How, Jester, got any jokes?" "Lost a bet, did ye?" The usual.

"Appearances can be deceiving!" he assured the room. "I may seem a fool, but I am in fact a great scholar and politician on a diplomatic mission."

He started juggling apples out of a bowl on the bar. The simple folk always went for that.

"So don't judge my position or begin your inquisition, for your false intuition may upset my disposition…"

Rhymes, too. The simple folk liked the rhymes and the juggling. Combine the two and they were putty. He might have to squeeze in a bawdy song before they left, but everyone would be happy.

And he was keeping their eyes off her. It was unlikely that anyone in this bilge-house would peg her a Princess - nay, a Queen - but they would without doubt take interest in a beautiful, high-born maid wandering the woods in little more than her undies, even if she was all slutched up like a ragamuffin.

Katherine was peering at a notice board by the door. He could see it bore only a crudely authored announcement of the impending wedding ceremony.

She laughed. Like she didn't believe it.

Luckily, the punters were watching him chucking apples about.

Most of them.

An old bottlebottom by the door had latched his eyes on her. "Any news from abroad, bonny stranger?"

This probably wasn't going to go well.

"Bonny..?" She had that look.

The Fool thought this old sot might not be long for this earth. He threw the apples, one after another, to the nearest punters and slid across the floor, placing himself between the Princess and her inquisitor.

"Non of much cheer, I'm afraid," he said. This didn't need to get any more difficult. "We were set upon by brigands on the way. We're just passing through."

The drunk stared. "That's a fine hat."

"And yours is a fine face, my friend!"

One of the punters at the bar spoke up. "Did ye see the graves on the way in?"

"That we did," he said, keeping himself between the Princess and the room.

"Mind 'em." The man speaking was about ten years older than the Fool. Also drunk. A lifetime bowling bails of hay to and fro had made a bull of him. He looked at the Fool not with threat, but with warning. "That's what happens to folks who bring the conflict here."

"The conflict?"

"There's no Elderhaime and Fairford here. Since the truce, there's only Fury."

"Fury." He had heard rumour of the man calling himself that name.

"Aye," said the bull man. He turned sadly back to his drink. "He's the King of these parts. Watch your step or you'll face his men. Or worse."

"Bandaged brigand bastard," spat another drinker.

Warning glares turned to the new speaker. A younger man, little more than a dreng. "Them bloody brigands pillaged our Kevin's last week," he continued, regardless. "He's got nowt left for winter now and he reckons they took his eldest daughter to peddle in Underton."

The Fool looked back at Katherine. The colour had drained from her face at the mention of bandages.

He had made a mistake.

He hadn't realised how serious things were, how much control the brigands had gained since the armies of Elderhaime and Fairford no longer patrolled the woods of the Mitland.

He wondered if any of these people wouldn't hand over the Princess to this "Fury" on the promise of whatever favour it might bring.

"It'll all change after the wedding," the Barkeep chimed in, placing two ales on the bar.

"Oh, here we go!" The bull man let out a groan. "The bloody royals are gunna save us now? It was them as started all this in the first place: Two kings fall in love with the same woman and spark off hundreds of years of war!"

"My point exactly!" The barkeep pushed forward a plate of bread and cheese. He was evidently something of a royalist.

"That was a royal argument that became a war. Think of the effect a royal marriage will have!"

The Fool looked at Katherine. He was sure they hadn't pegged her, but she now looked a strange mix of crushing terror and boiling rage.

She looked like she was about to spit out her own jaw.

Perhaps she needed to hear this? Couldn't hurt to let them talk, could it? Show her a few points of view she might not have considered? Give her the common touch. Though you do have to be careful who you touch in a place like this.

He walked back to the bar and picked up a tankard.

"Well, I think it's beautiful." An old woman, quiet until now, chucked her two-gobbetts worth in. "Two people who've never even met getting married in the name of peace? They're giving up their own lives for all of us!"

"What love did hew shall same renew!" called the Barkeep.

The Fool raised his tankard of ale. "I'll drink to that!"

He had barely got a couple of gulps in before she burst.

"What is wrong with you people?"

All eyes but the Fool's turned to Katherine. He gently put down his tankard.

He thought about tankards smashing into faces again, he thought about tables turning over and feet running for the door.

"Sitting here waxing lyrical about other people's lives!" she was still going. He turned to see the whole room looking at her, wide-eyed.

"You want changes? Well get off your... your... stools and, and... make them yourselves!"

The phrase "incandescent with rage" sprang to mind. It was like watching fireworks.

He thought about applauding, but she was already grabbing his arm and dragging him toward the door and out into the light.

"Peasants!" she hissed, storming back and forth across the road from the pub.

"You spilled my pint." He indicated the damp patch on his tunic.

"What do they know? Just a bunch of sots and knaves."

He could tell she needed a little time to herself. The old Rotter's need was greater than hers, anyway.

"…should stop blaming their problems on people they never even clapped eyes on…" She raged on as he walked to where the afflicted man sat by the path.

"Get this down your neck." He offered the man a tankard and some of the bread and cheese.

He had seen the old fella's reaction to charity before. He knew how it felt to be convinced that there was no one left to care in the world. And he knew how good it felt to have that belief proved wrong.

"Bless you, son!" The old man drank deep and shoved the bread in his gob.

Katherine still paced. Still wingeing.

The eldhad man eyed her between mouthfuls. "She a bit high-strung, that one?"

The Fool watched her. "Aye. It's some upper-class guilt or summat." He thought he should probably change the subject. Even caked in muck and fuming, Katherine had a certain royal air, a regal grace it was hard not to notice.

He shouldn't notice.

Distraction. "So, what brings you round this way? Not a good beggar's spot, I would've thought."

"No! You're about right at that! But I heard tell of this healer used to live on the hill on the edge of town. Supposed to be the best there ever was."

He had heard that about her too. "Really?"

"Yeah. They says she was the Queen's own personal nurse. Before all that unfortunate business."

Such an unfortunate business. The Fool tightened a strap on his leather gauntlet.

"They said she's the only person ever to cure someone of the Affliction. They said she could wake the dead if she wanted!"

They certainly said a lot about her. Quite the reputation. Some folk get all the good stories. Whether they're true or not.

"She's not there no more, though," the old beggar went on. "Just an old burnt-down house."

The Fool remembered the flames.

"So now I only see one possible cure for my ills." The afflicted man raised his tankard.

The Fool thought about the great healer who could raise the dead. Was there a chance -

He seemed to awake. He smiled. He knocked his tankard against the old man's.

"My kind of medicine," he said.

The Princess

"We don't need a healer!" She dragged her feet in the mud as the Fool hurried ahead. "Unless she can mend your addled mind."

"We need supplies," the Fool called back to her, "and I have a feeling there may be no better place to find them."

The path led them up the hill and through the tree line north of Crossford, beyond the border of the Holtlands.

The stories of the Holtlands would lead one to believe that you would be attacked by Fearies the very moment you set foot under the shadow of the trees but, of course, no attack came.

The Fool stomped on ahead, even as the way became more and more overgrown with bremels and the canopy overhead grew ever darker. The forest shutting out the sun so that none may see what dark business was afoot within its green folds.

"Wait!" she cried after him. Her dress snagged on thorns and branches whipped at her. "Wait for me, Fool!"

She was suddenly aware of the quiet. The woods were usually teeming with wild creatures of all shapes and sizes making their presence felt with calls and yammers of all varieties, but here she heard nothing.

"Why is it so quiet, Fool?" she called as she struggled to unsnare herself from the grabbing twigs.

He was at her side, soundless himself. "All I hear is you," he said.

He unhooked her dress from the bremelbush and held out his hand to her.

She took it with a frown.

She would have to do something about his insolence when they got home.

He led her a little too quickly through the wood, still climbing the hill, still rustling their way through the silence around them.

Until the trees parted.

She felt the hair on her arms prickle, though the air was still.

Here was a ruin.

A homestead of some sort, maybe a farm, or a woodcutter's lodge. It may have lain in a clearing once, but now the forest had reached back into its space, reclaiming the conquered land for itself.

Three stone walls still stood, but the roof had long since collapsed. From the look of the beams and the sooty smears on the stone, she would guess the building burnt years ago. Rubble lay all around and everywhere were trees and bushes making this old home their own.

Something was wrong here. She felt it like a cold hand on her heart.

Don't be silly. It's just an empty old house.

"A healer lived here?" she said.

"A Witch."

She thought about the Witches she had read about. They usually eat children. And live in houses in the woods.

"We are to get supplies here?" she raised an eyebrow at the Fool.

He shrugged and stepped through the space that would've been a door. "Hello?" he called.

"There's nobody here, Fool," she said. "Can't you feel it?"

"Feel what?"

She looked around at the encroaching wilderness. "This place is empty."

"Nobody'll mind if we have a peep around then, will they?" he said, disappearing behind broken walls.

"But the Rotter said there's nobody here!" They had wasted enough time. She needed to get home.

"Maybe he didn't look hard enough," the Fool suddenly sounded far away.

She looked around again, wondering which way was home.

She could leave him here, couldn't she? Just walk into the woods and find her own way?

But she couldn't. Thought of facing the long walk home without his idle chatter seemed unappealing, somehow. Being able to argue with him like nothing had changed was small comfort, but it was comfort she had to admit.

She shook that thought from her head and followed the Fool through the broken door. Best to get this over with. The sooner they found nothing in this ruin, the sooner they could get back on the road to Elderhaime.

She walked down the remains of a hallway. Rubble, fallen wood, masonry and silence all around. She heard the Fool call "Hello?" again.

She wondered why the house was burned. Maybe this Witch terrorised the townsfolk of Crossford with gramwords and misdeeds, and they put her house to the torch to protect themselves and their children?

Or maybe the superstitious townsfolk just took a dislike to an innocent woman who lived here and decided she was a Witch worth the burning.

She knew which seemed more likely.

She kicked over a stone and peered through another broken doorway. This room was more intact than the others. A few stones had fallen away around a window where some leafy greningen had crept through, and half the roof had come in, but she could see this was a kitchen of some sort. A wide wooden shelf ran along the far wall at waist height. She had seen the kitchen maids chopping vegetables and cleaning carcasses at work-surfaces such as this back home. There were hooks and nails on the surviving roof beams for hanging bundles of herbs and maybe jugs or pans. There was a stone kiln underneath the workshelf, and a chimney that rose through the wall behind and opened into a ragged, yawning hole a foot or so above her head.

She ran a hand along the wooden shelf and peered at the mossy residue on her fingers.

In wondering at this woodland kitchen, she remembered another story from her youth. Maybe bears lived here. Maybe this is where they made their broth after rising from their bear beds in another room she had yet to discover.

She smiled to herself.

And somebody spoke.

"You are not welcome here."

She almost soiled her skirts.

It wasn't bears.

Someone was there.

In the doorway.

Hooded and cloaked in black.

A Witch. Had to be the Witch.

The voice was low and hissing, distant and yet right in her ear.

She knew she had to say something.

She was thinking about Witches eating children.

"I… Er…"

The figure was moving towards her, drifting, as if its feet never touched the ground.

Runrunrunrunrunrun

"We're looking for the healer…"

It stopped.

It was so close she could've reached out and pulled its hood off.

If she wasn't scared rigid.

She turned her face away, only daring glance out of the corner of her eye.

It seemed to be scrutinising her.

She could only see darkness under the hood, but she felt as though she was being studied.

"There is no healer here," it hissed.

She really wanted to go home.

"That's not what I heard." The Fool's voice.

The Princess and the apparition before her both turned to see him perched in the broken window.

The Witch let out a gasp. "Jester?"

Katherine gaped as the black hood was pulled back by feminine hands, revealing the incredulous face of a woman. The voice had changed as well, to something altogether more human.

The Witch woman pushed dark hair out of her green eyes and laughed in disbelief.

Katherine looked at the Fool for answers.

He shrugged. "Princess Katherine of Elderhaime, may I present to you the lady Althea, Legendary white Witch and healer of Crossford."

Althea ran to the Fool. He hopped down from the ledge and welcomed her embrace.

The Witch

A day like any other.

She rose with the sun, as usual, though she wasn't sure how she knew the sun was rising. Her eyes just seemed to slide open at the exact moment, as if she could feel the light creeping across the ground above her. And, sure enough, the yellow dawn would slowly seep through the planks of the trap and she would know it was time to rise.

Today was a good day, as she did not rise from dreams of fire and suffocation. The days when she saw the rising sunlight as flames from above were her darkest.

She climbed out of bed and attended the animals. None had died in the night, which was always a good start. If you couldn't defeat death, at least you could keep him at bay for one more day.

In fact, the little Sefinch she had yet to name seemed in particularly fine fettle. He hopped from perch to perch in his tiny cage and trilled as she approached, her candle chasing the dark away. She thought he was ready. Strong little bird. She wondered if he'd needed her help at all.

The others were mostly unchanged, some slightly perked up, some slightly perked down.

Once they were all fed or made as comfortable as possible, she wrapped her shawl around herself, covering every inch of her body in darkness. Let any prying eyes see only a shadow, let their imaginations do the rest.

She lifted the Sefinch's cage and hauled it up the stairs to the trap.

There were two terrible moments in her every day. The first was waking to the realisation that she was still alone. That there was no one there in the dark beside her, waiting for her to just reach out her hand. Convincing herself that there was a reason to get out of bed and face the day was the first challenge of every morning.

The second terrible moment was here, squatting in the space at the top of the stairs. The tiny breath before she lifted the hatch. The instant she could see everyone who was waiting for her just outside, bows aimed down at her light-bedazzled eyes. The moment she could see his face, the moment she knew he'd come back to finish the job.

She let out a sigh, pressed her back against the trapdoor and pushed.

She looked out of the gap, her expectation of booted feet meeting the usual disappointment.

She wasn't disappointed. Was she? Did she want them to come back?

She pushed the hatch fully open. She placed the finch's cage gently on the ground and lifted herself out of her home.

She looked quickly around. No urchins from the village hiding in the ruins? No inquisitive beasts come sniffing in the night? The fallen beams and resolutely standing walls gave her no answer.

Her home was a part of the forest now.

She headed to the garden. Making her way through the tangled undergrowth, she passed her scarecrows. She bid them good day as they turned to watch her make her way along the path. They did their jobs well.

It was quiet in the garden, as always. She relished the peace. The silence was so palpable she felt that, if she were to speak, her voice might be snatched away from her mouth before it could reach any waiting ear. That was the way she liked it.

She thought about releasing the Sefinch here, but he may have struggled getting over the surrounding Stickleshrubs if he wasn't up to flying yet. Wouldn't want him impaling himself on a thorn on his first leap into the air.

She plucked some Turfwort for the stew and thought she would take the finch to see Mark. The sun was shining down now and she hadn't been up to see him for a while.

It was only a short walk. On the crest of the crag north of the hill. She sat down beside him and introduced the little bird. She picked some Sunlings from the grass and a few Bluefires from the tree that grew over him.

She placed them on the soil where he lay.

They used to come up here and look North, out over the Holtlands. Back when they thought they had got away from it all.

Back when they thought they had found peace.

She opened the Sefinch's cage and waited. She didn't think he would need coaxing, and she was right. He hopped onto the tiny doorstep of the cage and stopped for a second. She wondered if he was having his own worst moment then, imagining what terrors might wait out there in the world and measuring them against the safety of the cage.

He hopped forward and flew up to a branch of the Bluefire tree.

Just above the branch with the noose.

He looked at her with that little tilted head and she wondered how incomprehensible this all must be to him.

He was gone.

She watched the little red speck flutter out over the Holtlands until it was out of sight.

She needn't have worried.

She sat with Mark a little while longer. She used to talk to him about her day, tell him how she was filling her time, but her days seemed so empty now and she didn't want him to know.

She looked up at the old rope hanging from the branch above her and wondered.

Why not?

They needed her, didn't they? The animals? They wouldn't survive without her.

She would make them all better and then she would do it. Then she would be with him.

She whispered her love into the morning breeze and headed back home.

Back down the hatch, to her family of sick and injured creatures. Yes, they needed her, even if nobody else did.

She was cleaning out the stoat's hutch when she heard it.

A call from above.

Someone was in the ruins of her house.

The call came again: "Hello?"

Her heart stopped.

They were back.

They'd come for her.

No.

It was just some wanderer. Some vagrant. They came drifting this way sometimes when they heard stories of the Witch.

She would show them their Witch. She would give them what they wanted.

She dragged her shawl about herself again and crept up the stairs.

The Princess

There was a hatch in the floor.

A trapdoor that opened up in the apparently solid ground of the kitchen, revealing a stone staircase below.

The Witch held it open and invited them in.

"It's not much, but it's home."

Katherine wasn't convinced. Only moments ago, this woman was floating toward her like some fell creature, and now she was beckoning them into her underground lair? Who knew what terrors lay down those steps?

The Fool, of course, bounded straight down into the gloom.

She looked at the Witch and was struck again by her eyes. They were as green as any emerald she had ever seen.

She had seen three emeralds. And one of them had been very green.

"I didn't mean to scare you," said the Witch. She thought for a moment. "Well, I did. I meant to frighten you away, but... I didn't know it was you, your Highness."

Katherine nodded. So being royalty got her invited into a Witch's cavern? It really was a privilege.

"Won't you come in?" the Witch asked, smiling such a smile that Katherine found it difficult not to trust her. Probably some kind of spell.

But there was no such thing as magic.

"Good stew, Al!" came a cry from below.

"Don't eat it all, Jester!" replied the Witch.

Katherine could smell food. Something edible. Her need for sustenance overcame her misgivings, and she stepped onto the stairs.

As her eyes adjusted to the darkness, she saw a low-ceilinged room lit by candles. Opposite her was a bed and before that a tiny kitchen area, where stew bubbled in a pot over a stove. A thick, black pipe ran from the stove into the wall, spiriting the smoke away to who-knows-where.

The Fool sat on the bed, eating stew.

Between her and the Fool, the walls were covered with cages and hutches, floor to ceiling. Animals everywhere.

She stepped forward into the room, marvelling at the wildlife on display. It was as if all the animals of the forest had been captured and placed down here, the silence of the overworld giving way to the chattering and mewling of the menagerie beneath.

There were birds of brown (Andribbs, maybe?), and a large black one (definitely a Banpicker), she recognised a stoat from the stuffed one back in the library, a baby brock was sleeping on a bed of straw and was about the sweetest little thing she ever saw -

"These are my wards," said the Witch.

"Your wards?"

"The forest is a dangerous place. Sometimes they need help."

The Fool laughed through a slurp of stew. "You're healing animals?"

The Witch cast a glare in his direction. "All life is worth saving, Jester."

"You make them better?" asked Katherine.

"If they're ill, I try. If they are hurt I heal them as best I can and then turn them loose."

"So you are a healer, then?"

"Of a sort."

The Fool snorted again. "What about the dead ones? Do you awaken them?"

She ignored him. "I was just about to feed the brockling," she said to Katherine. "If you want…" she held out a tiny leather milkskin. Katherine had rarely seen such careful craftsmanship. The stitching was so small as to be nearly invisible, and the straw in the end was held in place by some kind of putty she could not place.

"Did you make this?" she said, taking it gently in her hand.

"Tricks of the trade," said the Witch.

"Where'd you get brockmilk from?" said the Fool. "You're braver than I am you been squeezing a brock's teat."

"It's cow's milk, Jester. I still head into the village when need be."

"Well," said the Fool. "Be careful you don't go breeding brocks the size of cows, then we'll all be brocken."

The Fool looked pleased with his joke. Katherine ignored him and was pleased to see the Witch did the same. "May I?" she asked, pointing to the brock's cage.

The Witch opened the cage door and lifted the tiny, fleshy, black and white bundle out. Brocks could grow to be as big as dogs, and twice as vicious, but this thing was little more than a handful. It mewled and wriggled as the Witch placed it in her palm.

"He's so small," she said. "I feel I might break him."

"He's tougher than he looks."

She held the velvety little life in her hand and nursed it with the bottle. He drew greedily on the straw like a sott with a wineskin.

She watched this tiny thing clinging on to its life and almost forgot about her Dad and the Fool and the horror and murder and this woman watching her with a strange, soft smile.

Almost.

"I thought you were dead, Al," said the Fool. The Witch didn't look at him, just kept watching the brockling suckle. "I avenged you. Well, I thought I did. A lot of things aren't what they seem at the moment."

"A lot of things," said Katherine.

"Where's Mark?" said the Fool.

The Witch still didn't look at him, but neither was she looking at the brockling anymore. Her eyes looked through the little creature to something distant, difficult to see. "Gone," she said. "That much is true."

The Fool looked at the ground, a spoon in his mouth. He licked the spoon clean. "Sorry," he said.

The Witch almost smiled and then she was back from wherever she drifted to. "How's your hand?" she asked the Fool.

"Fine." The Fool waved his un-gloved hand in the air. He always wore but one leather gauntlet on his right hand, painted red and green as his gaudy tunic all the way to his elbow.

Althea looked about to speak again, but the Fool got in first. "We saw an old geezer with the sickness in town."

Althea caressed the little brockling's belly. "I couldn't have helped him."

"You could've tried," said the Fool.

"I've lost the knack for people."

The Fool laughed, looking around. "You're living in a hole in the ground with a load of wild animals," he said. "I'd say you're about right at that."

Althea smiled again and the little brockling pushed the bottle away.

Katherine was surprised at how disappointed she was to have the little warm body taken out of her hand.

Althea put the tiny thing back in its straw bed and closed the cage.

Katherine handed her the milkskin. "So, you gave up medicine?" she asked.

The Witch pulled out a chair and sat down, between Katherine and the Fool. She picked up a bowl and reached for the stew ladle. She paused for a moment, and sighed. "It gave up on me. And I wanted to be left alone. Nobody comes looking for you if you're already dead."

The Fool looked hurt at this remark. His brow furrowed with what could've been grief or anger.

"Jester…" said Althea.

The Fool looked up at her with wide eyes. "You've eaten all my stew, you arsewarch."

The Witch

So King Duncan was dead.
Murdered in the mud by *him*.
History repeats.
The Jester's arrival had nudged a lot of forgotten thoughts that were now stirring in her head. It had been a long time.
Five, six years? Things had changed so much.
They never thought they'd get old, let alone die.
Now death was all she thought about.
So many were gone. Fallen away over the years, as leaves in the autumn. The only certainty in life is Death. And she'd started to long for him.
Katherine told her the whole sorry tale as they sat and drank tea, waiting for the Jester to return from the garden. He said he knew the way, said that the only reason they were there was because he thought her garden might yet grow and they needed supplies. She told him to take whatever they would need.
While he foraged, Katherine told her all. She told of the marriage proposal, the attack on the road to Fairford, the escape and also of her belief that King Warwick was behind it all.
The new Queen spoke whilst staring into the glow of the stove, sounding distant, as if recounting a bedtime tale she had heard once upon a time.
It didn't seem real. Particularly the part about Warwick. He had always been a good boy, hadn't he? He had helped them out so much.
But things change.
Everything decays. Even moral fibre.
She spoke of a bandaged man leading the brigands, and she thought that could only mean *him*. Why he wore bandages, she did not know, but she hoped it hurt.
It was all so familiar.

He died in the road. In the mud. While she watched and could do nothing.

History repeats.

And repeats.

The only certainty is death. After which there can be no life.

She thought it as if death was an infection. When our lives are first touched by death, he is with us from then on. He waits within us, biding his time. You carry death with you all your life.

There was only one question to be asked.

"What are you going to do?"

The Queen looked at her, finally. "I'm going to go home."

It was a strange thing to see Katherine - only recently a child to Althea's mind - now a grown woman. A woman forced to share her darkest hour with a seeming stranger.

Althea saw something in Katherine then, something she hadn't seen for a long time.

"I'm surprised I didn't recognise you," she said. "You have a look of your Mother."

Katherine's eyes darted to hers. "You knew my Mother?"

Althea tried a smile. "I used to work at the palace."

"Really? I don't recall…"

"I wasn't around that much. Always very busy."

Katherine looked back into the stove, as if that was the end of the conversation. Althea thought she must be accustomed to people avoiding talk about her Mother.

She wasn't surprised.

She thought maybe it wasn't her place to speak of such things.

"This man, Fury," - she found it hard to say the name - "he's been marauding the Mitlands since the Tyrant died. When your Father and King Warwick signed the truce, the soldiers and armies went home. The Holtlands were left wide open for his kind to take over. More innocent people have died in these parts during peacetime than during the war."

She realised how that sounded. Katherine still just stared into the fire.

Althea sighed. "It wasn't what they intended."

"I'll give them a war," said the young Queen. Quietly, calmly. "If trying for peace brings only more death, when I get home I will gather my armies to me and take my place as Folqueen of Sibland by force."

Katherine's eyes burned with refractions of flame.

Althea thought about it. All the power of Elderhaime, the oldest city in the Siblands, seat of the Lord of the Reeceland, the ability to summon all those loyal from Folksted, Richmere, Solsted, Brimmenhaime, Underton and anywhere else that swore fealty. All that might at the beck and call of a vengeful girl.

She feared for anyone who put themselves in Katherine's way.

"It's vengeance you seek, then?" she said.

Katherine looked up from the fire. "What else is there?"

Althea knew there were many answers you're supposed to give, so many things you are supposed to say. Lessons and lectures about the all-consuming nature of revenge, that when you walk with death in mind, you are also on his, that the Prince roams freely in the hearts of the vengeful...

But she couldn't say any of it.

Because she didn't believe it.

Once we are touched by Death, we carry Death with us.

And the only power greater than love is hatred for those who take our love away.

The Fool

Picking flipping tubers and herbs.
This was Fool's work for certain.
At least the sun was out.
And Al was still alive.
Shame about Mark, but still, one dead friend was better than two.
He kicked his way through the grass toward the garden. There were two crudely made scarecrows dressed in black up ahead. As he approached, they turned to look at him, their empty hoods following his movements. He smiled. It was an old trick of Mark's, most likely an underground pulley system connected to a rock he'd stepped on.
Mark knew his stuff. Best blacksmith he'd ever met. Some said he'd pulled stars from the sky to light his forge. That was about as true Al being able to raise the dead.
She was good, but she wasn't that good.
Mark would still be here otherwise.
He tried to think of the last time they were all together. Must've been at the castle. All standing 'round a bed. Bloody sheets. Some of them skriked.
That was just before -
He couldn't start thinking about that now.
Better to think of Mark in his prime, swinging Bloodgetter with two hands, carving through Fairford men like they weren't even there.
To a simple kid, it had looked like a good job. Something to aspire to.
He wondered if he would have felt the same if he had known where Mark would end up.
Where *he* would end up.
He kicked on through the greenblades.
He marvelled at the knot of Stickleshrubs that had sprung up like a wall around the garden. Al must've decided she

didn't want any prying eyes on her crops when she went underground. She must've sprinkled the Forspring tonic all around and let the shrubs grow wild.

He remembered using the tonic to bring the bristling bremelbushes out of the flowerbeds in the castle gardens. Bonwright the Gardener would chase him with a rake, but it was always worth it to get the team laughing. Saro and Blenheim and Al and Mark. Sometimes even King Duncan and Queen Amanda. And the Wolf, waiting in the shadows.

And Leila, of course.

But how could he drift away into memory when there was wort to be picked? He would not rest until all the wort in the world was his!

Come to me, wort, that you may meet your destiny in the faraway land of stew! Your sacrifice will not go unsung in the annals of kitchen eardlore!

Grasping in the dirt, he wondered if it was wise to leave Al and Katherine alone. Al was sharp as a gad, but she wouldn't know how much had been kept from Katherine. And who would? Why would anybody keep such things from a capable young woman?

Don't tell her.

So many people had said that about Katherine.

Don't mention it.

Until no one could bring themselves to do so.

They never spoke of -

What was that?

Could he hear a bell ringing?

He instinctively reached for Punch, but he'd left his rucksack back under the trapdoor.

Knackers.

It was clear as, well, a bell now. Someone was ringing the alarm in Crossford, way down at the foot of the hill.

"Finders!" he heard the distant cry. "The Finders are coming!"

He dropped his wort and bolted. Chancy happenstance for the wort.

He barrelled past the scarecrows, who watched him go, back through the trees toward the ruined house.

The bell rang and he ran faster.

Finders.

They were here already.

It was quicker than he expected.

He ran.

Had he got too sloppy in his old age?

He wasn't old. He was in his twenty-second year. Or thereabouts.

He ran.

Maybe he was past his prime.

They were already here.

He saw them.

He hated Finders. All grabbing fingers and slobber and tubes and long stretchy arms and cold grey skin and -

Two of them were running toward the ruins from the opposite side. He was going to meet them smack in the middle of the rubble that was once Althea and Mark's house.

He thought he could have two.

More were coming - he could hear them - so he'd have to be quick.

Still running flat out, his eyes darted for a weapon.

He scooped up a rock as he legged it into the ruin.

The Finders split up, one coming straight at him down what was once the hallway, the other disappearing off to his left.

One at a time was even easier.

The Finder ahead of him leapt forward, shrieking -

Gangly arms outstretched like a needy child -

He bricked it in the side of the head with his rock and it dropped.

"Find that," he spat.

He dived into the kitchen and tried the trap. It was locked.

"Open the door!" he shouted.

Thin, strong fingers grabbed his neck -

The second Finder was climbing through the kitchen window, just as he had earlier.

It had him.

It squeezed and pulled and he knew its tongue would be out soon.

The kiss of a finder is a blinder.

It dragged him half out of the window, hooting and squealing in glee.

It *thought* it had him.

He brought his rock up into its jaw, shattering bone and severing its lolling tubular tongue -

The hoots of triumph became a howl of agony and the Finder fell back through the window.

He sprawled on the floor and saw the trapdoor was open and Al and Katherine were reaching for him -

Behind them, three more finders were scuttling over the broken walls -

He threw himself forward and the trap snapped shut behind him.

The Princess

Monsters.
There were monsters now.
She had heard the bell ringing, very faintly, and they had both crept up the stairs to press their ears against the trap.
When they heard the Fool shout, Althea pulled the bolt, and they lifted the door open.
There was something attacking the Fool.
A monster.
Human in shape but impossibly thin, distorted and stretched, its mottled grey skin translucent and pulsating. Its spidery fingers scrabbled at the Fool's throat and its huge, white eyes bulged out of its face. Its drooling mouth fell open and what looked like two fat worms unfurled from within.
That was when the Fool smashed it in the face with a rock.
It fell away and he rolled into the trapdoor with them.
Althea locked the door again.
Monsters.
"How strong is that bolt?" asked the Fool, lying on the steps.
His answer came as the hatch above was wrenched upward, splintering the bolt. All three of them grabbed the hatch handle, using all their weight to hold it down.
"Not strong enough," said Althea.
The trapdoor lurched upward again.
She could hear them.
So many of them now.
Monsters.
She saw long fingers squeezing under the edges of the trap.
"There's another way out," said the Witch.
"Where?"
They were shouting.
The monsters where screaming.

Everything was so loud.

There couldn't be monsters.

"Behind the cages on the right wall. A bolt hole, it leads out at the bottom of the hill."

There were grey fingers and slimy tubes reaching for them as the hatch lifted another inch.

She didn't believe the tales.

"When were you going to tell us about that?"

"When it became relevant!"

"Well, how in the four corners do we get to it?"

They were getting louder. How many of them were there?

"I'll hold the door."

"No, she needs you. Get her home."

"Al, you can't hold it!"

"I can for a minute. When you get into the tunnel, you'll know what to do."

This bellowed conversation took place less than a foot from her head, but she barely registered it over the shrieks of the things above them. She wondered if she was dreaming.

Yes, this was all a dream and she would soon wake up in her bed in Elderhaime and tell her Mummy and Daddy about the funny dream she had. A dream of chaos and death and terror.

The Fool was dragging her down the stairs while Althea clung on to the trapdoor.

Wait.

That woman had been nice to her.

"We can't leave her!" Katherine shouted.

"Run!" cried Althea and she was gone.

She vanished. She and the trapdoor were yanked up into the daylight.

The Fool had heaved the stack of cages to one side.

There was darkness beyond.

A tunnel.

She looked back towards the light. She saw the creatures climbing down out of the sunshine. Impossibly long limbs reaching across the stairs.

The Fool grabbed up his rucksack, pushed her into the darkness and ran after her.

She ran, stumbling through blackness.

"Where is it?" she heard the Fool say behind her. "Where is it?"

She could hear the creatures shrieking and screaming down the tunnel at them. They would be on them soon.

"There!" she heard the Fool shout at the dark.

There was a sharp sound. A spark.

The tunnel lit up with incandescent flame running along the ground, back the way they came.

"Run, Princess!" the Fool's hand was in hers, pulling her away, but she wanted to see.

For an instant she saw the beasts illuminated like some unman boga from her childhood nightmares, long shadows cast on the walls and ceiling, arms and fingers reaching to take her away -

And then the roof caved in.

The light behind them roared, dazzling her for an instant before it was extinguished and the horrible, groping things were buried under rock and soil.

Monsters and magic.

What else were the tales right about?

She ran.

They ran through the darkness in search of light.

The Fool

'Course there was a bolthole.

Witches always needed an escape plan. You never knew when some pious goon was going to come and try to use your house as kindling.

The blasalt trick was something the Shadows would do in the good old days. Make sure no one can follow you down your escape route. A lump of flint at the end of a trail of blasalt leading to a keg of the same.

Mark always said that a well placed barrel of fire-powder could bring a fortress down, and Al had placed hers well.

Any finders in the tunnel were mushed under a mountain of stone and earth, and the rest were stuck on the other side of said mountain.

The tunnel spat them out at the foot of the hill, slightly east of Crossford.

He pulled Katherine down behind a gorse bush while they caught their breath.

"What were those things?" she gasped finally.

"Finders," he said. "Fell Baelic-spawn. The Brigands use them to hunt."

"They can't be," she said. "The Finders aren't real. Baelic the Bloody isn't real. It's all just stories."

He looked at her. "Then we've got nothing to worry about then. I'll just go and tell Althea we blew her house up for nowt. She will be relieved."

"The roof fell down! There was fire and light and the roof fell down! How?"

"Magic."

"There's no such thing as magic!"

"Truth to every tale, Princess," he said. "Tricks of the trade."

Why keep lying? Did he enjoy having secrets from her? Did he want her to see him as some mysterious hero wizard?

If that was the case, he'd have to get a new hat.

He just didn't have time to explain every little thing to her. That was it, surely?

Katherine looked like somebody had just asked her a really hard sum. She was trying to add all this up and not getting an answer she was happy with.

He hoped he hadn't broken her.

And they'd left Al.

"There was a lot of them, at least." He patted cave dust off his tunic. "That's good."

"Good?" Katherine looked like she wanted to go back to bed.

"They're much more dangerous on their own," he said. "They take out your eyes and leave you crawling."

She'd heard the tales, but he thought them worth another telling.

He smiled at the disgust on her face.

Was it wrong to find amusement in horror?

He thought it probably was.

He was pretty wrong.

He heard the rumbling then.

The sound of enormous cart wheels rolling through the mud and stone of the farway.

The Keepers.

He again pulled Katherine low to the ground, and peered through the underside of the bush.

There, about forty feet down the slope below them, was the Crossford road. And, heaving into view, was a Keeper dragging a cagecart, followed by about twenty Finders.

His blood boiled.

He gritted his teeth.

Al was in the cage.

She was alive, and apparently unhurt. She didn't look her cheeriest, but she was still wheezing which was something.

The Keeper slouched and stomped its way along the farway as the Finders screeched and squabbled in its wake.

Katherine's mouth was agape. "Hiders and Seekers, Finders and Keepers…" She seemed to wake up a little. "I thought they wanted us?"

"She must smell of us. They have very sensitive nebs."

She looked suddenly terrified.

"Don't worry," he said. "We're upwind." Just to be sure, he licked a finger on his un-gloved hand and raised it in the breeze.

He was right.

The cart rumbled on.

He watched Katherine watching the boga parading below them. The Finders thin and hunched, chattering and skittering like wolf-spiders, the Keepers with their huge, lolling heads and slumped shoulders. Like a baby as tall as a man and half as tall again. Black, dead eyes. Docile as cattle, though he knew they had fierce tempers when you wound them up.

They were an odd bunch and no mistake.

The Keeper trundled its cart along the way, looking for all the world like a giant gardener pulling a barrow out to field.

They stayed hidden until the Finders had been out of sight for a while. No sense in jumping up to give chase only to step on their heels.

Even after the beasts were gone, Katherine stared, as if she could see through the trees to the things that would be haunting her dreams for the foreseeable towardness. He'd seen that look before. She'd had a glimpse of something. The kind of thing that changed a person. Seeing your Dad murdered by another man is one thing, seeing your first boga is something else entirely. Men are supposed to kill. Monsters aren't supposed to exist.

He tried to remember the first time he saw some such. Maybe a huge brimdraca being hauled ashore from one of the ships at Underton harbour. He remembered the sun on blue scales and white teeth. And then the red when they cut it open. He wondered if it was really that big, or had he just been so small?

But he didn't have time for that. His brain was already turning over. Distances, times, plots and plans. He'd just walked back into an old friend's life and she'd already been taken by the Finders. Misery and pain seemed to follow him around.

He tried not to think of the word "curse".

He pulled himself to his feet, Punch at his side.

It had been a rough couple of days, but it was about to get rougher.

The Princess

They were all dead.

She stood at the foot of the steps and looked at the wrecked cages. Feathers and dust hung in the air.

They had come back to the ruined house for supplies. The Fool had assured her it was safe.

She had climbed down the stone steps into Althea's hiding place. Her home.

And everything was dead.

Those things.

Monsters.

Finders.

They had crawled out of a storybook and taken that poor Witch away and killed all the animals.

There were parts of Althea's wards strewn all over. The unman bastards. They'd even half-eaten one of their own. One of the ones the Fool had killed.

She saw what was once the little brockling. The tiny life she had held in her hand, so fragile and sweet. It looked like he'd been chewed up and spat out.

She wanted to weep.

She wanted to weep for all the needless death.

She wanted to weep with hate and rage and sorrow and why did he have to die?

Why did he have to die?

Why did I have to get him killed?

The tears loitered behind her eyes, never breaking forth.

She felt empty.

The Fool stepped down into the wrecked room.

"They killed them all," she said.

"They were only collecting people."

"They all died because of us. Because of me."

"They're only animals, Princess."

She looked at him.

It wasn't just the animals.

"And what does that make us? I have brought death in my wake, Fool. What does that make me?"

He didn't answer.

She knew. "It makes me a monster."

"The ones who did those things are monsters."

She looked around at the wreckage. A thought escaped her lips, unbidden: "Why do they hate me so much?"

"Because you're the Queen."

"That doesn't mean anything."

"It does if enough people believe it does."

She felt his gloved hand on her shoulder. "We should get a shimmy on."

"Where will they take her?"

He was tightening straps on his bag, now full of spoils from Althea's garden. "The Brigands must have a camp nearby. The Keepers'll take her there."

Katherine waited for him to elaborate. He didn't.

"And then what?"

He looked away, squinting in the light from the broken hatch. "Then they'll torture her to find out where we are."

Katherine thought about that. "Then… We should probably get moving."

The Fool looked at her like he didn't take her meaning.

"I have to get home," she said.

Now he just looked disappointed. "Althea just sacrificed herself for us."

"For me. So I could escape. We can go home and amass an army and destroy the Brigands and… those things once and for all. What Althea did is pointless if we just go and get caught anyway!"

"We won't get caught."

This wasn't going right. He was supposed to do as he was told.

"I can't take you home yet."

He was saying no to her. A peasant was defying her. Was she offended by a lowborn's insolence or upset because her friend was angry with her?

No, they weren't friends. He was a clown. A servant. How could they be friends?

"Fool! I order you - "

"I'm sorry, Kathy."

She was shocked into silence. He had never presumed such familiarity before. His eyes seemed to plead.

"I'm going after Al," he said. "You must decide where your allegiances lie."

He turned and walked up the steps into the light.

How dare he? How dare he disobey her? And no man but her Father had ever called her Kathy! Who was this Jester to behave in such a manner?

She realised she was alone.

In a ruined house.

In the woods.

Surrounded by death.

She ran after him.

Hitching up alongside him, she tried a different tack. "You would let me wander the woods alone?"

He didn't even look at her. Just kept stomping on through the mud.

"Just promise me you'll do as I say," he said.

Of all the nerve! "A Princess is to take orders from a Fool, is she?"

He smiled, as if sharing a joke with himself. "You're not a Princess, and I'm no fool."

Part Three:

The Hope and the Fury.

The Many Births of Baelic the Bloody

Extract from
"Myths and Legends of Old Firgenland"
by Lesung Cifesdaughter.

Once, many years ago, there was a wicked King who lived in the Magenhold and ruled over all the lands. He wanted nothing more than a son to continue his line, but his many wives only gave him daughters.

Finally, the wicked King went to the shrine of Ryneweard himself and pledged his soul to the darkness in exchange for the gift of a son.

The next child given unto him was indeed a son, but the darkness is not to be trusted and the child was born horribly deformed. A loathsome bundle of warts and muscle with red eyes and sharp, black teeth.

The Queen died of terrible injuries in childbirth, and the King took it upon himself to raise the horrific child alone.

The boy was named Baelic and the King presumed to treat him as any other child, though his many daughters were terrified of their brother and would not play with him lest he bit or scratched them.

The boy grew at an alarming rate, and was soon taller than even his eldest sister, Ferluf, though she was twelve years his senior.

In the first moon of Baelic's sixth summer, the King was woken by cries in the night. He ran to the nursery and saw that three of his youngest daughters lay dead. Their blood was on the walls and floor, and Baelic was performing an unspeakable act on poor Ferluf.

The King and his guards managed drag Baelic away and lock him in the Magenhold dungeon, for the King could not bring himself to slaughter his only son, no matter how monstrous.

Following the attack, Ferluf was with child. The babe came to fruit after less than two moons, and Ferluf did not survive the birth.

The King saw that this new child was as Baelic, monstrous and terrible, and put a knife through its face on the birth bed.

He still could not bring himself to do the same for his only son, however, and Baelic the Bloody lived on in the dungeon, his unearthly howls echoing up from the depths of the castle.

After a time, the King took to visiting his son. The King would stare through the bars of Baelic's cell, wondering at this eight-year old who stood taller and stronger than his best knight.

Some say in this time that Baelic began to talk to the King, though he had never spoken before. Some say the King arrived at his grim decision alone, but whatever the cause, the King began bringing things for Baelic. It started with animals: dogs, goats, sheep, cattle. The king brought them to his son one at a time and left them for nature to take its course.

Most of them were eaten, but some of them gave birth to unspeakable things, abhorrences that should never have been, creatures that the human mind would quail even to consider.

And that was before he started bringing him people.

The King would bring Handmaidens and vagrants and whores and criminals, and leave them in the care of his son.

He had his masons knock the dungeon walls through, so Baelic had the run of every cell. A fate worse than death it was to be sent to the dungeon in those dark days, for in that black labyrinth of cells, Baelic or one of his terrible offspring would eventually find you.

It was here that all the unman horrors of the world were born. Brittle the Banwarch, the Skriking Angshrikes, the Finders and the Keepers, all the wyrms, goblins, draca, boga and everything that slithers, creeps and crawls with evil in its heart slipped out of that dungeon on one fateful day.

The King had grown old and lost his mind to madness and, one day, he simply walked down to the dungeon and went in alone.

Some time later, a travelling merchant arrived at the Magenhold to find it in ruin and all its people slaughtered. Searching the ruins, the merchant found only two survivors. A young couple who had hidden when the monsters emerged, and survived once they'd left by eating the remains of their fellows. The hair on both their heads had turned white, and they would not speak of what they had seen or heard. When asked, they would cry out and fall to the floor as if in pain and terror, shrieking "The Prince is abroad!" over and over.

When the merchant returned with soldiers from Elderhaime, they found the dungeon door hanging off its hinges, the oak shredded as if by giant claws. The dungeon was empty, save for bones and darkness.

So, next time your Mother says to be home before dark, for the Prince is abroad, you know exactly what she means.

And the Prince is not alone.

The King

A man lay dying in the courtyard.

King Warwick raced down the marble steps to where the wounded knight lay, the Golden Crown of Elderhaime emblazoned on his tunic now soaked red.

"Have you sent for the healer?" the King asked.

The servant nodded. "On his way, M'lord."

Warwick knelt next to the Knight. His breath was short, bubbling from inside him.

"'Tis an ill wind blew him here, Your Majesty," said the servant. "He's not long for this world."

Warwick looked into the Knight's eyes, trying to hold him on this plane. "What happened, Sir Knight? You rode from Elderhaime?"

The Knight saw him for the first time. He tried to speak, but his breath was blood. There were four crossbow bolts in him.

"We think his horse carried him here unbidden," the servant ventured.

"What of the King? The Princess?" Warwick wanted to shake answers out of the dying man.

"Brigands... King Duncan is slain..." The Knight seemed to be drifting further and further away. "An age of chaos..."

"What of the Princess, good sir?" Warwick watched his eyes. Dark, brown eyes, seeming to grow darker. "The Princess, does she live?"

"I know not." His voice little more than a whisper now. "She was alone. Fool."

The Knight was gone with a cough.

Warwick thought it slightly rude to ride all this way only to insult your host with your dying breath, but perhaps that was not the Knight's intent.

Elderhaime scum.

He gently lowered the Knight's head to the ground. "Rest easy, my brother. Your bravery will not soon be forgotten."

He's the enemy.

No. He was a guard of King Duncan, and with his dying breath he had summoned help for Princess Katherine. This man was a hero.

A hero of Elderhaime is a villain of Fairford.

Shut up.

So, his Bride-to-be was alone? In the Holtlands? Hounded by Brigands? It was enough to make the blood boil.

"I have had my fill of these lawless knaves," he said.

The castle Healer approached.

"A little late for physic I think," said Warwick.

"Sorry, Sire."

"Bury this man with honours and let his name be sung with glory henceforth!" Warwick was using his King voice. It echoed off the stone walls of the courtyard. "Bring me my horse and armour, the hunt is on!"

The Healer raised a hand. "Er, sir? We don't know his name."

"Ah." Warwick looked at the dead, brave knight. "He shall, henceforth, be known as the Noble Nameless Knight. Make sure someone writes a song."

It seemed only fair that a man who brought such news should be remembered as well as possible.

Warwick's horse and armour were brought forth. Ferfost was the fastest stallion in the Fairford stables, black as the night and quick and fierce as the wind. Warwick had known him from birth, and they had rode together through mistide and good.

His armour was light, suitable for the ride ahead. As soon as his squire had tied the last clasp, Warwick hoisted himself into the saddle.

"Stay this madness!" came a cry from the staircase.

Felix was hurrying down the stairs to the courtyard.

He's a weakling. A coward.

"Madness, Felix?" Warwick reigned his horse. "King Duncan lies murdered and the Princess is lost to the mercy of scoundrels and the elements. Would you have me leave her to this?"

Felix walked towards him, arms open, imploring. "Nay, my King, but I would not have you cast yourself into the pit along with her."

Warwick looked down on his younger brother, so like their Father. He wondered for the tiniest fraction of a moment how Felix would cope should he not return.

That weakling will be the end of Fairford.

Then he remembered how cross he was.

"We have cowered before the men of the woods for long enough," he cried. "I will run no further!"

"At least take a battalion with you, or a squad of the guard!"

"I hunt better alone."

King Warwick of Fairford spurred his horse through the castle gates, leaving his brother standing in the dust.

Extract from Lord Felix Tyrantson's Diary:
Eight Years of Age

Second Stilnesday, Third Moon of Summer, 204
Today Dad came back. He was gone a very long time. He has been fighting the bad people from Elderhaime. He brought me a new sword and one for Warwick. Mine is called Trolltooth and has teeth from a Troll on the handle. Dad killed the troll himself. My sword is better than Warwick's one because his doesn't have troll teeth. Dad brought a new chambermaid home with him. He said she has been looking after him while he was away. She is nice. Her name is Sally. Dad is very tired and Sally helped him go to bed. Mum said she was happy to see him. She was crying and sometimes people cry because they are happy.

Third Sunday, Third Moon of Summer, 204
Today I played in the gardens with Warwick. He says I'm getting good at swords. He said he wished Dad hadn't come back. I think he was just mad because Trolltooth is better than his sword.

Third Moonday, Third Moon of Summer, 204
Dad didn't come to dinner tonight. Mum said he must've been ill because Sally was looking after him in his chamber. I heard Warwick shouting after I'd been sent to bed. I think he was angry at Dad. It's not Dad's fault he's ill.

First Ormennday, First Moon of Autumn, 204
There are lots of new servants now. There is Phillip and Gunnar and Edric and Waller. They are all nice and play swords with me sometimes. Mum says they take good care of her. Dad got mad about it and said she didn't need that many servants and she said she wasn't getting enough service before

and Dad hit her. I think he was mad because Sally works hard and Mum was saying she doesn't work hard. Warwick told me not to get too attached to the new servants, but I think they're doing a good job.

Second Moonday, First Moon of Autumn, 204
The servants are all dead. Sally drowned while she was pouring a bath for Dad, and the next day Phillip and Gunnar and Edric and Waller were all hanging from the walls. That's what happens to traitors and spies from Elderhaime, so Dad must have found out that they were doing bad things. I liked them. Especially Edric. But they must've been bad. We buried Sally and Dad was very angry. Mum didn't come to the funeral but I went to her chamber after and she was crying so I think she was just too sad to go. We will have to get all new servants now.

Fourth Ormennday, First Moon of Autumn, 204
My Mummy died. She fell out of the window in the tower. She was lying in the courtyard all in blood. I will miss her. Dad says that she drank too much wine and tripped up. I hope Belinda keeps her company.

The Princess

It would not come off.

She grabbed handfuls of bracken and tried to wipe herself clean, to no avail. She insisted that they try to find a stream to at least wash her hair, but the Fool kept walking.

So she followed. Through mud. Through leaves and bremels.

Still covered in slutch.

"The worst part" she said, "is I'm getting used to the smell."

The Fool turned to her for the first time in what seemed like hours. A familiar flippancy returned to his voice. "Keeps predators away. Or hides you from your prey."

"What, smelling of shite?"

The Fool raised an eyebrow. "That's no way for a Queen to talk in polite company."

"You're hardly polite. Since when do you refer to me as "Kathy"?"

"I always used to call you that, don't you remember?"

Did she recall? Perhaps there had been a time when it was acceptable for a courtier to call her by a pet name, but "Kathy" was a girl's name. Not a name for a woman. Or a Queen.

"Anyway," the Fool continued, "that's why dogs roll in filth and dead things. Anything that catches your scent thinks you're dead."

"Or made of shite."

He pointed at her, as if imparting some mystical wisdom. "Nobody expects an attack from summat that's already dead."

She thought for a second. "Or made of shite."

The Fool even managed a little smirk at this. She enjoyed a tiny moment of triumph.

She could talk exactly as she wanted.

This was all, of course, a pleasant distraction from the fact that they were walking determinedly into the lion's den. Was he distracting her? Again it was as if nothing else mattered while they bickered. As long as they could maintain their bungling, it was as if everything was normal.

As if they weren't following cart tracks to what the Fool estimated to be a brigand camp of two-hundred spears at least, into which they were to somehow mount an incursion in order to rescue a mysterious witch-woman she didn't even know.

Which begged a question.

"Fool…" She thought she sounded about to ask him for a song or a puppet show. "How do you know the witch?"

"Althea."

"Althea." Was the name familiar? It didn't feel it. "She said she worked at the castle, but I don't remember her."

"It was a while back." The Fool had scrunched his face up and hunched his shoulders again. He wasn't playing anymore. "I used to work with her husband."

Interesting. "Was he a fool too?" He shook his head. "How long have you been a fool?"

"All my life."

Katherine groaned. "You know what I mean. What were you before you were a fool?"

"Clever."

He was being "funny". But there was a question he surely could not dodge. A question she was almost ashamed she had never thought to ask. There must have been a time, surely, in their years together when she saw him as something more than his title? She couldn't think of one, so she had to ask.

"What's your name, Fool?"

She didn't really expect him to answer, and he didn't.

She also didn't expect to walk into the back of him as he stopped dead, though.

But she did.

She peered over the Fool's shoulder, her question forgotten as the Brigand camp stretched out before them.

The Fool indicated that they should crouch down into the bracken. From amongst the leaves she could see rows of tents filling the clearing, horses corralled at troughs, brigands milling hither and thither, blacksmiths turning blades at makeshift forges...

It was an army.

There were certainly more than two hundred.

The Monster

Every time Bowman touched his skin he wanted to poke his stupid eyes out.

Skin.

Not that he had any left.

His head was like a skinned potato. Raw and unappealing. Un-a-peel-ing. He would smile if it didn't hurt so much.

Bowman sloshed the ointment on as best he could, but he was no physician. He was, however, the only person Mister Fury could trust. He had to kill his physician because he suspected he was trying to murder him with a rare strain of bee.

He had many enemies. Many he didn't even know about. They were all waiting. Biding their time for that one moment of weakness. And he was never more vulnerable than when having his bandages changed.

How long had it been now? Months? Years?

That idiot.

He turned me into a monster.

The bandages had to be changed pretty regularly, as his head was essentially an open sore. It was strange how he remembered the agony of the burning, but the real pain came later, waking up alone, soaked in blood and water and vomiting in unconscionable, wracking despair.

He did it. That idiot. He burned me.

Bowman began easing the bandages back around Fury's pustule of a head.

If nothing else, this was frankly an inconvenience. There were plenty of matters which demanded his attention, and yet he had to take time out of every day to redress his wounds. It was a pain in the arse.

And the head.

You had to laugh.

Not actually laugh, as it hurt too much. But, still.

I bet he's laughing.

But not for long.

Bowman jabbed him with the pin trying to fasten the end and Fury nearly stabbed him to death with it. He was very proud of maintaining civility, though.

"Thank you, Bowman," he said, when he'd calmed down and stopped swearing. "You may send her in."

He'd been looking forward to this.

He'd put fresh bandages on, specially.

He'd arrived at the camp to the news that the Finders and Keepers had returned with an unexpected prize. Someone he thought he had already killed.

King Duncan the Dead's crown lay on the table before him, and behind it a tall mirror. He faced away from the entrance to the tent, so as to see her in the mirror when she was brought in. He enjoyed the notion that he didn't even need to turn to see her, she was that insignificant.

Althea was pushed in to the tent by Bowman and another of the men.

"Take the Witch's shawl and leave us," he commanded.

Bowman and the other man took Althea's shroud, revealing her slender frame outlined in an elegant black robe.

She had aged well. He let his eyes appraise her in the mirror.

She looked pleasingly bewildered. She wasn't crying or anything, which was a disappointment, but there was time to remedy that.

"Tis long since we met, Lady Althea. I thought you were dead."

She was looking at him. She would remember. Oh, how she would remember.

"I will not be offended if it escapes your recollection." He idly picked up Duncan's crown. This was going exactly as planned. "I am... changed somewhat now."

Althea squinted at him. He enjoyed her considering him. How terrifying and mysterious a form he must appear to her feminine eyes.

"You knew me by a different name, from a better time," he continued, placing Duncan's crown on his bandaged head. It hurt, but it was worth it for the look she gave him. "A time when the King of Fairford was not some romantic whiffet. I served the so-called Tyrant with every breath in my body, striking fear into the hearts of--

She laughed at him.

She pointed and laughed.

"Smeggy Ken, is that you?" Her eyes where wide, but it wasn't fear.

It all came back then, the insults, the humiliation. He wasn't that man any more. He leapt to his feet, forgetting all about the mirror.

"Nobody calls me that!" He strode towards her. "The days when your band of bunglers would mock my personal hygiene are long past, Witch! I am Mister Fury now!"

He lashed her face with the back of his hand and she fell. She needed to learn some respect.

When she looked up at him, he saw only hate.

"You were not so insolent when I burned down your house." There was the pain he sought. He could see her mind going back, back to those final moments. "Or when I left your husband crawling in the dirt with my blade in his belly."

She leapt at him. She was quick, but he was expecting it. He held her wrists and pushed her backwards with his bodyweight until he was pressing her down on the table.

This was more like it, the beautiful, noble Althea, squirming beneath him, on the verge of tears. He could get used to this.

"I can send you to him now, if you desire. Finish the job left undone by fire." She still struggled. He moved his face closer to hers. So close. "Or you can tell me where the Princess Harpy and that accursed idiot are hiding…"

A tiny thought formed. He wondered if a woman like Althea could ever grow to love a man like him. I mean, they got off on the wrong foot when he killed her husband, certainly, and now he was probably going to force himself on her, but he was pretty sure he could make her like it and women are nothing if not fickle.

"You are only delaying the inevitable," he hissed in her ear. "The Princess will die. And that insufferable Fool will pay for the innumerable times he has wronged me, humiliated me, foiled me -"

"Called you Smeggy Ken..."

She was laughing again. Laughing in his face.

Well, if that was her attitude.

He slammed her into the table again and put his hands around her throat. Still she laughed.

"You share his sense of humour, you shall also share his fate!" He could feel his skin peeling as he made his angry face under the bandages. What was the point when no one could see it anyway?

Oh, what was the point at all?

He banged Althea's head against the table and shouted "Guards!".

He threw her at Bowman's feet as they entered. She gasped for breath in between laughing.

People always laughed at him. They always had.

He'd show them.

"Give her to Rudesby." She wouldn't laugh at Rudesby. "Find out what she knows about the Princess and the Fool's whereabouts. Then kill her. Slowly. I'd do it myself if I wasn't so damned busy."

And she didn't keep laughing at me.

As they dragged Althea from the tent, she called out "Smeggy!" and dissolved into giggles again, her laughter disappearing into his army base. Reaching the ears of his soldiers. Echoing amongst his tents. Undermining everything he'd achieved.

None of this matters if they still laugh at me.

He heard Althea calling his old name as they took her away. How long before his men were whispering it behind his back, giggling to themselves as he passed? He thought he may have to kill them all before this was over.

It was then he realised he had flipped the table over and punched the mirror until his hand bled.

The Fool

There was a Fool who climbed a tree,
Just to see what he could see,
He made up rhymes,
To pass the time,
And -
There she was.
Two brigands were dragging Althea from one tent to another. She seemed to be laughing.
He was supposed to be the one who never took anything seriously.
This wasn't going to be easy.
They took her into a tent almost in the centre of the clearing, meaning he would have to get through half the camp to reach her and half the camp to escape.
Odds of about six-hundred to one against?
I've had worse.
Had he though?
Really?
He edged along the tree branch for a better look.
Any way you sliced it, this was a lot of spillends with swords. He reckoned only a fraction of them would be any use with a weapon, mostly just angry lost souls recruited from pubs and gutters or snatched on raids and given a green and brown tunic, but they still outnumbered him to a level to render their skill irrelevant. He couldn't fight every member of an army.
No, it was time for some good old fashioned sneaking. Wait until dark and then slip amongst them like a shadow.
Or a thief.
He almost smiled. In spite of the danger, one of his oldest friends a captive and an army between her and freedom, the Fool felt somehow happier than he had in a long time. Hiding up a tree, plotting a daring rescue, this felt like home.

If only the rest of his friends were there.

But they were gone.

He shook that memory from his head. Daydreaming would get him killed.

Maybe that was all he deserved?

Dismissing memories seemed to be second nature these days. He wondered if there was anything important he wasn't letting himself think about. Who knows what he might discover about himself if he just allowed his past to raise its head more than an inch before bashing it back down?

Anyway.

He swung down from the tree, straight into a gang of four Brigands.

They must've been patrolling right under him.

They were all armed.

A moment passed as he and they eyed each other.

They all had blades drawn, and Punch was still in the pack on his back.

The moment dragged just long enough to deduce that these were not the elite squad.

"'Ere!" said one, finally. "Where did you spring from?" He pointed his blade at the Fool.

"You could say I'm out of my tree." He smiled.

"What?"

"He's a Jester! It must be him the boss is after. A Jester and a Princess, right?"

This one must be hogging the intellect of the group.

"I am a Jester," he nodded. "But do you see a Princess?"

He couldn't believe they all started looking around, as if they'd simply missed her.

He hoped she'd stayed hidden.

"Where's the Princess, Jester?" The blade-pointer again.

He could see how this was going to turn out. "Look, chaps..." he moved forward slowly, arms and hands open, no threats. "I am a mere Fool, travelling the lands, plying my trade..."

"Prove it." That intellect. "Fool, are you? Then let us see. This is our court."

This was going to be easier than he thought. "I'm sorry?"

"Play for us, Fool."

It had been a long time since he had performed at swordgad. He gave them a big, resigned sigh. "If I must."

He took another step forward. They almost surrounded him now. Blades poised, mistrust in their eyes. He almost felt sorry for them.

"Right!" He cracked his knuckles. Two of his audience winced at the sound. "First of all, I want you all to meet a friend of mine: Mister Punch!"

He yanked the puppet out of his rucksack and held him aloft. The brigands eyed him warily.

"Say: 'Hello Mister Punch'." He was performing to the kids of the court now. Miniature noblefolk whose parents were off kissing the King's ring or philandering with chambermaids. This particular performance would have a unique punchline, however.

The Brigands looked at each other.

He was used to having to warm up a crowd. "C'mon, we haven't got all day!"

They chorused "Hello, Mister Punch" in awkward unison. Punchy could take it from here.

The puppet spoke. "Hail, ye shower of cutpurses!"

"Punchy!" The Fool gave him a warning look. He could tell the puppet wanted to go with some more confrontational material than they would perform for the weans. He wasn't sure it was wise, but comedy, like drama derives often from friction and discord.

The puppet ignored him. "I've never seen a more worthless scattering of venomous dung-beetles in all my life!"

The Fool knew it was time to start directing attention, so held Punch up to the face of the biggest member of the audience.

Punch was just getting started. "Take this carking beast of burden, for instance…"

The big brigand smiled uncomfortably. His mates laughed a little.

"Folk would pay for the privilege of witnessing such a travesty of nature!" The Fool waved Punch in front of the big brigand's face as the puppet continued his childish teasing. "Quick, put him in a cage and we'll make a fortune! People will gather round and clap their hands… over their eyes!"

The brigands were laughing. Cruelty amused them.

The Fool jumped back in. "That's it, chaps, he who laughs last thinks slowest. Now, I think Punchy has a few questions for you good fellows…"

He was now dead central, between all four of them.

He let Punch entertain, while he planned.

"Where can you find a dog with no legs?"

The big one would have to go down first, as he posed the greatest physical threat.

"Right where you left him!"

Probably a swift boot to the conkers followed by a bosh in the temple from Punch.

"What's brown and sticky?"

Next, it would be the brains. He would already be on the move, so maybe duck his blow or block with Punch.

One of the lesser brigands piped up. "Poo-poo?"

The Fool wondered if those would be the brigand's last words. And if they were fitting.

Punch corrected him "A stick. You need to get your mind out of the midden, sunshine."

A shot to the gut of the brains, double him over, take his blade and give him a knee to the bonce.

"What's white and creamy?"

They were getting into it now. Cruelty and crudity were their language.

"Cream!"

Once the brains was down and he had a sword as well as Punch, the remaining two should be pretty straight forward. The only concern was if they did the usual mid-level mercenary thing and just turned tail. He couldn't have them raising the alarm.

"What's big and roomy?"

He thought he would have to run at least one of them down.

The brigands chorused "A room!" They were suitably enthralled by the puppet's bungling.

"A BIG room, actually!"

He knew it was time, and Punch knew too.

"Now, let's talk a little bit about what you dangleberries have been up to today."

The brigands watched, expectant smiles all round. They weren't so far removed from the little noblekids.

"Your pets have caught a Witch, so you're gonna torture her until she tells you where the Boss and the Princess are, eh? Fool-proof plan, right?"

The brigands looked at each other. What did he just say?

The Fool couldn't fight every last member of the brigand army.

"But you see, you didn't take one little fact into account…" They looked from the puppet to him.

This lot would have to do for now.

Punch let him have the punchline.

"Nothing is Fool-proof," said the Fool.

The big brigand went down like a sack of spuds.

He heard the unmistakable crack of bone as Punch stoved his skull.

Brains was slower to react than the Fool had given him credit for, his weapon was barely raised before he had a fist in his gut.

The two lessers attacked at once, which was a pleasant surprise, but he knocked one blow aside with Punch and spun the other with Brains' sword, sending them bumbling into one another.

These two were just kids, really. Not much older than he had been when he first had a hildebill pressed into his hand.

They died together, pinned to the ground with their friend's blade.

He stood over four bodies. The thrill of combat fading to the familiar regret.

Who were these people he just ended? Who did they love? Who loved them? Who would lament them? He could never decide which was worse, to die alone and unmourned, or to leave the loved in pain.

He tried to convince himself he didn't enjoy what just happened. A voice from his past told him to take no pleasure in another's suffering. It wasn't honourable.

Was he honourable?

Was what he just did honourable?

Or was it just the latest chapter in his own, personal eardlore of lies and deceit and death?

"Tough crowd." Punch broke the silence.

He shushed the puppet.

"You always get maudlin after a killing," said the puppet.

The Fool pondered the fact that the person who knew him best in the world was a wooden head on a stick.

The Princess

She couldn't believe what she had just seen.

Or could she?

The past few days had been one unbelievable thing after another.

She wasn't used to it yet.

Once they had found the brigand camp they had retreated, following a little brook. The brook led them to a pool at the foot of a mossy rockface. The Fool had hurriedly supped a couple of handfuls of water and told her to stay put while he went to get the lay of the land.

Seemed he was determined to abandon her in this wilderness.

She did want to try to clean herself up, though. A mask of filth may be fine disguise for an animal, but she thought it might be nice to feel like a person again.

As soon as the Fool was gone, she had climbed out of her tattered garments and into the pool.

She soaked her dress, wrung it and lay it out on a rock to dry. It looked almost forlorn lying there, like the sloughed skin of some overdressed creature.

She wondered why Princesses didn't wear armour.

Because they're supposed to stay behind walls and moats and hide in towers, not wander the wilds dodging death and all his agents.

There was a time she would've believed the very title of Princess would be enough to protect her. No one would dare harm royalty, surely?

The world was full of surprises.

She undid the complicated weaving of her hair and let it down. Her girl had spent so long preparing it for the wedding. Little knots and plaits circled her head as if she were already crowned. It was a strange relief to destroy all that hard work and let her blonde locks fall free.

She washed her hair, combing filth out as best she could with her fingers. What she wouldn't give for her whale-bone comb and a bristlebrush.

The pool was deep enough to stand in with only her shoulders breaking the surface and she allowed herself to float there for a while, peering up at the blue sky through the leaves above.

She closed her eyes.

Before she was even asleep, she jerked up from a half-formed dream about bandaged hands reaching out of the darkness.

Probably not a good idea to be nodding off, anyway. Not with about five-hundred villains going about their business less than a mile away from her.

When she was dressed again - still damp, but rather damply clothed than naked to the elements and wandering eyes - she had wandered after the Fool.

He had said to stay put, but she had only done so in order to bathe. He couldn't tell her what to do. And she had a right to know what was going on.

Who in the four corners does he think he is?

She had followed the brook back through the woods in the direction of the brigand camp, thinking about the Fool. Who was he? Where had he come from? She had known him long but not, it seemed, really known him at all.

She remembered her Father introducing them, she thought. She must've been about twelve, the Fool fourteen, fifteen? Her Dad had seemed so sad, and the Fool cheered everyone up.

Thinking about it now, her Mum must not have been long gone. Her Dad gave her the Fool like a toy. A distraction to help her forget.

Had it worked?

She thought about her Dad. Dead in the mud.

When she heard voices through the trees, she dropped into the bracken and crawled forward, suddenly aware that she had no idea what to do if she was discovered.

It was the Fool.

He wasn't alone.

He was talking with some brigands.

He was laughing with some brigands.

She knew it. That bastard. His conspiracy revealed. He was a consort of the enemy.

Traitor.

She felt the tears behind her eyes again. Her Dad had trusted that man. Perhaps even loved him, and he had betrayed him.

She clenched her fists so hard her nails dug into her palms.

And still she didn't weep.

She couldn't quite hear what was being said, but it was almost like the Fool was performing one of his routines for the gang of outlaws.

That was strange, admittedly.

Maybe he was providing some entertainment while they plotted their next --

Oh, wait.

Nope, he'd just killed all four of them in a flurry of movement.

It can't have lasted more than a couple of seconds. The Fool stood over four dead people.

Her mind stumbled and her heart lurched. She turned and ran through the woods.

She couldn't believe what she had just seen.

Or could she?

She sat on the rock by the pool, absently combing her fingers through her hair.

Who was he?

A Fool. A Fool who conjured flying contraptions from dress clothes.

A Fool who could kill four men single-handed in the blink of an eye.

Six years she had known him. Six years he had bungled and played in the court. Six years the familiar jingle of his bells would echo through the halls of Elderhaime.

She'd never seen him kill anyone before.

She would've remembered.

"I'm climbing trees while you're doing your hair!"

He was back. Acting as if nothing had happened.

An act she thought they both could play.

"Some of us are not as accustomed to stench as you." She glared at him. "Did you have any trouble?"

"Trouble? No. No trouble."

He was an exceptional liar. There wasn't so much as a hint of murder about him. He may as well have just returned from the pantry.

"Did you see anything?" she said.

The Fool was kicking stones. Thinking. "They've got Al in a tent in the middle of the camp."

Katherine wrung her hair one last time. "So what's your great plan?"

"Haven't really got that far, yet." He was frowning into the distance, as if he could scowl his thoughts into cohesion.

"I thought you were good at improvising."

"Yeah, but improvisation without inspiration; that's how you wind up with a shoddy routine."

Katherine stood up to shake out her hair. "Well you'd better think of something." She flicked her hair off her shoulders and it cascaded down her back. She needed something to tie it up with. "I want to go home."

She just wasn't sure if she wanted him to take her home anymore.

She realised he wasn't talking.

She looked at him.

He was staring at her, as if he had never seen her before.

He took a slow step towards her.

The way he was looking at her. Had she left a button undone?

"What?" she checked herself. All sealed up.

He still stared.

He moved closer.

She felt strange. "What is it?"

He had never looked at her this way before. She felt naked under his gaze. His eyes scoured her features with an intensity that made her quail.

He was so close to her now.

This man just killed four people.

"Stop looking at me that way…" She had to look away from his eyes.

He was right there. Inches away.

His face looked down into hers.

He gently lifted her chin, drawing her eyes back to his.

"What…" Why couldn't she catch her breath?

The Fool slowly brushed a strand of hair from her face. He gently ran his hand through her locks.

She could only manage a whisper. "Fool…"

The Fool plucked a single hair from her head.

She yelped and stepped back.

Whatever spell she had been under was broken.

"You oaf! What did you do that for?"

He held the hair up between his thumb and fore-finger, scrutinising it as if it was the most important thing in the world.

"I'm gonna need more of these."

The King

He rode hard.

The Crossford road led over the Fairfold and through the Holtlands, then turned north at Crossford. There he would follow the route towards the Bergstall until the road rose upward to the Lip. Here, his way turned west into the Fothwood and on to the Elderfarway and the approach to Elderhaime.

This was the most direct route between Elderhaime and Fairford, so Duncan's procession must've been ambushed somewhere along it. He followed the road towards Elderhaime, hoping he would stumble on the scene of the battle.

He wondered if Felix was right. He moved quicker alone, but these vagabonds had already put one King to the blade. They would surely not balk at trying to lay him low also, should their paths cross.

He could not allow fear to govern him now. There was an innocent abroad in the wilderness, and it was his duty as her betrothed, nay as a man, to protect her.

He spurred his horse on through the mud and the trees.

This wasn't what he'd had in mind.

The wedding was supposed to be a beacon. A shining light of peace for everyone in the Siblands to crowd around and follow.

But he had drawn King Duncan out onto a lonely road and let him be killed like an animal.

It was his fault.

He had to save Princess Katherine.

He could feel his dream of peace slipping away. If she was dead, the war that had bubbled underground for so many years would finally spill out and engulf them all.

Or Elderhaime would be cowed and defeated once and for all.

This wasn't about politics anymore. A young girl was lost in the woods. She was probably scared and cold and alone.

That was all that mattered right now.

He had passed Crossford and rounded the Lip when he saw the first corpse. Brown cloak over green tunic. Brigand.

He spat.

There were more up ahead.

The trees reached out over the road, forming a long, green tunnel.

Banpickers leapt into the branches above as he approached. He was interrupting a fine meal, no doubt.

Some of the bodies were brigands, but they were mostly royal guard. Many were missing helmets and chainmail, lost to the scavengers.

The banpickers were not the only carrion birds that had been at work here.

Ferfost stirred, uneasy.

Warwick put a hand on the horse's mane and peered around into the darkness of the Fothwood.

They had what they wanted. Surely the brigands that survived were long gone?

He removed his helmet and tilted his head to the silence.

Nothing but the calls of the birds above him.

He could see carriages up ahead. Smashed and broken, wheels removed and any gilding cut away.

He kicked Ferfost forward.

The dead lay all around, abandoned where they fell.

The King was amongst them.

The Princess was not.

He reigned Ferfost in and dismounted, shin-deep into the stirred-up mud.

Duncan lay on his back. The pickers had taken his eyes.

King Warwick of Fairford wept then, to see so noble a man meet such an ignoble end.

King Duncan's crown was gone.

They took his crown.

You weep at your enemy's grave.

The voice was louder out here in the wild. Clearer. The voice was not his own, though it echoed in his head.

He pushed it from his mind and looked around. The banpickers had begun to settle on the bodies again.

He wished he hadn't ridden out alone now. All these people needed burying and he didn't have time.

Instead, he started dragging them all out of the road, covering them over with cloaks or branches as best he could. He waved the pickers away and they perched above again, glaring at him with their black eyes. They would return once he was gone, and the wolves would follow soon enough.

He gathered as many rocks as he could and piled them over King Duncan's body. It was the closest he could get to building a tomb.

He slammed the tip of his sword into the ground beside the makeshift cairn and knelt. He clasped the hilt to his forehead and swore a warrior's oath.

"Let the dead be my witness. I swear they shall be avenged, lest I join them in the next world."

He placed a hand on the cold stone.

"I will find her, my Leige."

The Fool

The Princess must be in position by now.
He notched an arrow.
From here he had a clear view of the row of Keepers' carts. The hulking great beasts were kipping in the moonlight, slumped against the Finders' cages. Each cage held at least one Finder.
They almost looked peaceful.
He took aim.
He thought about Katherine.
What kind of protection was this? Chucking her straight into the lion's den?
It was safer than being here. This entire camp was about to wake up and come after him.
She was safer where she was.
He pulled the bow taught.
Wasn't she?
She was just a girl.
No. She was a Queen.
His Queen.
He loosed the arrow -
She'd be fine.
The arrow thumped into the arse of one of the sleeping Keepers. It immediately bellowed in rage and pain, hauling itself to its feet like a grumpy, giant baby.
He smiled and loosed another arrow.
In moments, everything went barmy. Keepers raging into each other, falling over tents, destroying everything. The Finders were awake, shrieking and rattling their cages.
They probably knew he was there. They could smell him.
The camp was waking up now. Brigands were approaching. He watched one get pulped in the face by a flailing Keeper. He laughed for a moment, before he heard

that old voice from his past telling him to never take pleasure in another's pain.

It was pretty funny though.

Anyway.

He scoured the gathering crowds, looking for one particular face.

Or one particular lack of face.

It seemed they were destined to do this dance again and again. No matter how many times it seemed the minstrels had put up their lutes, the song just started anew.

One of them would have to die, and he was pretty sure which one he wanted it to be.

There.

He saw him. Stalking through the tents toward the massive barney the Keepers were causing.

The Fool moved through the trees, drawing parallel with the bandaged bastard.

He saw him looking at the site of the commotion, then turn back towards his own tent.

Towards Althea's tent.

He may have been a pathetic, cowardly worm of a man, but he wasn't completely gadwise.

Better get his attention.

The Fool bounced a rock off the bandaged head, quick-smart, and made sure he was sitting cross-legged and carefree on a log when his target turned around.

Never let them catch you sweating.

"YOU!" shrieked the bandaged bastard, and the Fool's suspicions were confirmed. He had had his back to them when he killed Duncan, but the Fool was sure he knew the voice.

And here he was. Somebody else he thought had died in flames.

"How, Smeggy."

Kenneth had undoubtedly been waiting for this meeting for a long time. He didn't speak, he seethed.

"My name. Is Mister. Fury."

He didn't waste any time drawing his sword and barrelling at the Fool like a maniac, screaming bloody murder.

The Fool hopped off the log and sidestepped easily, tripping him as he passed.

Never let rage be your fuel.

Ken sprawled on the floor. The Fool hadn't even drawn Punch yet.

"You maggot!" Ken scrambled to his feet, tucking his bandages in.

"Maggot, am I?" The Fool stepped onto the log, and twirled his way across it like a ballerina. There is nothing more infuriating than nonchalance in battle. "Well, then I make you a catch, having baited you away from your prisoner."

"I'll see you hung, drawn and quartered for what you have done to me!" Ken hurled himself forward again -

This time, the Fool spun on his heel, kicked Ken in the arse as he passed, plucked Punch from his rucksack and returned to face his foeman.

His foeman. It was strange to finally think of Smeggy Ken in such a way. He'd always just been a bit of a nuisance. An arsewarch. A bloodtick in his boot.

Then he started killing my friends.

They circled each other.

Ken held back this time. He was learning.

"You're looking well, Ken." The Fool gestured to the bandages. "This is definitely an improvement."

"I will end you tonight, you and your two wenches!"

Ken launched into another enraged attack, blow after blow swinging wide or knocked aside by Punch.

He wasn't learning very quickly.

It amused the Fool to render his rage so impotent, and the angrier Ken got, the easier it was to hold him at bay.

"You should relax a bit, Smeggy." The Fool dodged another swipe of Ken's sword. "All this rage and frustration can't be healthy."

Ken struck again and Punch parried.

"And this 'Mister Fury' thing. Not sending a very positive message, is it?"

Ken was red-faced and breathless. The Fool bopped him with Punch, gently on the bonce.

"What about 'Mister Cuddly'? 'Mister Firm-but-fair'?"

Ken's face was so red with rage, the Fool reckoned he'd be able to fry an egg on his forehead, given half a chance.

"Or even plain old Smeggy Ken?"

That did it.

"Don't call me that!" Ken launched himself forward with such ferocity that the Fool didn't have to put much force into his swing. Punch connected with the back of Ken's head and he fell.

They had played enough.

There was no honour in humiliating your enemy, but Ken was a special case.

He deserved it.

None fear ridicule so much as the ridiculous.

And the Fool had always had a tenuous relationship with honour.

He picked up Ken's sword.

He stood over him.

Ken rolled onto his back, looking up. His rage turned to fear.

"I'm going to kill you, Ken." He pressed the sword into Ken's neck, just under the bandages. "I've paid the price for underestimating you. Now you will pay the price for the wrong you have done me - "

This man. This worm of a man.

How many years had they put up with him? How many times had he let Ken go, given him another chance?

He leaned in close.

"- and her."

"Oi! Stay your hand, Fool!"

Idiot. He'd got too preoccupied with Ken. He forgot where they were. Dunnelhead.

He turned his head to see a group of brigands. Twenty feet away. Headcount around sixteen. At least two bows.

"Put up your sword," a voice demanded.

Too far to run for the trees. Too many to fight.

Should've stuck to the plan.

Did he even have a plan? Or had he just decided he wanted to humiliate and murder funny old Ken?

He was breaking his promise.

He dropped the sword.

The Princess

He used her hair for a bowstring.

He fashioned a bow out of a yew branch and a tiny thread woven from strands of her hair.

When he had finished, he had twanged the string and smiled at her. He was very pleased with himself.

"A bow made with strands of your royal hair… ness. That's poetic that is. You gave up a little bit of yourself."

"You mean you stole a little bit of myself."

In spite of her disdain, she had been quite impressed. The bow looked sturdy enough, and he had also sharpened some sticks into makeshift arrows.

He had told her that her tiny sacrifice would bring good luck, and they were going to need a lot of that.

Hiding in the darkened undergrowth at the edge of the brigand camp, she was inclined to agree.

He'd given her a short sword and lied about where he got it from. He said he found it. She had seen it fall from the dead hand of one of the brigands.

She looked at the dead man's blade. It was dull in edge and sheen. Probably more use to club than to cleave.

She peered out through the leaves.

Darkness had fallen fast, and the camp was now lit by fires and torches.

Wait for the signal, he had told her.

Until yesterday, she had thought this man a lovable idiot.

Lovable? Hardly. A likable idiot.

In the past few hours… she didn't know what she thought him anymore.

A magician? A vagabond? A murderer?

And now she was trusting to his strategy in a life-or-death situation she didn't even need to be in.

She could leave now. Just head home.

The Fool could probably handle things himself, from what she'd seen that day.

But he might not. And the witch Althea might die, and she was kind to her when no one else was. And they had sort of got Althea's home destroyed and got all her animals killed, so there was recompense for that to consider.

She sighed.

Why was it suddenly her job to go prancing into mercenary groups?

Because her Dad was dead.

Because she was Queen now.

And with Royalty came duty.

But it wasn't fair.

But what was?

She saw the signal. And heard it.

The bellow of some huge animal, and a rising commotion on the far side of the camp.

Her muscles turned to stone under her skin.

Can't move.

According to plan, the Brigands began to head toward the sounds.

Leaving her a clear path to the tent they had Althea in.

The moment stretched out ahead and behind her. What if she missed her chance? What if she got caught?

What if she succeeded?

She took a deep breath.

"I just wanted to go home." She said it aloud, ensuring that the world knew this was not her idea.

She decided. "Right."

She gripped the sword tighter.

She stepped out from under the trees.

The first few steps were the hardest, feeling painfully apparent without foliage between her and any searching eyes, but it seemed all eyes were on the increasingly raucous disturbance across the camp.

Crouching next to tents and hurrying between shadows, she couldn't see what was happening, but she could hear what sounded like fighting. Cracking wood and clashing steel. The brigands were all moving in that direction, and she soon found it surprisingly easy to avoid their gaze.

"Keep low and stay in the dark," the Fool had told her. It really was that simple.

Until she turned a corner to see two brigands hurrying towards her.

They saw her.

They must have.

She crouched back into the shadows as they approached. She was only before them for a moment, but it must've been enough.

She could hear one of them talking.

"...I mean, I understand the safety aspect, obviously."

They came closer.

"It's just the design I can't understand."

Katherine held her breath. She could hear the clatter of their armour. She drew her sword back to arm's length.

"In a battle situation you want full use of your peripheral vision, right?"

They were upon her. She prepared to strike.

"But I find these helmets so restrictive. You can only see directly in front of you."

They passed her. They carried on their way.

"I'm always afraid I might miss something, y'know?"

Katherine waited until she could hear the brigand no more, and heaved a huge sigh of relief.

She hadn't failed yet, and that was a triumph.

The Witch

She had thought so much about dying. About going to join her love in whatever afterlife turned out to be the true one.

Not long after she had buried him, she had gone up to the crag where his grave lay and thrown a rope over a bough of their Bluefire tree.

She would've done it. She climbed on the boulder at the foot of the tree and tied the noose, ready.

He had been her life, so without him there was only death.

Before she could do it, she heard something. An animal was crying.

She found the baby bibblecap hiding under a bush. The poor thing was terrified. Broken leg. Looked like it had been in a fight with a brock or somesuch. And bibblecaps were such docile, stupid creatures. It feebly attempted to gore her with its tiny tusks, but she had managed to heave it out into the light.

Tomorrow, she had thought. *I'll do it tomorrow, when this poor thing is better.*

But there was always some defenceless animal in need of her help, so she had lived on for nigh-on three years.

Now she wished she'd gone on her own terms.

Seeing the end of her own rope seemed more appealing than seeing the end of some of these torture tools.

It wasn't the first time she'd been pained, of course.

There had been a couple of brief instances in the old days, usually by some dribbling pervert just waiting for someone to cram a blade between his shoulders, but this was different.

Rudesby hadn't started yet, but she was already uncomfortable.

This wasn't just because she was tied to a rack with her wrists and ankles in manacles.

Rudesby had entered the tent some time after she was in position and started readying his tools and a small furnace, all the while engaging her in light conversation. Though he had the physical demeanour of a weasel, he had the manner of a polite barkeep.

"So, you're a white witch, then?" He was placing tools in the furnace to heat. "That's braw, that really is."

He opened a leather pouch and unfurled a roll of linen. Within were saws and pliers of various sizes.

She didn't feel like talking.

"I was into healing, myself, y'know?" It seemed he didn't need her to talk. Not yet, anyway. She was pretty sure he would become more insistent before too long.

"Just took a different path. Funny where our choices take us. We all have our decisions to make. You, for instance, are gonna have to decide whether to spill your guts metaphorically -" he slid a glowing hot poker from the furnace and brandished it at her - "or literally."

She watched the luminous tip of the poker.

This is bloody typical.

Within hours of the Jester showing up, she was about to be tortured to death by the most boring maniac in the four corners.

At least she would see Mark soon. But there would probably be a considerable amount of pain before that.

She wondered if he would be angry with her. She had tried so hard, he would know that, wouldn't he? She just couldn't go on without him.

Sounds outside the tent.

Something was causing a commotion in the camp.

She decided to try her luck. "What's happening out there?"

Rudesby leaned in close over her, but all she could see was the poker.

"You think it's somebody coming to rescue you? Not likely. There isn't a warrior in the land could infiltrate this camp."

The racket outside was getting louder.

"No man alive could get past our guards, and none would dare try."

It was beginning to sound like a fight. Steel on steel, running feet. Was that the sound of a carriage?

Rudesby heard it too. He drew away from her slightly, tilting an ear. "So… no rescuing going on today."

There was shouting now. And the cries of Finders.

"You are here until we say otherwise…" Rudesby was still speaking absently, his attention outside. Was he trying to convince her or himself?

He walked to the entrance flap of the tent. Shadows hurried past outside.

"Absolutely no chance whatsoever—"

"I think I get it," she said.

"Good."

She was sure she could hear a carriage.

Rudesby turned to look at her. "Didn't want you to get your hope—"

It was at this point that Rudesby fell to the ground.

His fall was most likely caused by two enormous shire horses which ploughed into the tent.

The horses pulled a cart carrying a cage. The same that had brought her here.

The cart was driven by a Princess.

Or was it a Queen?

The horses pulled up a few feet short of her, snorting and scratching the earth.

Rudesby sat up, bloodied by hoof and wheel. He noticed he had impaled himself on his hot poker. He looked at Althea, said "Famous last words, eh?" and lay back down.

Althea looked up at Katherine, who waved "hello" and jumped down from the cart.

"Hope I'm not interrupting?" she said.

"No, by all means…" Althea offered her wrists and Katherine unlatched the manacles. "Thank you."

"Don't thank me yet." She ran back to the cart. "We still have to get out."

Althea just had one more thing to do. "One moment."

She walked to the furnace and used all her might to turn it over, scattering hot coals over Rudesby's body.

They left the painer's tent in flames.

The Fool

Ken was smirking at him now.

"Never much for a stand-up fight, were you, Ken?" said the Fool.

Ken climbed to his feet. "It is not the manner of the fight, but the outcome which is remembered."

He drew a dagger from his belt.

The Fool knew that blade.

Crimson handle with the golden Crown of Elderhaime carved into the pommel.

It was Duncan's.

He'd seen him open letters with it.

It was the blade that killed The King.

It was the blade that killed his friend.

"Your King is dead." Ken knew he recognised it. "As you will soon be."

Why had he toyed with him so long? Why hadn't he just killed him? He was not fuelled by rage, but his own malice would be his undoing. That voice from his past would be tutting at him by now. Tutting and shaking his head.

Had he learned nothing?

Ken pushed the knife to his throat.

"And your precious Princess with you."

The blade was cold.

He thought about how little pressure it takes for a gad to puncture skin and flesh and muscle -

He just hoped she got Al and got out.

He felt the pressure -

I'm sorry. I really cocked this up.

He closed his eyes -

And heard a scream.

Two shirehorses were barrelling through the crowd of brigands, dragging a cart behind them.

Ken was distracted for a second -

The Fool knocked the knife out of Ken's hands and headbutted him in the face.

He heard the familiar crunch of a nosebreaker, and Ken went down like a bucket in a well.

The cart was upon him -

He instinctively raised a hand as it passed -

And there she was.

For an instant, all he could feel was the soft warmth of her hand in his.

Then he was heaved off his feet and up onto the cart.

And they were off - the cart tearing towards the treeline.

She plucked him from the jaws of death. At the hands of Smeggy Ken, no less.

Couldn't give her too much credit, though. She might get cocky. Wouldn't want that. She was hard enough to put up with already.

He realised he was still holding Katherine's hand. He had landed on one knee before her.

He sprang to his feet as the cart raced on, turning her tender grip into a manly handshake. "Well done, Your Majesty!"

Althea was snapping the reins and shouting at the horses as the cart raced for the edge of the clearing. He slapped a hand on her shoulder. "Successful rescue, I think!"

Althea shouted back at him. "Full marks for the rescue, but lets see how the escape goes, eh?"

Katherine was staring over the back of the bouncing cart. "They are after us."

He looked and, sure enough, there were a fair few brigands on horseback gaining ground behind them. Ken must be so terribly vexed.

"Knackers," he said.

The cart rattled out of the clearing and down a wooded way.

Branches and leaves rushed past them.

Althea whipped the reins harder and the wind pulled at his hat. "You shouldn't've come after me!" Althea cried. "I let them take me so you'd be safe!"

He needed to take stock of their assets.

A bow with no arrows. A cart -

Wait, what did she just say? "Oh, so it's fine for you to save me, but I can't return the favour?" he shouted into the wind.

Was that a Finder? Yes, there was a Finder in the cage at the rear of the cart -

"I wasn't saving you, Jester, I was saving her!" Althea nodded at the Princess.

Mister Punch. He was always an asset -

"What?" said Katherine. The Fool wasn't sure if she resented the implication that she needed saving, or being referred to as "her".

Katherine stumbled as the cart hit a divot. These roads weren't the best kept.

Althea was still shouting. "So, now that you've brought her back into harm's way, what's the next step of the plan?"

He looked back. In spite of their speed, the brigands were lighter and faster. They were closing the gap. He saw bows being raised.

They were about fifty yards back.

He looked ahead. They were heading south. Surely they must be near -

He had a plan. "Go fast."

It was more of a collection of ideas than an actual coherent plan, but it was a start. That's how all his plans started. It was also how most of them remained, but that wasn't the point.

He grabbed Katherine, pulling her under a low bough that would've taken her head off at the speed they were going.

She brushed his hands off her.

"Princess," he said, "It's time to put that lucky bow to use." He handed it to her.

She looked like he'd just passed her a severed head.

"I've never… I don't have any arrows," she said.

The cart rattled and lurched as Althea whipped the reins even harder, calling out "Sorry!" to the galloping horses.

The Fool was already climbing up over the roof of the cage, to the rear of the cart. He called out to Katherine: "Improvise!"

A brigand's arrow buried itself in the top of the cart near the Princess. He was very pleased with the timing. To the untrained eye, vigilance can seem like prescience.

Katherine's eyes lit up as she caught his meaning. She wrenched the arrow free, nocked it and loosed it in one swift motion.

He would've been impressed if the arrow hadn't pinged wide and spun into the trees.

She looked sheepish and he shook his head in dismay. He turned back to climbing over the cage. The Finder was bouncing off the cage walls beneath him as the carriage rocked, long fingers reaching up between the wooden bars, desperate to get at him.

The Brigands were twenty yards back now. Gaining all the time.

Arrows flying past him. Some finding the wood of the cart, most whistling wide. He was right about the brigands' training. They couldn't hit a Baroness' bum.

That wouldn't matter for long. Accuracy is of no consequence at a distance of inches.

He leaned down over the back of the cage and unlatched the lock.

Ten yards. He could almost smell them.

The brigands spurred their horses to close the final distance.

The cage door swung open -

The Finder scuttled forth, clawing for him -

He smashed Punch into its repellent face and it fell back -

Into the path of the brigands, scattering them. Some of the horses fell, some broke off into the woods, one pulled level to the cart.

Its rider leaped onto the side of the cage, scrabbling for purchase on the wood -

Katherine plucked another stray arrow from its mark and stabbed the brigand repeatedly in the hand.

The cart bounced over him as he fell under the wheels -

The Fool tried to remember if Katherine had ever killed anyone before.

Her face said this was the first time.

Althea lashed the horses and apologised even more profusely.

Up ahead, the Fool saw the bank of the River Thurgan. They were closer than he thought.

The remaining brigands were regrouping their horses behind them, regaining the ground lost in their collision with the Finder.

Ken was with them now.

The Fool was scrabbling back over the cage to Althea and Katherine, the wind whipping at his face.

"Get in the cage!" he cried.

Althea looked over her shoulder. "What?"

"I said get in the cage, both of you!"

He took the reins from Althea, giving her his best "Do as I say" look. She started climbing back over the cage.

They were almost at the river, and the brigands were almost upon them.

Almost.

Up ahead, the way took a sharp right turn at the top of a steep embankment.

Katherine was less receptive to his commanding look. She would learn.

"Princess, get in the cage! Now!"

She looked like she was going to argue for a moment, but then he saw something unexpected there in her blue eyes.

Trust.

Her eyes said "If you say so."

She trusted him.

He wasn't sure why that made him feel as if he could leap off the back of the cart and talk all the brigands in to making friends with them, but it did.

He wasn't going to try, though.

He didn't have long to unhook the horses.

He looked at the muddy road racing underneath him and thought about how much it would hurt to plant his face into it at this speed.

He leapt between the horses, feet on their pounding flanks, arms over their backs. He wasn't much for horsecraft, so he just undid every buckle and knot he could find.

He felt them come loose -

He leapt back onto the cart as the horses pulled clear.

The cart began to slow -

He was too late.

He saw a brigand leap from his horse behind them, landing half in and half out of the door of the cage -

And he saw Althea and Katherine calmly lift him, one on each arm, and dump him out onto the way.

The brigand's friends rode over him as he rolled. Ken led the charge.

He felt a warm swell of pride in his ladies. They killed that brigand right up and no mistake.

He only had a moment to ponder the peculiarity of applauding murder, however, as they had all but reached the river.

He swung himself out, leaning over the side of the cart.

He looked at the riverbank -

He looked at the brigands -

He held Punch out, ready -

The Puppet looked at him. "Is this going to hurt?"

"Shh."

Another second and they'd be over the bank -

Now or never.

He swung Punch with the full weight of his body -

Punch connected with the cartwheel, knocking it from its axle -

The axle - and the whole corner of the cart - ploughed into the dirt.

He clung on as the cart span to a halt, teetering at the very brink of the slope. The river churned thirty feet below.

The brigands were on them -

He quickly swung down into the cage, where Althea and Katherine waited.

"Now what? Are we to cage ourselves-"

He interrupted Katherine's questions: "Stand over there." He pointed them both to the front of the cage and they stepped into position.

He turned and closed the cage door behind him. Ken was right there. The brigands were aiming their bows.

Perfect.

The Fool raised his gloved hand to Ken, two fingers extended.

Their eyes connected -

The Fool smiled.

He turned and threw his body at the wall of the cage.

The delicate balance of the cart was upset. It held on for a moment, and fell.

He wondered if this was his best plan as they rolled down the slope, a jumble of limbs and screams. His usual definition of a successful plan was one which didn't kill anyone he liked, so this one was fair enough so far.

It was all worth it to see the look on Ken's face, he assured himself. Well, the look in his eyes. Couldn't see much of his mush lately. So much the better.

The cart slapped into the water, and he was relieved to feel buoyancy. The river was carrying them away.

He managed to get the cage door open again, and helped Al and Katherine out before the water rose too high.

Clinging to the roof of the cage, they rode the cart through rocks and rapids.

Althea shouted in his ear. "Still think it's a successful rescue?"

"You're alive, aren't you?"

The Witch

They swam ashore when the cart started sinking.

They found themselves on a long, rolling moor, shrouded in silent mist. She knew where they were.

She shivered and pulled her wet shawl closer around her.

"This is a darkling place." She said to the Jester. "I can feel it."

In truth, she could feel nothing beyond the familiar paranoia of one afraid of the dark. As with those moments of terror back in the mornings when she woke from uncertain nightmares, it was the unfamiliarity in these lands that truly afeared her. What malevolent eyes might be gazing on them from out of that blackness? What evil machinations moving against them in the shadows? And, from what she had heard tell, such fears were not unfounded.

She didn't want to die out here.

"It is pretty atmospheric, innit?" The Jester did not seem to share her trepidation.

Even if he was scared, she wouldn't be able to tell. She had not often seen him rattled.

"We must not linger here," she said.

"Well, let's get a shimmy on then."

"Which way home?" asked Katherine. She looked as frightened and bedraggled as Althea felt.

The Jester thought for a moment.

He licked a finger.

He picked his nose.

Althea and Katherine groaned.

He pointed into the darkness with his snotty finger. "That way."

She laughed at him. He hadn't changed.

She thought how gadwise it would seem, to follow such a man into the wilderness. How an appearance can deceive unintentionally or otherwise. How one can only spend so long in an assumed role before the role assumes you.

Acting the fool.

"What are you laughing at?" he had caught her gaze.

She shook her head. "Once again you waltz into my life and completely banjax everything, Jester. Kidnapped, tortured, half-drowned, lost in the middle of who-knows-where…"

"Just like old times, eh?"

"That's why I was laughing."

He grinned at her. And the sadness she had lived with for years sneaked back upon her.

The things that never change can only remind us of the the things that do.

He saw the need to change the subject: "And I know where. We are on the Dunmoors."

Katherine's eyes were wide. "The Dunmoors?" She had heard the tales too, no doubt.

"The Haunted Dunmoors. Feared and shunned by all but the bravest and most foolish." He was enjoying this. "They say that the moors are plagued by the restless spirits of lost children. Unable to find their way home…"

Althea gave him a nudge. "Behave yourself, Jester." The journey would be toil enough without a traumatised Princess in tow.

And she felt her own fear rising.

But that was ridiculous. She knew the truth behind the legends of the Dunmoors. Didn't she? What was it the Jester said?

Truth in every tale.

He wasn't finished yet. "Many an unwary traveller has been lured into the darkness by the sobbing of a weeping child," he leaned in close to Katherine. "Never to be seen again…"

"Shut up!" Katherine punched him in the arm. He recoiled in mock agony, clutching the wound.

"Alright! No need to get rowdy."

Althea noticed something then. Something she felt she had seen before, but had not fully understood. Something that could be a greater threat to the fragile hope of peace than any amount of chaos and destruction. A force so powerful that death itself could not tear it asunder.

Oh dear.

Part Four:
The Learned and the Learning.

Brittle the Banwarch and the Lost Children of the Haunted Dunmoors

Extract from
"Myths and Legends of Old Firgenland"
by Lesung Cifesdaughter.

In a village called Crofton, on the western edge of the Dunmoors, there lived a boy called Tord. He lived with his mother and his father, who was a great hunter.

According to the village tradition, every birthday after their fifth, the children of the village were taken out on the moors to hunt.

On Tord's seventh birthday, just as the two preceding years, his mother told him to beware of the evil Baelic-spawn named Brittle the Banwarch, who lived on the moors and stole away unwary children. Tord said he would be careful and off he went with his Father.

They travelled with a small group of hunters, looking for deer and rabbits and whatever else they could find. Tord had to return with at least one kill every year, for a child was not allowed back into Crofton empty handed.

After a hard day's hunt, they made camp on the moor and lit a fire. They ate stew and sang songs.

That night, Tord was woken by a strange sound. He looked up to see a hand reaching into the tent he and his father shared. A thin, pale hand with long, bony fingers, it grabbed his sleeping father's head and the fingers were long enough to wrap around his neck.

His Father was dragged out into the darkness and Tord looked out of the tent to see Brittle the Banwarch, so tall and thin and pale, walk from tent to tent and pluck out the sleeping men in silence, carrying them by their broken necks like chickens for the cleaver.

Tord ran to try to get on a horse, but Brittle had already killed them all, slitting them from throat to belly.

Tord hid behind the body of one of the horses and watched as Brittle collected the last man and looked about to leave the camp. The monster stopped at the edge of the path and sniffed the air. He could smell Tord, and he turned and strode towards the dead horses.

Brittle peered around with his red eyes but Tord was nowhere to be seen, for he had climbed inside the belly of one of the horses to hide. Brittle could not see nor smell Tord, so went on about his ghastly business.

Tord climbed out of the horse's belly and headed for home as fast as he could. While he was out in the wild, he came across a lone deer and killed it with his bare hands.

So it was that Tord returned home, alone, covered in blood and bearing his kill.

As this story passed into legend, so the traditions of Crofton changed. When a child reaches their seventh birthday, they are taken out onto the moors, to the spot where Tord's father made camp, and abandoned. They must find their way home with a kill or not at all.

Most return home within a few days, but some are never seen again.

Travellers on the moors tell of small shadows moving in the dark and low whispering on the wind. Some suggest that Brittle the Banwarch has, over the years, amassed an army of Ghost Children to do his vile bidding.

They say if you travel the Dunmoors at night and hear the lonely weeping of a lost child, it is best to ignore it, lest you wander from the path and find yourself at the mercy of Brittle the Banwarch and the Lost Children of the Dunmoors.

Extract from Lord Felix Tyrantson's Diary: Ten Years of Age

Second Dorenday, Second Moon of Winter, 206
He's at it again. I can hear them now, in his chambers. He takes two or three at a time in there. Warwick says he's just a lonely old man. He says he feels sorry for him. I don't. I know why he's lonely. I know what I saw. And no amount of chambermaids in his bedroom will make him feel better.

Third Moonday, Second Moon of Winter, 206
Dad was really angry today. Soldiers from Elderhaime are sneaking around in our country and doing bad things like setting fires and turning horses loose. Dad says you can't fight a war against what you can't see. He says it's better to fight in the open, these people are cowards. Warwick thinks it's a group of about five or six people hiding in the woods. They are causing a lot of trouble for only that many. Dad sent his Enforcers and Warwick out to get them.
It was snowing today.

Fourth Stilnesday, Third Moon of Winter, 206
Dad kicked me down the stairs today. Just like Belinda all those years ago. He was so angry because the Green Shadows sank some of his boats. He was going to attack Underton from the river and come at Elderhaime castle from behind, he says, but they sneaked out in the night and set the ships on fire and sank them. I'm not supposed to call them The Green Shadows, that's what the peasants call them and they are just superstitious. So he kicked me down the stairs.
He kicked me down the stairs. Just like Belinda.
I'm lucky I wasn't in the tower, or I'd be down on the courtyard just like Mum.

The Princess

She had never killed anyone before.

She tried to convince herself that the men she threw into the road had survived, but she could still hear the snapping bones as they hit the ground, the dull smacks as hooves trampled them.

She was a murderer.

Was it murder in war? She was unclear on the distinction. Truce or no, Elderhaime and Fairford were technically still at war, and these men were at the service of this Mister Fury, who was most likely working for King Warwick, so she was a warrior now, surely?

A Warrior Queen.

Daddy would be so proud.

But what would Mummy say?

Neither of them would say anything. They're gone.

She poked at the fire with a stick.

Through the flames, she watched Althea. The Witch seemed distant. They had told her about her home and the animals in the cages, and she had just nodded and sighed, as if she had already known. As if it was an inevitability.

She thought again about the Witches in the tales and legends. Althea was disappointingly un-gnarled and severely lacking in warts. Her back bore no hunch and her skin was a healthy tan rather than a sickly green.

Also, she had yet to see this Witch weave any magic. The firey collapse of the tunnel had been impressive, but was it magic? She was fairly sure that Witches were supposed to be magical, but as yet none had been turned to toad, nor had any been stricken with the sickness, neither had Althea summoned any demons or imps to fornicate with.

All told, Althea the White Witch of Crossford was something of an anti-climax.

But all had yet to be told.

"You said you knew my Mother?" she asked of the Witch.

Althea started, as if she'd forgotten Katherine existed. She smiled. "Your parents were very kind to me, a long time ago."

We are all servants of history. Especially those with no knowledge of it.

"I barely remember my mother. She's only been gone six years, but nobody ever speaks of her. It's as if she never existed."

She tried to picture her. Her face there in the light of the flames, but as in her dreams, it eluded her.

"Jester never spoke of her?" Althea looked surprised.

He never spoke to her of anything of substance.

"The Fool only has secrets from me. And he tells me only lies…"

"Ignorance is bliss, Princess." He stepped into the firelight, a dead boar over his shoulder and the bow on his back. She hadn't seen him approach, or heard his bells ringing.

He didn't have his hat on. His matted brown hair fell in a his eyes. Eyes that gave a warning she refused to heed.

"He even shrouds himself in secrecy," she continued to Althea. "Come, Fool, entertain us with something other than frivolities. Tell us your tale."

He cast the boar down by the fire. "My life is no story worth the telling."

She wasn't in the mood for his secrets. "Tell us what you did to so infuriate that bandaged brigand."

"You obviously haven't spent enough time with him," said Althea.

The Fool sat down, cross-legged.

She was getting a taste for it now. Perhaps if she could get one little truth from him, the rest would follow? "Come, Fool. He just wants to kill me, but you seem to have him especially vexed."

"I set fire to him and dropped him out of a window." He looked her straight in the eye. "It was a few months back, now."

She didn't know what to say.

He looked from her to Althea. Both were silent. "Good chat."

He pulled a knife from his boot and, just for an instant, she was afraid.

He raised the knife and threw it.

It stuck into the ground at her feet.

"I killed it, you carve it."

So easy to kill for your own benefit.

She felt an emptiness climb from her stomach and settle in the back of her throat. A hollow she knew could only be filled with screams.

She would not scream.

"He killed my Dad."

"Took a King's knife to end a King's life." The Fool shrugged. "Poetic. I'll drop him from a higher window next time."

Queens don't cry. They make big decisions and stand proud and noble and don't falter and quail and she wanted her Dad.

And he was gone because of her.

"It was my fault." She would not weep.

"It wasn't your job to protect him." The Fool wouldn't look at her.

"He wouldn't've been out in the woods if I hadn't gone stropping off..."

He was dead because she wouldn't do as she was told.

It was Althea who finally spoke. "I know how you feel," she said. "But you cannot allow misplaced guilt to poison your heart. There is no one to blame but the one who chose whether a man lived or died."

Katherine looked up at her.

Althea seemed to search for her next words deep inside herself, hauling them up from beneath years of pain.

"My husband had a Blacksmith's shop in Crossford, but Mark wouldn't forge for the Brigands or pay their 'taxes'. They outnumbered him. Tore him down with hooks."

"Ken never was one for a stand-up fight," said the Fool. "Mark would've tarred and feathered him in single combat."

"He went out to face them. They killed my husband and burned my house down while I hid. Ken saw me go in the house. He thought I burned, but I escaped through the tunnel."

"That's why I burned him," said the Fool. "I thought he burned you."

She smiled weakly at the Fool, but turned back to Katherine. "My husband was killed by a cruel coward. Killed for being brave. And there isn't a day goes by that a don't blame myself, but you know what? I blame Kenneth Bronwenson even more."

"Smeggy Ken," said the Fool.

So this man had taken her Father, Althea's husband and driven the Fool to burn him alive. What horrors had he visited on yet others? And here he wandered the Holtlands freely, oppressing and exploiting workers and farmers at will? Althea spoke of taxes. Taxes are only to be levied by the supreme monarch for the better running of the lands, not to be taken at sword-point to line the purses of cut-throats.

There was a difference, wasn't there? Royal taxes weren't stealing, were they?

Things were going to have to change. Perhaps open war on Fairford was not the answer. Perhaps when she returned home, she should rally the troops and scour the Holtlands for these vagabonds. Hunt them one at a time like animals, or maybe burn the entire forest around them?

Perhaps she should have a word with the royal bankers as well, just to be sure.

Things had to change.

She knew nothing of battle or war. Or even hunting. The only person she knew who seemed to understand these ways was…

"Fool," she ventured. "You said you used to work with Althea's man… as a blacksmith?"

"No."

"What, then?" He gave her the look again. She ignored it again. "Who are you, really?"

He leaned forward. "Just a Fool, Princess." He scooped up the dead boar and threw it in her lap.

As she protested, he waved the hilt of the knife in front of her. "He's not getting any fresher."

The King

The trail ended here.

He watched the river roll past and pondered.

They had left the brigand camp, he was quite certain. A chase had ensued, the tracks had been easy to follow, and they had ended in the river. The churned, beaten earth on the slope down to the water told so.

The Brigands had split up, some moving south along the river bank and some returning to the camp.

All this meant that the Princess was either drowned and lost, or had ridden the river to the Dunmoors, which meant she was lost also.

You lost her.

Not yet.

You did all this.

He knew it wasn't true.

Well done. You did what I never could.

"Shut up, Dad." He tugged the reins and Ferfost began picking his way through the woods, along the river.

For years I fought Duncan to no avail. You've managed to wipe out his line in a matter of days.

No.

And all in your misguided quest for peace.

It's not misguided.

You tried so hard not to be me, and you've ended up a better tyrant than I ever was.

I'm no tyrant.

You are my son. Stop trying to be something you are not. Seize this opportunity.

I'm not like you.

Take Elderhaime. They have no King, no leader. The Princess is as good as dead out here. Take Elderhaime and you can truly unite the Sibling Lands. Under your banner.

If I took their lands by force, the only unity would be against me.

So, find the Princess. Make sure she is dead. Then lament her death with them and tell them peace is what she would've wanted. You'll be the only royal left in Sibland. The plebs will have no choice but to name you the Folking.

Warwick looked down at the brigands' tracks as Ferfost stepped through the undergrowth.

He knew his father had no voice anymore. He knew there was no voice but his own.

I know she's there.
She always is.
Standing by the bed, drifting just out of sight.
I'm trying to reach for her, but she's shying away. She fears my touch.
Don't go.
Don't leave us.
She has to.
He says she doesn't.
He's never been there before, but he always has.
He reaches for her too, and he's quicker than me.
There's blood now.
And bandages.
He's here for my Dad.
Don't hurt him. Please.
They want to take everything away from me.
The bandaged face leans over the bed.
He wants me too.
I claw at the bandages.
They come apart in my hands and underneath...
Oh, underneath...

The Princess

She awoke from the dream to the sound of whispers.

For a moment she thought her dream had followed her into waking, but as she tilted an ear to the darkness, she heard it again.

Whispers on the wind. Voices in the mist.

She looked around.

The Fool and Althea both lay nearby, around the dead fire. Both still asleep.

More whispers.

It sounds like children.

The Lost Children.

She didn't believe the tales.

But how many tales had she seen to be true now?

Were there shadows moving in the fog?

She stared into the dark, waiting for something to catch the moonlight.

Something did.

"Fool!" she hissed.

They were out there.

Small, dark figures flitting hither and thither in the shadows.

Many of them.

The Fool did not stir.

"Fool!" Louder this time.

The Fool still did not wake, but Mister Punch did. The Fool was clutching the puppet in his sleep and it raised, seemingly of its own volition.

The Puppet spoke. "What's wrong, Majesty?"

"Wake up! Something's here…"

Punch seemed to notice the shapes and sounds in the mist. "Crikey!" The puppet headbutted the Fool in the gut. "Wake up, Boss! Trouble!"

The Fool did not open his eyes. "I know."

The sounds were even closer know, and accompanied by the creak of leather and the rustle of chainmail.

And still the whispers.

The Fool finally opened his eyes.

All the stories of her childhood were creeping back into her mind. The Lost Children of the Moors, Brittle the Banwarch, Gargrin the Blood Bather, the Hateful Wyrm of Blackwold, they were all out there in the dark, ready to spirit her away.

The tales were all true.

The Fool was on his feet now, and Althea was awake.

Katherine stood and backed slowly toward the Fool.

The whispers were all around them. She felt if she could only listen a little harder she would surely hear their words.

The three of them stood back to back, each bracing themselves for what may come.

It's all real.

All of it.

The fog seemed to close in about them, bringing whatever it hid ever nearer.

She clung to the Fool's arm.

The mist parted.

It was as if a curtain lifted in front of her, revealing the whisperers.

They were children.

Or very small people.

Fearies? More like dwarves.

A throng of small, dark silhouettes surrounding them.

Black, hooded figures of various sizes.

Katherine thought of the first time she saw Althea, and a courage rose within her. It would take more than a dark costume to frighten her now.

She looked to the Fool. He seemed to be smiling, but that could just as easily mean they were in grave danger as they were safe.

One of the figures stepped forward, removed a black hood and knelt before Katherine.

She thought it could've been worse.

It was a boy of about fifteen years.

He spoke, his head bowed. "Lady Katherine of Elderhaime, my master bids you welcome to the Dunmoors." He looked up. He had a handsome, childish face. "He is expecting you."

Who was? "What? Expecting…? I didn't even know I was…"

This was getting confusing. She looked at the Fool again. He was still smiling and he raised an eyebrow at her befuddlement.

The boy continued. "Tis lucky we found you. The moors are no place for wanderers."

"But they're a fine playground for children?" the Fool laughed.

The boy's face darkened as he looked to the Fool. "This is no game." He rose to his feet, turning his attention back to Katherine. "Follow me, please."

He strode through the line of children, girls and boys, all dressed in the same dark tunic, hooded and cloaked in black. Most seemed to be armed with shortswords or other, more peculiar weapons.

Althea and the Fool were already following the boy.

"So that's it, is it?" she called after them. "A gaggle of little ticks sneak up on us in the night and we just follow them home?"

The Fool and Althea looked back at her. They waited.

It was all true.

There were Lost Children on the moors.

She imagined them leading her to Brittle the Banwarch's lair, where she would be hung on a hook and skinned and butchered.

But she didn't believe the tales.

She didn't.

She wasn't going to let them scare her.

She wasn't going to be fooled.

Katherine eyed the children as she passed. Each one solemn-faced, staring straight ahead.

The one closest to her was a girl of no more than eight years old.

"Does your mother know where you are?" She asked, incredulous.

The girl looked her in the eye.

The girl nodded.

The Fool

"My Master is expecting you," the kid had said.
I bet he is.
He had heard the stories about the Children of the Moors, both the common and the secret ones, and he had his own expectations.

Though knowledge of their whereabouts was beyond even *him*, surely?

How long had it been?

Too long.

Al sidled up to him. "Master?"

"You don't have to call me that, Al."

She elbowed him in the ribs. He knew she was thinking the same thing as him, but neither of them felt like saying it.

They were led over the dark moors by the little kitlings, Katherine continually asking where they were going, what was going on, were they there yet. He could've voiced his suspicions, but where was the fun in that?

As they followed the wee dreng and his cohorts, he was put in mind of another group of little warriors. A gang of bare-foot vagabonds who thought they owned the streets of Underton.

He thought of them stealing apples and bread from unwary marketeers.

He thought of them sitting on the harbour wall and watching the ships sailing for Etheldrealm and the Calanlands.

He thought of the friends they found and the adventures they went on.

Then he thought of how the friends grew up and apart and all the terrible things they did and the worse things that were done to them so he stopped thinking.

The Dunmoors rolled on into the night, lit by the stars. They had wandered out of the fog and, with the clear sky, he fancied he could see deep black shapes looming to the east.

That would be the southern Eastrod mountains, with the Stonefold at their feet. North of there, somewhere in the darkness, the Thurgan river would be creeping down from the peaks. And North of that was the Fairfold.

Their way had brought them so far east that the way to Fairford and King Warwick was easier than their way home.

From the Dunmoors back to Elderhaime, they would have to cross swamps and negotiate woods and perhaps even scale the Lip.

If they were heading to Fairford, it was a straight ride over moorland, the rocky waste of the Stonefold and onto the meadowy expanse of the Fairfold.

Simple as a bibblecap hunt.

He was pretty sure the Princess wouldn't see it that way, though.

And perhaps even he wasn't certain of the welcome they would receive.

He wondered if he was even right about the welcome they would find here on the moors.

He heard the Princess gasp and looked ahead.

It seemed the sky, speckled with stars, had somehow fallen to the ground in front of them. Or else it had leaked, streaming down blackness and scattered lights upon the Dunmoors.

It was a lake. Clear, still water reflecting the night sky. The Dunmere.

He had never been here before.

"Beautiful," said the Princess.

He looked at her. Her face was lit by stars and wonder, and he could only grunt agreement.

They reached the edge of the water. He could see an island out in the centre of the lake. Dark buildings rose from it, difficult to make out.

There was no sign of a bridge or a boat.

"Is that where we're heading?" he asked.

"Honanmor. The hall of our master," said the boy leader.

"Are we supposed to swim across?"

He didn't reply, he just looked out at the lake and blew a long, high whistle.

Then nothing.

The lake was still and silent.

"Are there sheepdogs out there?" the Fool asked. "An isle of sheepdogs?"

The little dreng said nothing.

Just kept looking at the lake.

"What are we waiting for?"

The dreng finally turned to him. "Didn't your Master teach you patience?"

There was something in the kid's eyes that gave the Fool pause. Only for a moment. "I don't have a Master, lad, I'm me own man."

The Princess coughed her disagreement.

"You don't count," he said to her. "You're a Princess -"

"Queen."

"Queen. That's different."

"How so?" she folded her arms.

"Well," he said. "A Master is like a teacher. Nobody ever learned anything from royalty."

"Really?" It was dark, but he could see the look on her face. "Well, I'll have to change that."

He shrugged. "Suppose a Queen could be everyone's Master."

The still waters were broken by ripples.

There was a boat coming.

It came almost silently out of the darkness.

A ferry. A raft. A wide square of wood being punted by a lone ferryman.

He looked at the kid.

The kid smiled. "Patience."

The ferry was big enough for all of them, but there was a strange, forced proximity. He felt like an ancient Oten, towering over the tiny people.

When they reached the island, the ferryman (Or boy. Or girl. Couldn't really tell in those hoods) tied up the raft and went silently into a little shack by the water.

The dreng led them on, up a stone path.

They passed long, low wooden buildings. Small faces peered from some of the windows, and there were whispers in the shadows.

The children began to break off and disappear into these buildings as they passed, until only the patient dreng leader was left.

The island was a hill rising from the lake. At its peak stood a lone building like a barn, looking down over the barracks below. For that is what he thought they must be. Barracks for an army of children.

Their guide led them to the peak of the hill and pushed open a pair of oaken double doors at the front of the barn.

The Fool was about to say something about the kid making them kip with the horses, but as soon as he stepped through the door he saw they were in a hall. A great hall, even.

It was warm and dry, with no gaps in the woodwork. And there were no horses.

"My Master will be with you shortly," said the kid. He bowed politely and shut himself out.

The Fool peered around in the candle-light. The high ceiling and wooden walls were lit by sconces and chandeliers. He saw a long, narrow table stretching the centre of the hall.

It was a better set up than he expected. "Nice digs for malevolent spirits."

Katherine was still cross. "They're not ghosts, they're just a rabble of urchins!"

A voice boomed across the hall. "Those urchins may have saved your life, your Majesty."

It had been a long time since the Fool had heard that voice outside of past words echoing in his head.

He emerged from the shadows in the corner of the hall, looking much as he ever had. Perhaps greyer, perhaps a little more stooped, perhaps slightly longer in the beard, but still the same old Master.

He walked the length of the table towards them. "I would expect a Queen to speak more diplomatically in foreign courts."

Katherine was taken aback. "My apologies, Mister...?"

The Fool smiled. "Wolf."

Katherine looked at him. "What?"

"He's The Wolf."

The Fool stepped forward with a low bow. "Master."

The Wolf returned the bow, before clapping a hand on the Fool's shoulder. The Fool pulled the old man into an embrace.

How long had it been?

The Wolf held him again at arm's length, seeming to survey him. He felt as if those ancient blue eyes saw everything that had transpired. He felt as if they peered through every memory the Fool had amassed since he and Wolf had parted last.

The Wolf smiled at him.

"They say only fools and the irretrievably lost venture onto the High Moors." He turned to Katherine and Althea. "Your company is made up of both, I deem."

Althea stepped forward, bowing as the Fool did. He was happy she remembered the old formalities.

"My lady," said The Wolf, "It is always a pleasure to be graced with your presence." He bowed to her.

"As it is yours, Hildewulf. It is long since we met."

The Dog of War. Not a particularly noble name, but not all nobility is born to it. And not all names fit the bearer.

"Too long," said The Wolf.

Katherine was wearing a frown like a tragic mask. "You all know each other," she said. It wasn't a question.

Wolf turned to her with a smile. "Queen Katherine of Elderhaime..."

"You know me?" She backed away a little, looking from the Fool, to Althea and back to this stranger, looking for answers. "Wait… How do you know I'm Queen? How did… Who in the four corners *are* you?"

"My name is Hildewulf."

"There's nothing he doesn't know," said the Fool.

"No one can make that claim, Jester."

He was smiling. It made him look for all the world like some mischievous old uncle. Or the Fool imagined that's what a mischievous old uncle would look like. He wondered if he'd ever had an uncle. And if he did, had he been mischievous?

Anyway.

The old man took Katherine's hand in a gentle grasp. "I bid you welcome to Honanmor, Your Majesty." He bowed to her. She looked confused. "For tonight at least, my home is yours."

The Princess

The Children of the Moors, The Little Lost Ones, The Tiny Ghosts.
They were just a gaggle of kitlings.
Led by a strange old man.
Yet another tale turned out to be both true and not so. The tale depends on the teller, she supposed.
When they had arrived, Wolf had refused all questions, insisting they rest first.
He had shown them down wooden corridors by candlelight, to a hall of individual rooms. She was reminded of the servants' corridor back in the castle.
They were each given a room and each room had a bed.
An actual bed.
A thin, hard bed, but still much more comfortable than some forest floor.
The rooms also had food.
A plate of cheese and cold salted meat was waiting on a tiny table. And water. There was a jug of water.
For a moment, alone in this strange room, she thought maybe this was too good to be true. Here on the Haunted Dunmoors, to find hospitality of this kind was against all expectations.
But all she knew of the moors were tales.
And she didn't believe the tales.
This man, The Wolf. The Fool and Althea seemed to trust him.
But could she even trust them?
She hardly knew anything about any of them.
They had kept her safe, hadn't they?
She didn't know.
She thought she would struggle to sleep, but woke in the morning from a rare absence of the dream. This was the first peaceful night she could remember.

She woke to a knock on the door.

When she dressed and answered it, she saw Althea, the Fool and Wolf.

They asked her to join them on a walk.

If there was something afoot, they must all be in it together.

When they stepped outside, she was amazed to see the sun high in the sky.

"You slept the day away," said the Fool.

"I must've been tired." She tried to remember the last time she slept properly. Even in her warm bed back in the castle, she had only fitful slumbers.

She must've been *very* tired.

And now she was awake.

Wolf showed them around his little island world.

"The legends of The Children of the High Moors are essentially true," he said. He was older than her father, but he had a life in him, a light in his eyes. Bright blue eyes, framed by his long grey hair. He wore a long, deep red robe that was dense with embroidery long faded and tarnished. His clothes looked as old as he did, but robbed him of none of his grandeur.

He went on. "The local villagers abandon their children on the moors at the age of seven as a right of passage."

"That's terrible," she said.

She thought she knew a little of how abandonment felt. And she was recently acquainted with the sensation of being lost and lonely in the wild.

But she was a Princess. Now a Queen. Could she ever know these children's pain?

Did she want to?

They walked past a courtyard at the back of the great hall. High wooden walls all around. Children were regimented throughout the yard, dressed in white and armed with long sticks.

Althea and the Fool walked a little behind, either silently or speaking too quietly to be heard.

The Children were training. They were all ages between seven and young adulthood. A girl who appeared the eldest walked among the rows of little ones, murmuring encouragement and chiding failure. They swung their sticks, thrusting and parrying as one to her orders.

This was an army.

Wolf stopped walking, looking out over the courtyard. "The ones who want to go home, we guide to safety. The others come here."

"They don't all want to go home?"

"Being abandoned in the dark by those you love and trust can make you see your home in a different light."

All she wanted was to go home. Would she feel the same knowing she was abandoned?

"So what is it that you do here?" she asked.

"The children are welcome to stay until their sixteenth year. They are schooled in sciences, ethics, arts, languages…"

Katherine pointed to the training session before them. "War?"

Wolf smiled. "The martial art."

"And what happens when they reach sixteen?"

"They take what they have learned out into the world," he leaned towards her, as if imparting some secret. "I'm trying to create an army of individuals. Armed with knowledge and temperance."

She pointed again. "And big sticks?"

He laughed, wagging a finger at her. "Violence is rarely necessary, often avoidable, and ultimately inevitable."

She tried to think about that. It sounded like some nonsense the Fool would come out with, but coming from this old man it seemed loaded with wisdom.

He had to be a wizard of some sort.

He looked like one.

Althea might not look like a Witch, but Wolf made her think a kindly old Wizard had stepped from a storybook.

She wondered why Witches in the books were terrifying and ugly, whilst Wizards were kind and wise.

Maybe magic affected men and women differently.

She watched the girl walk amongst the training children.

"Why are you doing all this?" she asked Wolf.

"I have been a teacher all my life, but I am only one man." He was watching the kids swinging their sticks in unison. "Each of these children has the chance to change lives, to show people that we have a choice, whether we know it yet or not."

She waited for him to elaborate. He didn't. "What choice?"

He just smiled at her. "If you'll excuse me a moment."

Wolf stepped away from Katherine and walked out amongst the sparring children. He approached the older girl and they exchanged quiet words. After a moment, Wolf turned away with a bow and the girl addressed the children.

"That's enough for today, everyone."

How old was she? Katherine thought she was at most a couple of years the girl's senior, and here this young thing was, talking and acting like a little warlord.

The girl continued. "Now, if anyone's interested, preparations will be made in the main hall for the entertainment of our guests…"

A gasp of excitement came from the assembled ranks.

"Now, remember the company we are in." The girl locked eyes on a particularly scruffy boy who couldn't have been more than nine. "I'm talking to you, Jonas."

There were giggles and Jonas feigned hurt.

"And have fun."

There was a palpable intake of breath, as if the kids were about to jump in to a frozen lake.

The girl was having fun tormenting them. She paused for longer than strictly necessary, looking around the pained faces in front of her. Some of the younger kids were hopping from foot to foot in anticipation.

She finally relented. "Dismissed!"

The children broke ranks and were suddenly running and shouting everywhere.

Just like children should.

The Wolf turned to Katherine and shrugged as they swarmed around and past him like a tide.

The Boy

He danced with a Princess that night.

Like in a tale.

She was a Queen, really, 'cos her Dad died, but she hadn't been crowned yet.

What does a title matter anyway?

He hoped Tia saw.

Was that weird? He wanted Tia to see them dancing together and wish it was her.

When the Master sent them out onto the moors, he knew it was a diplomatic mission, but also that time was of the essence. He didn't have time for pleasantries out there, but things were different when they were home in the hall and the band was playing.

She stood a little away from the dancing, watching her Jester fooling and playing with the Littlies. She was smiling, but she seemed sad.

Near everyone in that hall knew what it was like to lose their parents, but he was pretty sure his were still alive.

And he had a new family.

She reminded him of the new kids, standing there. Every time some new Littlie came in on their seventh, a bit sniffley, a bit scared, and stood in the corner trying to pluck up the courage to get involved. Sometimes they would conjure the moxie themselves, other times one of the older kids had to go and give them a nudge.

He decided she needed nudging.

Also, he didn't think she liked him much when they first met, so this was his chance to make amends.

"Your Majesty," he gave her a polite bow, as is only fitting for a Queen. "My name is Garrick, we met on the moors…"

She eyed him with something approaching a grin. "You look different. Maybe because you're smiling."

He felt himself turning red.

He was just a simple boy from Crofton and she was everything a Princess should be. She was beauty and grace and her skin was soft and she was kind.

But you can't say that to a Queen.

He maintained decorum, as he'd been taught so many times in etiquette class.

"I must apologise for my unstudied diplomacy and the curtness of my earlier instructions."

She raised an eyebrow at his words.

"Would you do me the honour-" he continued- "of allowing me to compensate for my previous surliness via the medium of dance."

He was quite pleased with that line. He thought it sounded pretty accomplished, even though he was getting a bit sweaty and uncomfortable.

She took his hand.

"You'd better be good" she said.

You'd better be good.

He didn't think he'd ever been so happy, excited and scared at the same time.

They danced a jig, and it was fun. His fear soon fell away and he was just dancing with a girl. Like he used to with Tia.

The Princess was only a couple of years older than him, after all.

He wondered for a moment if a royal could ever fall in love with an orphan of the moor. Could a lowborn lowlife climb that high? He thought about how much good you could do if you were a King. You could solve all the problems in the land just by giving orders.

They were dancing to a slow one. The Littlies always got bored when the music slowed down.

"There's a girl watching us," said the Princess.

It was Tia, of course. Arms folded. Looking mad.

"That's just Tia," he said.

"Is she your sweetheart?"

Obviously Princess Queens didn't need to bother about etiquette.

"There's nothing sweet about her," he said. He felt guilty as soon as he said it.

The Princess stepped back from him, holding his shoulders and looking in his eyes.

"You shouldn't be at odds. Life's too short for squabbles. Some people live their entire lives without… anyone to dance with. So when you find someone, you should probably give them a jig."

She beckoned Tia over.

You have to come when a Queen calls.

"I think I'm in your spot" she said to Tia.

When the Princess turned away, Tia kicked him in the shin.

She put her arms around his neck, scowling into his eyes.

And he danced with his best friend for the rest of the night.

The Witch

"They're just children." She shook her head.

She watched them all dancing and larking in the centre of the hall. The table had been moved and a band had formed at one end of the room, playing lutes and fiddles with surprising skill. Some banged pots and boxes for the reeling jigs, and a few even took to singing for the more well-known songs.

Katherine was dancing with the young lad that brought them in, while Jester fought play-battles with the younger children on what was now a dance floor.

"You say 'just children'." The Wolf was sitting beside her at the edge of the hall. "As if they are less than us."

So much innocence, she thought. The world won't let that last. She supped her ale. "I think Jester and the Princess belong here."

"An adult is merely a child with no hope left," said Wolf, imparting lessons as usual. "Children are possibilities. Any of them could be anything they want to be."

"Or anything you want them to be?" she looked at him.

"They are free to leave, Althea. I would return them to their parents' doors, they need only ask."

"How long have you been out here?"

"I'd been coming here for a couple of years on and off up until we all left Elderhaime."

Around the time Katherine's mother left. That was when it all fell apart. Everyone drifted away from the King and his lonely daughter.

All except the Jester.

"This place has been here for much longer than any of us, however." Wolf was still teaching. "It's unclear exactly when Honanmor went up, but there is a legend that says the first lord of this hall was a man named Tord."

That name rang a bell. "The kid from the Banwarch story?"

He nodded. "Tord saw the tradition of abandonment that he had inadvertently started and took it upon himself to offer safe haven to children who couldn't - or didn't want to - find their way home. But, of course, that's just another story."

"So how did you get the job?"

"Before me, it was a couple of old nobles by the name of Smolt were masters of Honanmor. I stumbled upon this place on my travels. Returned from time to time. The Smolts decided on retirement around the time the Green Shadows disbanded."

She hadn't heard that name in a long time. It conjured images of bravery, loyalty and youthful stupidity in her mind.

The good old days.

It was easier to remember them than the bad ones.

"We abandoned them, didn't we?" she said. "Duncan, the Jester, Katherine?"

"We had done all we could," said Wolf. "And I knew we would reunite when the need called."

"Not all of us," she said.

The Wolf was silent for a moment. "I mourned him," he said finally.

For a second, Althea was angry. Where were they all? When she really needed them? When Mark needed them? They could've saved him.

She could've saved him.

But she didn't.

And the anger subsided to the usual level of sadness. The constant weight of death in her heart.

"Me too," she said.

The Jester was now trying to teach Katherine to waltz. They were laughing and smiling.

There it is again.

"If they're not careful this'll all end in tears." She pointed at them, whirling across the floor. "Jester knows Katherine must marry Warwick, for all our sakes, but she will not see."

Katherine was flicking ale at the Jester now.

"And in time, she will see only him." Althea took another swig from her tankard.

The Jester was now chasing the Princess around a table with a mug of ale, followed by a parade of children.

"You do not believe that Warwick is responsible for Duncan's death?" said Wolf.

"I don't know," she said. "It's been so long. He'll be a man now, and the man can be very different to the boy."

"True enough. But if the Queen decides against a unifying marriage, I don't think it will be for the reason you suggest. You put too much stock in our Foolish friend's charm." He leaned forward. "Do not underestimate our young Queen."

She thought for a minute. "I'll wager ten silf that she doesn't marry Warwick." Her look was a challenge.

"Only ten?"

"Twenty."

Wolf reached across the table, offering her his hand. "Done."

Katherine and the Fool were throwing ale at one another, much to the delight of the children.

Althea shook his hand and sat back, watching the ongoing chaos in the hall.

She sighed. "We could've stayed in Elderhaime. But the Queen was gone, the Shadows were no more, we just wanted to be alone for a change." She supped her ale. "Mark and I, we stopped caring about anyone or anything else. Duty to crown and land is nothing against a decree of the heart. Love is the most self-serving of all human foibles."

The Wolf leaned towards her again, a twinkle in his eye.

"Not so. You overlook the single greatest expression of love: sacrifice." He was teaching again. "The truly selfless act, to give up everything for another, is an act of love untarnished by self-gratification."

She thought of Mark hurrying her into the trapdoor.
But what about you?

I'll be fine. Whatever happens don't come out until I come for you.

When the fire started to creep through the boards above her head, she had run down the escape tunnel.

He had sacrificed himself for her and she couldn't even save him.

She knew she would've torn the world in two to bring him back, sacrificed the lives of untold numbers in her raging grief. But that would've been no selfless act. She loved him. She missed him. She wanted him back. When she realised he was truly gone, there was nothing left in the world for her.

If Katherine and the Jester fell in love, they would sooner leave the Siblands to another thousand years of war than give each other up.

She watched them dancing and playing with the children. *And who could blame them?*

The Fool

It was late.

He wasn't sure how late, but it was.

They probably should've turned in a while back, but the ale was flowing and the kids were having a nice time. The littluns had all been sent to bed early on, and the older ones were allowed to have a pint before bed.

He and Katherine had had a few more than one.

He tried to remember if he'd ever seen her drunk before. He hadn't just got her drunk for the first time in her life, had he?

So much for his promise.

He carried her to her room.

They had been given quarters by Wolf. Was nice to sleep in a bed again.

After he put her to bed.

Put her to bed and leave the room.

Go and sleep.

Elsewhere.

Somewhere else.

An elsewhere some.

They were arm in arm, but he was as good as carrying her.

He'd lost his hat.

And Punch. Punch wouldn't be happy he missed the party.

Had he been there?

Punch.

Where was his hat?

Where were they going?

Her room.

That's right.

And then to his.

Him.

Not her.

He kicked open the door and they staggered through into the tiny wooden chamber.

Katherine immediately flopped face-first onto the bed.

"Lodgings fit for a queen!" he cheered.

Katherine groaned. "Don't say that!"

He sat on the bed beside her. "What? You are Queen. This is your Queendom."

She rolled over, looking up at him. "Can't I just be Kathy again?"

She looked pretty. He tried not to notice. Had to stop noticing that. "You're still Queen, no matter what we call you."

She squirmed over and rested her head in his lap, still looking up at him. "And what does that make you?"

He shouldn't be here.

"Will you still be my Fool, no matter what we call you?" she reached up to run a hand through his hair. She mustn't have been used to seeing it.

"Always." He closed his eyes.

He shouldn't be drunk with a drunk Princess. Or Queen. A girl he'd known since she was a child. Since HE was a child.

She stroked his face. "Just a Fool. A Fool who keeps company with witches and warlords and can fight his way through legions of brigands…"

He knew where this was going.

Somewhere he didn't want it to go.

Well, a different somewhere he didn't want it to go.

One of the somewheres he wasn't supposed to want to go to, the other he really didn't.

He shouldn't be in here.

He made for the door.

She almost slipped off the bed. "How could a Fool be capable of all the things I've seen in the past couple of days..?"

The Fool opened the door.

How indeed?

He spoke without turning to face her. "Wolf taught me everything I know."

There was a long moment before Katherine started laughing. "So that's what he's doing here; making an army of Fools?"

He thought of the first time he'd seen the old man, back on the streets of Underton, running and running and running back under the arch and nobody there to help but him.

That was only the first time Wolf saved his life.

"I was little more than a budding vagabond when I met him," he said. "He showed me that I could be more."

Katherine was still laughing. He supposed it was the only logical response to the events of the past couple of days.

"From cutpurse to jester?" she giggled. "An interesting choice!"

Jester. Long since he was anything else.

He thought of Mark and Saro and Blenheim and Althea and King Duncan and Queen Amanda and Leila and even Wolf, all laughing. Laughing at some barmy joke of his. Some bunglery.

He thought of Duncan telling the guards "This boy's just a fool."

He thought of naming Mister Punch.

"They always used to call me the Little Jester." He turned to her, and she saw something in his eyes that stopped her laughing. "Your Father thought it amusing to actually make me one."

He thought of telling her everything. About The Wolf in Underton, about Leila and the betrayal of Jolias Arch, about the Green Shadows and their sorry end, about Althea and Mark, about Saro and Blenheim in the woods, everything.

But he knew if he began to tell her, he wouldn't be able to stop until his whole sorry life were laid before her like a tapestry of blood and lies.

Truths so long buried take time to unearth.

So he told her nothing.

"Get some kip, Princess."
He left the room, closing the door behind him.
"Queen!" she shouted.

I know she's there.
I can't see her.
She's not alone.
There's something else.
Children.
Children in the dark around the bed.
Lost.
I reach for her.
I'm afraid.
The bells ring.
And he burns.
He burns and bandages himself.
Raw skin and teeth bared.
She runs.
I can never see her face.
Do I even remember it?
He steps forward from the darkness.
I want to run. Run after her.
I can't move.
He has the knife. He wears the crown.
He asks me to marry him.

The Princess

Her head hurt.

Not like being hit or banging it or anything. This was a dull throb deep behind her eyes, even before she opened them.

Her first hangover.

A cold light crept through the window, and she remembered where she was.

She was in a weird settlement of children run by a weird old man. It was quite weird.

She sat up.

After her restful night before, the dream had come back stronger and stranger. As usual, she couldn't quite remember it, but she could still feel the dread and loss that it had gripped her with.

They had to leave. Last night had been wonderful fun, she remembered dancing and laughing a lot, but they had to leave.

She wanted to go home.

The Fool brought her to her chamber.

Did he?

She had the vague recollection of proximity, of intimacy.

That Fool probably took advantage of her.

No.

No. It wasn't like that.

She almost got through to him, but she pushed too hard.

He said things. Things she barely remembered and understood even less.

That's why they had to leave. They had to get back to Elderhaime, where she could be Queen and he could be the court Jester again, and she wouldn't have to worry about getting drunk with him and strange feelings manifesting themselves.

There was a jug of water on the table. She drank straight from the jug.

A thick black cloak had been folded at the foot of the bed. She wrapped it around herself and stepped out of the door.

She looked for a moment at the Fool's door opposite hers. She wondered what the courtiers would think of a Fool entering a Queen's bed chamber. Was it worse for a Queen to enter a Fool's chamber?

Politics.

She pulled the cloak up around her ears and stepped out into the early morning mists.

The island was quiet, shrouded. The dew on the grass wet her feet as she walked.

She wasn't sure where she was walking to.

And what of it? If she wanted a Fool in her chamber, wasn't she Queen? With her father now gone, there was nobody to force her into the arms of a man she didn't want.

Not that she wanted the Fool, of course.

Just, she could.

If she wanted.

She walked around to the main hall. She could hear children training with their sticks in the courtyard. It was a full-time job for them, obviously.

It was time to go home. Time to call the scattered forces of Elderhaime to her. Time to scour the Holtlands as she marched on Fairford. Time to show King Warwick he proposed to the wrong maid. If the people wanted unity, they would get it under her rule.

Her.

Alone.

A political marriage proposal was bad enough, but corrupting such a declaration of love by using it as bait for an assassination was unforgivable. He obviously didn't understand love at all.

Did she?

Did she understand love?

She peered into the great hall. It had been cleared since the night before, and now a line of six children twirled slowly across the floor, moving with a strange synchronicity.

Katherine watched them move as one, mopping the floor in a silent ballet.

She asked one of them what they had done to deserve cleaning duties instead of training with the others.

"It's just our turn," was his reply.

She wandered back outside, heading down to the river bank.

"Just our turn," the boy said. Even children are not safe from the intrusion of duty. And these children were here by choice. Would they not rather be playing tig or chasing butterflies or some other juvenile pursuit?

Down by the lakeside was a brittle old stickleshrub, curled over by the wind. On a long, protruding branch sat a beautiful song bird. She could hear its trilling melody from afar and quietly approached.

She marvelled at its rainbow belly and blue feathers. It ruffled itself and puffed out its chest.

Katherine tried to remember its name from her books, but couldn't place it. She thought Althea would know its name.

The bird hopped a little further along its perch.

It was a strange sight, this little speck of beauty amongst the grey moors and the misery that seemed to surround her.

Somehow, it gave her hope.

The bird didn't have to worry about duty or birthright or any such thing. He just had to sit there and sing and then fly away whenever he felt like it.

Oh, for the life of a bird.

She noticed the ripples hit the bank of the lake all too late.

There was a Finder.

Coming out of the water.

She had been watching the bird so intently she didn't see it until it was almost on her.

A Finder.

It smashed through the branch and the bird flew away, the lucky thing.

It was on her before she could scream.

She'd hadn't seen one this close before.

It had a long, thin hand around her throat.

Her feet were off the ground.

And then she was lying on her back.

It was so heavy for such a wiry, sinewy creature.

She scratched at its face, but it clasped her wrists and pinned her down.

At least it let go of her throat.

She was screaming, she realised. Her own voice sounded distant as the translucent grey skin of its face split open and its tongue lolled forth.

It was a forked tongue.

No, it was a pair of fat, slimy, pink tubes that snaked out of its mouth and onto her face.

She remembered the tales.

She remembered being told that blind beggars had been caught by Finders.

She remembered what the Fool had said.

They take out your eyes and leave you crawling.

Where was he? He was supposed to be protecting her.

The tubes slathered up past her nose.

She screwed up her eyes tightly and wondered what being blind would be like. And how long she would live afterwards.

The tubes fixed over her eyelids.

She was still screaming.

She wondered if this was how she would be remembered. Katherine the Lost and Blinded and Dead.

It was sucking out her eyes.

And then it wasn't.

It let her go. Its weight was lifted.

She opened her eyes to see a hand, clad in chainmail, dragging the Finder off her by its tongue.

It was a Knight, armoured and helmeted.

A Knight had saved her.

The stories were true.

"Unhand her, foul beast!" came his commanding cry.

She scrabbled backwards, blinking her eyes to make sure they hadn't come loose.

A Knight in shining armour. Well, the armour was slightly mucky, but you can't have everything.

She was in a tale.

This couldn't be real.

The Knight ripped out the Finder's tongue and punched it in its reptilian face.

The Finder puked blood. They left parts like that out of the tales, she thought.

"Princess!" The Fool, Althea, Wolf and some of the children were running down the hill towards her.

The Knight fought with such skill and strength, she was mesmerised. Every attack the Finder made was dodged or parried, and every one of the Knight's blows hit its mark.

The Fool was at her side, kneeling. "Are you hurt?"

Katherine shook her head, still transfixed by the battle before her.

The Fool stood up to join the fray, but Wolf grabbed his elbow.

The Knight finally drew a long sword. A blade of unparalleled craftsmanship, Katherine noted. Funny how an instrument of death could be a thing of beauty.

The Finder had no protection against the blade, and was soon running out of limbs.

What, mere moments ago, was an unspeakable terror emerging from the river to terrorise her, was now a pitiful, wounded animal skulking on the ground before its assailant.

It whimpered and rolled onto its back.

There was quite a crowd gathered now, many of the children had run down from the courtyard, but the Knight seemed oblivious to his audience.

The Knight knelt beside the dying finder.

He removed his helmet, but Katherine could only see a mess of black hair.

He spoke to the beast. "Must those born from misery live and die in misery?"

The Knight stroked the face of the Finder and it nuzzled his gloved hand, feebly.

"Poor thing." He drove his sword into the Finder's heart. It shrieked and shuddered and died.

The Knight got to his feet, and gently pushed the Finder's body with his foot. It rolled down the bank, into the lake.

The Knight turned, sheathing his sword, and finally seemed to notice the gathered crowd.

The Fool spoke first. "King Warwick."

Katherine looked at him. The Fool, Althea, Wolf and the assembled children were all down on one knee.

She looked back at the Knight. Her saviour.

He was handsome. Jet black hair over a kind face that was all sharp edges. Soft grey eyes over high cheek bones.

He seemed a little embarrassed.

"Hello." He raised a gauntlet.

All she could think was: *Bollocks.*

Part Five:
The Found and the Lost.

Extract from Lord Felix Tyrantson's Diary:
Twelve Years of Age

Fourth Dorenday, Third Moon of Summer, 208
I talked to him today. He had been drinking, but it was a calm day. He didn't hit me or threaten me, really. I asked him about Belinda.

He didn't remember at first. He didn't know who I was talking about. When I told him she was my cat, he laughed at me.

He said that was why I'd never be King. I'm not a soldier like Warwick. I'm too old to keep playing at swords and weeping over pets. He said I'm weak.

It's not my fault I'm skinny. Warwick is bigger than me. Maybe I'll grow.

He said the only advantage I have is my mind. He says I'm a schemer. He's a warrior and a schemer, Warwick got one part and I got the other.

The only thing that matters is power. If you don't have it, then the only thing that matters is getting it.

He said he watched me catch that rabbit in the snare I made. He said it made him proud.

He said he killed Belinda because he could.

I didn't ask why he killed my mother.

If only you could make a snare for the whole world, he said.

If only.

The King

He had found her.

She was more beautiful than he had heard, than he had even hoped. Hair so golden and eyes so blue and skin so soft and pale.

But she was afraid and confused.

And angry.

They weren't supposed to meet like this.

He looked at himself and thought he must seem almost an unman to her, covered in the bladewine of some Baelic-spawn, the mud of the road and other, older blood that was harder to explain.

He stepped forward. She drew herself up and he saw a thousand thoughts in her blue eyes.

He could think of only one way to bring her peace.

He drew his knife.

Her eyes went wide.

He knelt before her.

He presented the knife to her, hilt first.

"Your Highness, I am responsible for the death of your father. Had I not asked for your hand in marriage - had I not invited you to Fairford - your caravan would not have been abroad in the Fothwood and your father and his brave guards and nobles would yet live." He kept his head lowered and his eyes closed.

He could hear a murmur amongst the others. The Hildewulf was there, and Althea the Healer. And the Jester, of course. He thought they must be all that remains of the legendary Green Shadows that haunted Fairford so in his youth.

"How do you know about my father?" the Queen asked.

He knew how it looked.

"One of your brave knights survived long enough to get to Fairford." He looked up at her, finally. Her eyes were fixed on the knife he still held out to her. "I found the caravan on the Elderfarway. I buried the King as best I could."

"How did you find us?"

"I tracked the brigands. Though they dared not cross the River Thurgan, they sent their Finders across. I followed."

There was a long silence. He could hear her breathing as ragged as his. "How can we trust you?" she said at last.

"You can't. I intended none of this, Highness, but I caused it all. I offer my knife…" he raised it again. "That you may enact a punishment befitting my crime. Your Father is dead because of me."

She took the knife.

Her soft, gentle fingers lifted it from his grasp.

He lowered his head.

"It is your fault," she said.

He really hoped she wasn't going to kill him. Of course, he deserved it, and to offer himself was the right thing to do, but he would rather not die. There was so much he had left to do.

"But it wasn't just your fault," she continued. "Rise, King Warwick, and look me in the eye."

He did so.

She pointed his knife at his nose. "You can live, for now. But if I find out you had more to do with this than you're letting on, or if you do anything… weird… I will kill you." Her eyes were blue fire and he knew she was serious.

She gave him his knife back.

"Thank you, your Highness," he said.

"My name is Katherine." She offered her hand. He bowed to kiss it.

"And I am Warwick."

She looked at him with a frown, as one might scrutinise a parchment written in a foreign tongue.

"Can we get off our knees now?" It was the Jester.

Warwick turned to the gathered crowd. "Of course, my friends, please rise! How rude of me."

They got to their feet.

He turned back to Katherine. "I had entertained such fears, but you are safe and in good company, I deem!"

The Jester, Hildewulf and Althea approached, and he stepped forward to meet them. "My heart soars to see you united once more!" He shook hands with the Jester and Hildewulf and bowed to Althea.

Katherine sighed. "You know them all as well?"

He knew them. "We are... old enemies. From the days of my father."

"I need to get out more," she said, looking away.

Warwick remembered it well. The Jester had been but a boy at the time, and Warwick not much more. If his part in the sabotage of Fairford's fleet had been known, his father would've hanged him in the courtyard, son or not.

He remembered the realisation that he had been born onto the wrong side of a war. He remembered his many run-ins with the Green Shadows and how they carried themselves with dignity and honour, while he was garrisoned with Bronwenson and his cut-throats. He remembered wondering how one could so admire his enemies and so despise his allies.

"Well, my Queen," said the Jester, "If you're not gonna do a murder out here, shall we get in and murder some breakfast? Cos I certainly could."

The Princess

Who was this man?

A King in name, born into the family of her sworn enemy. She had blamed him for the death of her father, and yet here he was, sitting opposite her at the long table in the hall of Honanmor, scoffing eggs and bacon like any traveller long abroad.

How did she get here?

Mere days ago she was lamenting her time locked within castle walls, her lonely routine of waking, dressing, reading, wandering, maybe riding through the gardens or onto the Reeceland if she had accompaniment.

Now she was in a wooden fort on an island on a lake in the haunted Dunmoors of Fairford, and she had battled with monsters and brigands and watched her father die and done killing of her own.

And now she broke bread with her enemy. A Tyrantson.

He had saved her. Hadn't he? The Finder had almost plucked her eyes from her head but he had appeared like a hero of legend, in the very nick of time.

But she had only his word that he didn't send the beast in the first place.

She watched as the Fool talked his usual frivolities. He and the King were reminiscing about some old adventure, though she heard only vague words through the net of her thoughts. Battles and blazes and derring-do, no doubt. Althea and Wolf seemed to be watching her.

Could she trust these people?

Did she even know any of them?

She obviously only knew the Fool as much as he wanted her to. She had come to see a different Fool these past few days, one which Althea, Wolf and even Warwick Tyrantson seemed to know intimately.

Who are they?

From what she could gather, they had all been part of some gang or team, wandering the wilds and causing havoc for the Tyrant King. She wondered how different that was from what the Bandaged Bastard was doing now.

A conspiracy. Years in the making.

The tales might say this fortuitous meeting of old friends was fate, but she didn't believe the tales.

She wondered if she could trust them. Any of them.

At this point they were her only hope of getting home. Beyond that, she wasn't sure.

She couldn't help thinking of something she said to her Dad: "I will not be a bargaining chip."

Was that all she was? An accessory to peace? Or worse? She thought of the Fool's warnings back in Crossford. How much would Elderhaime pay in ransom for her? What political leverage could be executed with a Queen as a hostage?

She couldn't trust anyone.

Everyone wanted her because of what she was. They weren't her friends.

Were they?

She wasn't even sure of herself anymore, let alone this gaggle of seeming strangers.

A child dressed in black brought more bacon to the table, but Katherine had lost her appetite.

Someone at the table spoke to her.

It was Warwick.

"My Queen?"

She realised she hadn't responded.

"Yes?" she said.

"We were saying a better route back to Elderhaime may be to cross the Thurwund west of here and head through the Hardwater to the Underfarway."

The Fool grinned. "And then we can climb the Lip, if you're feeling up to it?"

"Climb..?" she remembered looking out from The Longing Cliff, the sensation of emptiness below her. The infinite misstep of falling.

"It would be the quickest and safest way back up to the Reeceland." Wolf spoke now. She felt like they were ganging up on her. Only Althea remained silent.

"Safest? Climbing a sheer, two-hundred foot rock face?" she looked at each of them.

"It's more like four hundred," said Warwick.

"And that's after we wade through miles of treacherous marshland," the Fool was enjoying this, of course. "And then miles of dense, unassailable woodland."

"It may be the only way to avoid the vagabonds who hunt you." Warwick spoke earnestly. "They sent out more Finders, it is only a matter of time before they catch your scent."

"You do stink," the Fool said to her.

Warwick looked at him, open mouthed. "You speak that way to your Queen?" He looked like he might punch the Fool.

The Fool shrugged.

Katherine raised a hand before anything else could be said. "Enough. If this is what you advise, then so be it."

"It is settled, then," said Warwick. "I shall escort you for as long as you need me."

Great.

She would go with them. She remembered her map studies, and she thought she could find her way from the Hardwater Fens to the Underfarway herself.

She would go with them, but she didn't know how long she would stay with them.

The Witch

That put the cat amongst the pigeons.

Not only did Warwick turn up and rescue the Princess, he was every bit as noble, handsome and gentle as a Prince from a tale. Perhaps those twenty silf would go to Wolf after all.

And maybe it would seem less of a curse for Katherine to be betrothed to such a man?

No. She knew that Warwick's suitability would only mildly sweeten the bitter tonic, and Katherine needed no excuse to spit it out.

Yes, King Warwick was a fine match, but that wasn't going to make this any easier. If she was correct, Katherine was on the verge of giving her heart to another, and once love took hold, all chance of peace was lost.

Althea pulled her cloak around her in the morning chill.

A crowd had gathered on the slope outside the hall of Honanmor. She perched on horseback alongside the Jester and Warwick. The children gathered around.

Her horse was a brown mare named Guthrinca. Althea was uncomfortable in the saddle, and horses could always tell. She'd had a few words, but the beast was stubborn and aloof.

She wouldn't be surprised if she was thrown before the day was done. She couldn't really blame the animal. Who would want someone riding around all day on their back like a dead weight? Everyone wants to rid themselves of their burden.

They awaited the Queen.

When she emerged from the great doors along with Wolf, her appearance was less regal and more akin to the waifs and strays around her. Cloaked and hooded in black.

The Wolf spoke. "It seems the ranks of the Lost Children have a new addition!"

The children laughed and cheered for Katherine.

For a flickering moment, she seemed lost. But she smiled and bowed low to her young subjects.

She'll do fine.

The Jester was impatient. "Come 'ead, Princess. We need to get a shimmy on if we're gonna get you home."

She descended the steps towards them. Warwick smiled down from his horse. "Ready when you are, Your Majesty."

Althea watched Katherine smiling and bowing and waving at the mass of children as she passed them. They loved her already, as would the nations of Fairford and Elderhaime if given the chance.

She was born to it, like it or not.

As Katherine reached her horse, the young man who had found them on the moors stepped forward to help her into the saddle.

He danced with her the night before. Another of the Queen's admirers. They would be queuing up before long.

There was a girl standing behind him, trying not to look angry. Young love.

The Queen thanked the boy with a kiss on his forehead. He looked like he might faint. The girl looked like she might burst.

So, not everyone was a fan of the new Queen.

The Wolf stepped to Althea's side and held forth a small wooden cage. A yellow bird fluttered within. A merecandle, in case of emergencies. Much faster than a pigeon.

She took it gladly, nodding her thanks to Wolf. She knew there would be a compartment in the base of the cage containing a tiny scroll and capsule for attaching to the bird's leg.

She poked a finger through the cage and the merecandle hopped up to perch on it. She introduced herself and the little bundle of feathers ruffled up.

Her thoughts went to the menagerie she'd left behind. Torn apart by Finders. She had kept them alive and they had returned the favour. But what reason did she have now?

Get Katherine to safety. That was a job worth the doing. And once it was done, perhaps Althea could finally be free.

Yes, when this was all over she would go to Mark, under their Bluefire tree. For once and all.

"I hope you won't need him." Wolf said.

"Me too."

He handed her a bed roll which she knew would also contain blades, food and whatever other provisions he could spare.

"I would come with you, but I fear I should not leave the children alone with Finders abroad," he said.

She reached down to take his hand. "These children need you more than we do, old man."

He smiled at her. "I sincerely hope so."

Althea thought the Finders would be most likely to follow them away from the fort, but she knew this shower of innocents should not be left unguarded.

One of the smallest children, a boy of about seven, ran out from the crowd and pulled at the Jester's trouser leg. She watched as the child held out a familiar red-and-green tri-pronged hat.

"Thanks Ozzy!" cried the Jester, taking it from him. "Thought I'd lost that."

The little boy watched with a grin as the Jester squeezed the hat onto his head and shook it, ringing the bells.

"I don't think you're a fool," said the boy. "You're just silly."

Althea smiled. She hoped he was right.

The boy ran off into the crowd.

Everyone was ready. They were to set out on what would hopefully be the last leg of their journey.

Warwick rounded his mount and called to the children, "Farewell, my friends! We ride to Elderhaime!"

The Jester produced a rusty old miniature bugle and blasted a feeble, elongated, raspy quack from it. She laughed.

He'd had that thing for years, but it was only seen on special occasions.

The Jester spurred his horse into a gallop and tore away from the hall, almost falling from his saddle with rehearsed precision.

The children laughed and applauded his idiocy, and Althea couldn't help but smile.

They kicked their horses into a trot and headed after him.

Just ahead of her, she heard Warwick speak to Katherine. "It's a full-time job with him, isn't it? Fooling?"

"You have no idea," the Queen replied.

Finally.

They were talking.

About him.

The Fool

So they were going home.

And he was coming with them.

Warwick had always been a good lad. Back in the Shadow days, they wouldn't've done half as much damage to the Tyrant's plots without the help of the Tyrant's own first born.

He wondered if, once they got back to the castle, Warwick would be sleeping over.

He thought maybe they could have the wedding at Elderhaime. A wedding and a funeral for Duncan at the same time. Life and death. Hope and despair. Sugar and shite.

We'll see.

It was what he wanted, wasn't it?

It was what everyone wanted. For the King of Fairford and the Queen of Elderhaime to be bound together in a symbolic gesture of their willingness to unite the Sundered Sibling Lands forever.

It was definitely what he wanted.

He wanted to see her bound to another man forever.

Why wouldn't he want that?

They rode over the moors, through the grey mists and on towards Crofton. The town was a dense gathering of wooden houses perched on the edge of the Dunmoors, crowding along the east bank of the Thurwund. He thought the buildings seemed to lean out over the water, as if peering into the depths in search of something they dropped.

Crofton was a market town, but if you were in the market for anything other than fish there was scant supply. It was a handy stop on the river twixt Brimmenhaime and Underton, but not much else.

A covered bridge just north of the town was their means of crossing the Thurwund, and he was chuffed not to have to approach Crofton itself. Not only could the Brigands' hunt have already led them there, but the thought of a town that abandoned little uns as a rite of passage set his teeth on edge.

If he were to set foot in Crofton, the town would probably be afire by sundown.

Parents were supposed to keep their kids close, guard them from harm and watch them grow up. Not abandon them, not leave them alone on the moors or the streets or in a castle or in the woods or anywhere. Someone once told him that wherever your parents left you was where you would stay.

The Fool had been left in the gutter.

Left to die or fend for himself.

He chose to fend.

Best they move past Crofton, sharpish.

As they approached the bridge, he became acutely aware of the bottleneck they were walking into. The bridge was around a hundred feet long and about eight feet wide. Enough for two of them to ride abreast.

A wooden tunnel, over water, with guarded gates at either end.

As they approached he could see that the guard on the near side was asleep. Or dead. The bridge gate was open.

"Asleep or dead?" the Fool called to his companions.

Warwick drew his sword.

They were on a dirt farway in open ground and the town lay a quarter mile to the West. There was nowhere for an attack to spring from here, was there?

There was always somewhere.

He leaned down in the saddle and picked up a pebble, which he bounced off the bridge guard's head.

The man woke with a cry.

Asleep, then.

Warwick sheathed his sword with a frown.

"How, good sire!" the Fool called to the startled man.

The bridge guard stood up, straightening his chainmail. "How yerself."

"Sorry to disturb you, you're obviously a very busy fellow, but may we trouble you to make use of yon overwater farway?"

"A Silf apiece."

Ripoff. The Fool was just about to offer a fistful of bloody teeth as alternative payment when Warwick spoke.

"Do you know to whom you speak, sir?" the King asked the guard.

Warwick wasn't going to tell him, was he? The Fool threw a warning glance at the King.

"Someone who has to pay a Silfring to cross this bridge, just like everyone else," said the Guard. "Pretty shiny armour or no."

The Fool was certain this smug get would've come down with a severe bout of "pretty shiny gauntlet in face" if Althea hadn't tossed him a small bag of coins.

"Keep the change," said the Witch.

Warwick was still bristling as the horses passed the guard and clopped onto the bridge.

The Fool glimpsed black water through the boards creaking beneath his horse's hooves. Warwick rode beside him, then Althea and Katherine brought up the rear.

"You probably shouldn't be telling everyone who we are, my lord," he said to the King.

"Jester, these are our people, mine and Lady Katherine's. They look upon us as we look upon them: as our family."

The Fool made a "polite disagreement" sound. "Maybe in the homelands, but out here things are a bit different." He looked down through the boards again. "This river isn't called the Thurwund for nowt. It slices the Siblands clear in two, we're in no man's land here and many have allegiance only to themselves. All they'll see when you announce your royalty is a money pouch."

Warwick nodded. "All the more reason we must unite the lands. These people are isolated and disenfranchised when they should be the heart of the Kingdom." He turned in his saddle to address Katherine. "My lady, don't you think—"

He didn't finish his question because of the spear that came up through a gap in the floorboards and stuck his horse through the neck.

It was a conversation killer.

The King

He landed on his feet.

Ferfost hadn't thrown him since he was a colt, so he knew something was amiss.

The horse was screaming.

A Longar had been thrust up through the floorboards and into Ferfost's neck.

In one movement, Warwick swept his sword from its sheath and split the shaft of the spear.

Ferfost lolled forward onto the boards, driving the speargad even further home.

Warwick was dimly aware that the other horses were panicking.

It only took a second to know that Ferfost would die. His blood was pouring through the gaps in the planks and Warwick saw the boat below. Two men on one narrow boat. About ten, fifteen feet down? The sounds from behind told him there was at least one more boat.

"Ho, up there!" came a call from beneath them.

The gates fifty feet behind them creaked shut.

He turned to see the ones ahead being pushed closed by two more guards.

They were trapped in a hundred foot tunnel of wood, at the mercy of the spearmen below.

Longars were jabbing up in front of Katherine and Althea's horses as they reared in alarm.

"Ho, up there!" came the call again.

"Ho yourself!" The Jester was out of his saddle and perched like an eagle halfway up the wall, his puppet drawn.

Ferfost's eye was white and wide. He was going to die slowly, afraid and in pain.

The voice called again: "Give us all your money and jewels or we'll kill you all."

Just a robbery. They obviously didn't know who they had just snared. The Jester was right to silence Warwick's royal announcement, or they might be facing a kidnapping.

Ferfost was still shrieking and trying to stand.

"How are we supposed to give you our jewels when you're way down there?" called the Jester.

A hatch opened next to Warwick.

A square window lifted outward in the wall, almost directly opposite where the Jester perched. Daylight spilled in. There was a sack suspended from a pulley system just outside.

"Put your money and jewels and weapons in the sack and then we'll open the gates and you can be on your way." They must do this a lot.

Ferfost's crying was reducing to a bubbling bleating as his hooves found no purchase on the boards.

Warwick walked to his struggling horse. He placed a hand on his flank, looked him in the eye and then quickly pushed his sword through his friend's head.

"Sorry," he said.

"Do we have an accord?" called the voice.

The Jester looked at Warwick.

"What are you doing?" hissed Katherine.

Warwick pointed downward and then held up a hand with four fingers raised. The Jester nodded.

Warwick thought for a moment. Then nodded back at the Jester.

"Just give us a moment to gather our things," called the Jester.

Warwick pulled at a knapsack on Ferfost's saddle, and dragged out a long coil of rope.

"Ten foot?" he mouthed to the Jester.

The Jester nodded again, smiling as he saw the rope.

He heard Katherine and Althea whispering urgently, but there was no time for questions.

He fed the rope out and threw one end to the Jester, still perched on the wall.

He sliced the rope around the thirty foot mark.

The Jester tied his end around his waist.

Warwick did the same.

He backed up to the hatch.

"Open a window," he told the Jester.

The Jester heaved his puppet at the wooden wall beside him, knocking the rotten planks free.

There were now two windows facing each other in the walls of the bridge.

Warwick and the Jester looked at each other and both stepped backwards into the air.

Falling was a strange sensation, but it was only a moment before the rope snapped taught and he swung inward to the underside of the bridge.

He saw them.

Four men on two narrow boats, little more than canoes. They weren't even wearing armour. They were peasants. Three were holding Longar shafts aloft and the third was holding a rope attached to the sack-pulley. None of them seemed to be expecting to die.

They both hit the boat at the same time.

The Jester landed a two-footed kick into the chest of one of the pikemen, sending him sprawling into the water

Warwick could've had the head off the pulley man. He must've been the one who killed Ferfost. He deserved to die, didn't he?

Kill him kill him kill him

But Warwick swung his sword pommel first, knocking the man down into his boat.

Someone on the bridge made a perfectly timed cut of the rope, and Warwick and the Jester landed in the first boat. Warwick on his feet, the Jester on his arse.

The two men in the boat behind them were agog.

"How, ye craven Herbrogs!" cried the Jester, climbing to his feet. "You owe us a horse."

Warwick leapt between the two boats, and the peasants staggered back.

He smashed the Longar from the hands of the first and punched him in the face.

He went down, bleeding.

The last man dropped his pike into the Thurwund and raised his palms. "Sorry," he said, his eyes wide. "I needed the money."

The Princess

It had all happened so fast.

She had seen Warwick's horse rear up, spilling him to the ground, she had seen him land like a cat and suddenly his sword was out and the horse was scraping around in a pool of blood.

She might have thought Warwick killed his horse. Just for a moment. The spearpoints that came up through the floor in front of both her horse and Althea's put paid to that.

She had watched as the Fool talked to the men below, saw Warwick put his horse out of its misery, and watched them whispering and tying ropes around themselves.

Althea had told her they were up to something foolish.

The Witch had slid a sword, hilt-first, over her shoulder into her hand. She told her to be ready to move.

She had looked back at her. She had smiled a smile of encouragement, as one you might give to a child about to get in the saddle for the first time.

The Fool had smashed a hole in the wall and he and Warwick had leapt out of either side of the bridge.

The rope had twanged tight, blocking their way.

Althea had kicked her horse forward, raised her sword and slashed the rope clean in two. Both halves whipped out of the windows and out of sight, the very instant the Witch's horse had leapt the corpse of Warwick's.

Katherine's horse and the Fool's riderless nag had followed suit.

When they had reached the gates at the end of the tunnel, they found them barred shut on the outside. Katherine had hopped from the saddle and stuck Wolf's sword through the crack in the door, lifting the bar from within.

When they were free, their captors had already fled.

The Fool and Warwick brought prisoners up the riverbank. Three men. Warwick took the Fool's horse and rode the rest of them down.

And here they were.

Five men in total.

On their knees, unarmed and afraid.

Their friend the bridgeguard from the east bank was long gone, as was the one the Fool had knocked into the Thurwund.

Warwick had gone back into the bridge to grieve his dead horse. She thought he must be a particularly tender man. He had mourned a Finder he himself put to the sword and now he knelt next to the corpse of a steed.

She wondered if there was enough compassion left in her for such actions. All she seemed to feel was rage and confusion.

She still hadn't cried for her Father.

There just wasn't time.

These men had presumed to rob her. What right did they have to take from her? From anyone?

When Warwick emerged from the bridge, he walked to where the prisoners knelt. She wondered if he had cried.

They were on a grassy belt that ran parallel to the river. The worn dirt track slithered out of the bridge and off to the north, fading fairly rapidly before it reached the wall of gnarled, black trees indicating the southern edge of the Hardwater Fens.

That way did not look inviting.

"Well," Warwick said to the kneeling men. "Before we start, let's do some introductions."

The Fool gave him an imploring look, but Warwick continued. "I am King Warwick of Fairford, and this is Queen Katherine of Elderhaime."

The men looked confused.

"What happened to King Duncan?" asked one.

"He was killed by a treacherous wretch like you," she sneered.

Warwick raised a hand. "My Queen, please. We do not yet know what misfortune led these men to this end."

"They're not men."

"That remains to be seen." He widened those grey eyes at her. "Please?"

She could keep her peace for a few minutes, she thought. She nodded.

Warwick nodded thanks and turned back to the kneeling men. He knelt himself and looked the nearest in the eye. He spoke quietly. "What's your name, my friend?"

The man looked scared out of his wits. She could scarce believe these cowards had the gall to carry out such bold thievery.

"Martin, my Lord," he stammered.

"Martin, why did you kill my horse?" Warwick was not threatening or angry, but seemed completely emotionless. Somehow she found this all the more unsettling, and it seemed to have the same effect on the men.

"I didn't!" the man called Martin pleaded. "It was Algar!"

"I'm sorry my lord!" wept another man. He had dried blood on his face from where Warwick had hit him. "I meant not to hurt the nag, just spook it, like."

"You need to work on your Longar thrust, Algar. You know the 'gar' in your name means spear?" The man looked confused. Warwick turned back to Martin. "Martin, what I meant was:" he leaned in close to the frightened man's face. "You all seem like decent enough gentlemen…"

She couldn't help a laugh at this, but Warwick flashed her a look that silenced her. Maybe this was what it was like to meet the Tyrant? Not a roaring madman, but a calm, calculated inquisitor. There was something in that look that frightened her.

Warwick continued. "What drove you to take up spears and robbery?"

Martin couldn't look Warwick in the eye. He shrugged his shoulders like a scolded child. "Dunno."

"We had to," said the man next to him. He was older than the rest, grey bearded beneath the muck. "Crofton's good as dead."

Warwick turned to this new speaker. "How so?"

"Brigands squeezed the bloody life out of it, your liege."

Katherine wondered if the old rodent had deliberately misspoken his deference.

The old man went on: "Every shop, every tavern, every farmstead, every blacksmith has for stump up every last gobbet they earn or face the gad of Fury's bill."

"Fury?" the Fool perked up at that name.

"Aye, Sir Gleeware, you ken he?"

The Fool smiled. "Aye, we ken Ken."

"Aye, well, that arsewarch and his drengs have brought nowt but mistide likes of which we never seen. Nay trade fars this way nay more, by farway or brim. Floaters from Brimmenhaime are few an' far twixt, an them from the bay don't tarry if they haven't to."

He was starting to lose her. Some of the old speech was still used by everyday folk, but she hadn't heard this much in one mouthful since an old nanny she'd had as a child.

The old man looked at Warwick. "People are clemt. So we took it 'pon ourselves for to feed 'em."

"By stealing from passers by?" said the King.

"Them as look as they can spare some."

Warwick sighed. He was looking at the old man like he was a puzzle to be solved. "Well," he said, standing up. "I think we can come to some arrangement. Excuse us a moment."

Warwick stepped away from the men, waving Katherine, the Fool and Althea to follow him. They gathered around him a short way away.

"What arrangement?" said Katherine. "They tried to kill us. That's treason."

"They threatened to kill us. That's different," said Warwick.

"Still treason. You know damn well both our Fathers would have strung them up for this."

Warwick gave her those sad grey eyes again.

"Perhaps that's why we should be merciful."

"Do you really want to hang them, Your Majesty?" Althea said. "The Fool is the only one here under your royal command. Would you make him your executioner? Would you have him kill unarmed men?"

Katherine looked at the Fool. "I'm sure it wouldn't be the first time."

The Fool shrugged.

"We should give them the horses," said Warwick.

She couldn't believe what she was hearing. "What?"

"We will have no use of them on the Hardwater."

"And I wouldn't want to hoist them up the Lip," said the Fool.

"They killed your horse," she said to Warwick. "And you want to give them more?"

"I don't believe they intended to kill Ferfost."

"No, they just intended to rob us."

"My lady, they had no choice."

"There's always a choice!"

"But not always an easy one. The choice between committing thievery or letting your family starve, for instance..."

"But, they're just like the Brigands..."

"No, my lady," said Warwick. "The Brigands only destroy. These people were, in their own simple way, trying to save their town. Their families. Their own little corner of the world." Those eyes again. Sadness and hope. "Katherine, they were trying to do our job."

"Oh, come on! You're saying this was our fault?"

"Perhaps ours, perhaps our Fathers'. If the lands were united, a central, unified force could clear the Brigands from the Holtlands in a matter of months. Perhaps then people wouldn't be afraid to travel the farways and brims round these parts and formerly honest men wouldn't be hiding under bridges waving Longars around. I will not speak of marriage in such darkling times, Your Majesty, but we must at least learn to *work* together."

He turned away, seeming almost angry. A small shudder went through Katherine as she again felt the Tyrant's presence.

Warwick approached the men, who were all still kneeling. "On your feet."

They stood.

"Here's the accord," he walked in front of them like centurion of some tiny, bedraggled remnant of a great force. "You can take the horses, the saddles, anything my friends and I don't need for the journey ahead."

The men's mouths hung open.

Katherine shook her head. A compassionate Tyrantson wasn't the most bizarre thing she'd seen recently, but it was close. What was it her Dad and the Fool kept saying about him? "He is not his father's son."

"You can also take the carcass in the bridge for meat and rendering."

She couldn't contain her incredulity at that. "You're going to let them eat your horse?"

Warwick turned to her. "My horse is gone. What's back there is meat. If he can help feed but one starving mouth, then Ferfost's death has not been in vain."

Warwick turned back to the men.

"This is… most gracious of you, my Lord," said the old man, his thick dialect all but gone. So, she thought, Warwick had earned this man's true deference with mercy and honour. Perhaps he was doing something right after all.

As the old man and his companions all bowed their heads to the King, Warwick spoke again. "There is something you must do for me in return, however…"

All five men looked up and babbled their assent.

"I will make it my very purpose in life to unite these lands and remove all trace of Brigand scum from the Holtlands, the Dunholt and wherever else they may try to hide if you promise me that, next time I pass this way, the toll on this bridge is a Silf… and nothing more."

He smiled at them.

"And stop abandoning your kids on the Dunmoors!" the Fool butted in.

Warwick looked at him with a raised eyebrow. The Fool and Althea nodded in unison. Warwick shrugged and turned back to the men. "And stop that as well. I'll hear about it if it carries on, and I'll make sure all the lost children find their way home."

That last part would have sounded like a pleasant idea to most people, but in Crofton there were countless ghost stories about Lost Children returning home from years on the moors, un-aged and inhuman, possessed by various evil boga. She watched the men shudder at the thought and wondered if she'd met any of their children in the hall at Honanmor.

"My lord," the old man spoke. "Did I hear ye say you were heading into the Fens?"

"You did at that. We're bound for the Lip."

The old man's eyes were wide. "Ye'll never make it that far."

The Fool

The old geezer could talk.

The others called him Gomolfax.

As they prepared the horses, Warwick, Althea and Katherine packed everything they needed. The Fool let Gomolfax talk.

Too many people were too quick to dismiss an old man's words as ravings, but he knew there was wisdom in experience and truth in every tale. Not always a lot, but still…

The old man had tried weaving a story for Warwick, but the King simply clasped a hand on his shoulder and said "We have heard the tales, my friend. Our way is still north."

The Fool knew it wouldn't take much to get the old man going again, so he waited for the others to go about their business and approached him.

"I haven't heard the tales," he lied. "Why won't we make it to the Lip?"

He had, in truth, heard many stories about the Hardwater Fens - and even spun a few himself after crossing them - but he was interested to hear what terrors were currently reputed to lurk within its watery bounds.

The old man leaned in close. He smelled of mud and piss and disappointment. The Fool hoped he would one day reach Gomolfax's age, but smelling of bluefires and satisfaction.

"Be watchful, Gleeware," said the old man. "Dimnes roams free pon the Fens. The Prince is abroad, you mark me."

"I mark you. What's out there?"

Gomolfax's eyes widened. "You no ken the tale of Jinny Greenteeth? The Eldhad hag o' the Hardwater?"

"Yeah, I have heard that one. She's a witch who seduces men and eats babies and stuff, right? Looks young and beautiful but is a wretched hag underneath? Lives in swamps?"

"Not any swamp, lad. This swamp. Greenteeth was ran into the Hardwater by the Hildemen of Crofton, way back. She'd been using gramword and Rynecraft to have her way with the Lord of the town. He cast her out."

Althea, stripping her saddle nearby, had heard this. "It doesn't take dark magic to turn a man's head," she said. "Poor girl."

She'd had her fair share of fear and mistrust over the years, thought the Fool. How many towns had she been hounded out of before she found her way to Elderhaime castle and Duncan's court? And then she found no peace even when she and her man should've been happy ever after.

He wondered if there were any tales about Wizards being chased into a marsh.

Gomolfax eyed Althea, then bowed his head respectfully. "As may be, ma'am, but not long after she went into the fens, people started going missing."

"Taken by the swamp?" asked the Fool, though he knew the answer.

"Nay, lad, taken by her. Some say she's a tornghast, unresting 'til her vengeance is done. Others say she still lives, even after all these years, through some pact with Ryneweard himself, feeding on the bladewine of those luckless enough to wander into her realm."

Ryneweard? You could tell you were witnessing a great yarn-spinner when the name of the Darkness himself was bandied.

He clapped Gomolfax on the shoulder. "Well, we may have to have words with old Jinny and the King of Despair, should our paths cross!"

The old man shook his head. "It's not she alone you must mind. There's all manner of wretched Baelic-spawn in the fens. Beware the Angshrikes: if you hear them call in the night you'll be dead before dawn. And the Fearies'll draw you out into the swamp with lights and song and then drown you and take your body and you'll wander home with the Dreadlight in your eyes and murder your whole family."

"Fearies?" Katherine's attention had been caught and she spoke up now.

"Scary Fairies," said the Fool.

"And don't forget the mile-long Mordraca who, if they don't swallow ye whole, will prick you with such poison yer head'll swell and swell and swell 'til it bursts." The old man gave quite a performance. The Fool couldn't have delivered the warning any better himself. Gomolfax spoke what would seem nonsense to most with a seriousness the Fool found almost noble. He had seen warriors speak of their battles in such a manner. He wondered...

"Have you seen them?" Katherine spoke the Fool's mind.

Gomolfax looked out at the Queen from under a furrowed brow. "Maybe I have at that, Majesty. And maybe I haven't. But when you look out from a camp fire, into the dark and see huge glassy unman eyes staring back at you, you start to wonder."

This intrigued the Fool. "What was it?"

Gomolfax seemed to suddenly lose interest. "Nay ken. Could find nowt then or following morn. I still see those eyes, though." He tapped a finger against his temple. "Every night."

The Witch

So not only did Croftonians abandon their children on the moors, they chased Witches into the swamp and left them for dead. How many of her sisters had been run out of rotten towns like this? And how many more ordinary women were branded Witches simply because they caught the eye of the menfolk? Men were forever looking for someone to blame for their own weakness. Jinny Greenteeth had discovered the hard way why Witches tended to favour the wilderness over so-called "civilisation".

The equipment they needed was all unpacked from the saddles and strapped to their backs. A couple of tents, some small pots and pans, a lot of rope, some mutton and a water canteen each was about all they had. She held Wolf's little birdcage in front of her like a lantern, the merecandle's yellow plumage not quite living up to its name.

She looked at the path ahead of them.

The grass crept up to the twisted trunks ahead, a throng it seemed they would have to cut their way through. Beyond that, the marsh stretched away into grey mist and mystery. She thought if the mist were to clear she might see the trees of the Dunholt on the far side of the swamp, and perhaps the Lip and the plateau rising beyond them, and even the gentle slope of the green Reeceland rolling up to the Magen Crag and the white teeth of the Northrod Mountains reaching up from the horizon.

But all she saw was mist.

The sight would fill a traveller with foreboding even without the mutterings of the old man.

Goodbyes were said. King Warwick reminded the Crofton men of their bargain and set forth. The Jester waited 'til Katherine was out of earshot, but Althea heard what he said to the departing men.

He told them they were lucky to be alive.

"You should thank whatever fates you believe in, gents," he said. "be glad the King was here and that he got to you all first, because I would've killed every one of you. If I hadn't fallen on me arse in that boat."

The Crofton men laughed as if trying to convince themselves he was making fun. She thought they knew as well as she did that this was no jest.

When they reached the wall of twisted trees running the edge of the Hardwater, it became apparent this was no ordinary hedgerow. Thick, intertwined bremelbushes, packed so densely together that peering at them was like peeping into an oubliette. She was fairly certain these bushes had been grown with a Forspring tonic of some sort. Bremels didn't grow into such twisted knots unbidden.

"They should hang the gardener," said the Jester.

"Is this here to keep us out, or to keep something else in?" asked Katherine.

"Bit of both, I reckon."

King Warwick drew his sword. It seemed to be his response to many problems.

"There used to be a path here," said the King. "There will be again." He smiled and began hacking away at the branches.

Althea and Katherine drew blades and joined him.

The mesh of thorns was only about twenty feet deep, but it took them over an hour to cut through to the opposite side, and that whole time was spent with mottled wooden talons seeming to grasp at their skin and pluck at their clothes, the trees fighting back against these intruders in their midst.

When they were finally through, they were exhausted - apart from the Jester who had refused a blade, complaining of javelin elbow.

Warwick sheathed his sword and leaned on his knees, breathing deep.

Something happened then that Althea did not expect. Something that tickled her gently with hope.

Katherine offered the King her waterskin.

The King looked her in the eye and said "Thank you."
Katherine shrugged.
Warwick drank.
And like that, the moment passed.

It was the first civil act Katherine had made towards Warwick since not stabbing him when they first met.

It was a start.

She looked out over the veiled bog.

"So these are the Hardwater Fens?" said Katherine. "The tales say the water is so thick you can walk on it."

"You could say that of some people I know," said the Jester.

"Is it true?"

"Yeah, I knew this lad in Underton once-"

"About the marsh, Fool."

He shrugged. "Not as such…"

Warwick spoke up: "I believe the name originally came from the bogs being so quick, they are hard to get out of. I presume that's also where most of the tales of marsh boga come from. Men fall into the quick and are pulled under the mud in seconds, never to be seen again."

Althea had always thought it was simply because the Fens were a body of water you could walk across. Hardwater.

She didn't speak up, though. What did it matter the name of the place? All that mattered was their passage.

"It's a rubbish name," said the Jester. "I think we should call them the Harsh Marshes. When you two get married, can you get them to put that on all the maps?"

Both Katherine and Warwick visibly blushed at the mention of their seemingly abandoned arrangement. Warwick was suddenly very interested in his sword - picking at imagined imperfections on its blade - while Katherine verbally hurried away from the Jester's indiscretion: "So how do we get across?" she asked.

Warwick stood up, holding out one of the coils of rope. "We tie ourselves together. And be very careful."

"Aye," said the Jester. "The whole swamp is covered with little cluds of earth sticking out of the water like stepping stones. Whosoever leads us will test each sod first, and everyone behind will step exactly where he steps. If anyone falls in, the others haul them out. It won't be Hardwater, it'll be piss-easywater."

"A much finer name," Warwick grinned. "I'm sure we can get that on the maps."

The Fool

He wasn't jealous.

It didn't bother him.

What did he have to be jealous about? He was devoted to a higher cause. He knew that Katherine must marry Warwick in order to unite the Siblands.

So it didn't make him grit his teeth when Warwick stumbled and Katherine caught his hand and pulled him to her.

Warwick led the line, then Katherine, then Althea and finally the Fool brought up the rear. All tied together round the waist like a chain of criminal coalhackers on their way to Colhydel to spend their days scraping light-giving darkness out of the very heart of the world.

No, it didn't bother him at all when Katherine said "Don't want your armour to get rusty," and she and Warwick shared a little smile and laugh and he could see a tiny spark ignite.

No, he was happy. Warwick was a handsome, noble man. Katherine could've done much worse with all the inbreeding that goes on in royal families. She could've ended up with some offal-faced Baelic-spawn.

But did he insult her by thinking such things? She was not so shallow as to be wooed by a handsome knight in tight armour, was she? No she was much more stubborn than that. She probably hadn't even noticed Warwick's faraway eyes and strong arms and thick, flowing locks the bastard the bastard the bastard.

Anyway.

He didn't care.

He kept his eyes on his feet as they stepped from clud to sod, and occasionally lifted his head to survey the misty land around them. They would be an easy target if anyone (or anything) were to spot them, but the mist concealed them as well as any potential attackers. Or so he hoped.

He thought about the last time he crossed this way, and the men who had disappeared into the murk in mere seconds.

He looked back at his feet and thought about green, rotten hands reaching out of the water for his ankles.

He didn't even mind when Warwick took his armour off.

"Built for riding into battle, not for traversing a swamp!" said the King jovially as he lashed the various plates together and strapped them to his back.

He didn't mind that Warwick's short-sleeved tunic drew extra attention to his arms, not to mention his athletic torso the brightboy bastard bastard.

That was no way to think of the King. Or, he supposed, an old friend. He thought of Warwick as he had been back then: troubled, fierce and earnest. He hadn't changed all that much, but his troubles had. In those days he was troubled with attempting to do good in spite of his father's will. Now he was just troubled with attempting to do good.

And, in a bad world, to do good can be the hardest thing.

The mists drew in around them as they went, like cobwebs drifting on the wind. A chill rose in the air.

There was a sound -

A sound like distant howling.

They all stopped dead -

"What's that?" said Katherine.

"That," said Warwick, "is a wolf, if I'm not much mistaken."

More howls joined in the call.

Warwick had tilted an ear to the breeze. "They're away in the Dunholt," he said. "They're not so gadwise as to enter the swamp."

"Are you sure it's not Angshrikes?" said Katherine with a laugh.

"Oh, you'd know an Angshrike if you heard one," said the Fool.

She stopped laughing. "Are they real?" She peered back at the Fool. She was little more than a shape in the mist to him. "Are the stories true?"

"Truth in every tale, highness," he shrugged. "So we better get a shimmy on."

They shuffled forward again, the howls still echoing around them.

"I've seen the truth behind a few stories this past few days," said Katherine as they walked. "Finders and Keepers, the Holtland Brigands, the Lost Children of the Dunmoors. None were exactly as the stories told."

"Well," spoke Althea. "Stories change with the telling, and some stories require embellishment. To explain the unexplainable."

"Lies, you mean?" said Katherine. "People should only believe what their eyes tell them."

"Lies can be used for good or ill, Highness," said Althea. "It all depends on the liesayer."

Liesayer. The Fool smiled at this. There were many names for the trade he had fallen into, the thing he masqueraded as. Fool, Jester, Jangler, Dysig, Sott, Gadwiseman, Spillend, Footler, Bungler, Pleganner, Gleeman, Gleeware, Liesayer and on and on. He had heard them all at one time or another. As title or insult, in mirth or in spite, but perhaps Liesayer was the one that suited him best.

But he wasn't just the liesayer.

He was the lie.

It was with this in his mind that he fell into the swamp.

He wasn't sure how it happened. Maybe a loose clud, a slip of his boot, or maybe Jinny had reached up from the mud to grab his ankle, but whatever the circumstance, he was immediately submerged in the thick, syrupy muck that passed for water in this place.

He opened his eyes to blackness. If Jinny or the Mordraca was coming for him, there was no chance he'd see them in this quagmire. It was like he'd fallen into cold treacle. He was going to need to breathe soon, and that might be a problem.

He felt the Hardwater sucking at him, but he couldn't be sure which way was up or down. He was suspended in darkness like a babe in the womb.

It could almost be cosy if it wasn't so cold.

Yeah, he could do with a breath now.

Right now.

He was suddenly aware that his legs were kicking in air.

He was sinking into some unknown world below the swamp, a forgotten cavern magically concealed beneath the thick, murky water. Oh, what wonders awaited him in this undiscovered —

Nope.

They were pulling him out of the Hardwater legs-first. He had landed upside down and was being backwards born into the same old familiar world.

He would've sighed if he could breathe.

He felt hands grabbing his belt and he was heaved free with a slurping pop.

He looked around in the dazzling light to see that Katherine and Warwick had yanked him from the muck. Together, they had pulled him out by his trousers. Their first united triumph. Maybe he could get these two together after all.

It didn't bother him.

It really didn't.

"It's a good job I don't have any dignity to lose." he gasped.

He looked down and saw the bog was about to claim his beloved tri-prong. It had slurped it off his bonce and was about to swallow it whole.

He reached out and caught it before it disappeared.

"Gimme that, you thieving bog bastard."

He yanked the hat free and slapped it back on his head.

He turned to his saviours. Warwick and Katherine knelt on the green knoll beside him, Althea stood behind them.

He slapped Katherine and Warwick's faces with his muddy hands. "Thanks, everyone." He pinched their cheeks, as you would a beloved child. "Oh, you two…"

He stood up, leaving them kneeling with mucky smears on their faces.

"Well, don't just sit there, this Fen's not gonna cross itself."

The Witch

"Al!" She heard the Jester calling her. "Don't go too far!"

She picked up a twisted burr of driftwood and added it to the pile cradled in her arm.

Aside from the Jester's tumble into the muck, their passage across the Hardwater had been blessedly uneventful. They had reached the northern edge of the swamp just before dusk and King Warwick had deemed it better to make camp rather than brave the Dunholt after dark.

So here she wandered, scooping soggy logs from the soft ground.

She looked around her. The black branches and twisted roots of the Dunholt seemed to reach out over the mire, while the swamp crept away between the trunks of the trees. The only solid ground was the camp site they had chosen. A grassy bank at the mouth of the Fenbrim, where the river eased its way into the marsh.

She thought about the next stage of the journey. She had never climbed The Lip before. She wondered if it was true that you died before you hit the ground.

She looked out north, into the mist, and fancied that she saw the faint, looming outline of the cliff against the darkening sky. She thought about stepping off it. How grand an undoing, to fly to your rest.

"Al."

That was not the Jester.

She felt her stomach drop. The voice had come from the gloom of the wooded swampland just in front of her.

She tilted her ear, trying to hear over the common trickling, chirping marsh noise.

Did she imagine it?

A voice had said her name. A weak, croaking voice. Hadn't it?

She stood, clutching her firewood.

Listening.
Until she heard it again.
"Al."
Her blood roared in her ears as her heart pounded. The voice was rough and small, as if it hadn't been used in years. As if…
"Al."
It couldn't be.
Could it?
She began to creep forward.
"Hello?"
"Al."
She stumbled down the bank and moved along a narrow gully. There was no Hardwater here, just mud and water like anywhere else.
She had heard it. It was real.
Someone was calling to her.
"Al."
It was louder now. More urgent.
So many thoughts ran through her head:
Go back. Get help. Shout them. Go on. Find out. See for yourself.
It's him.
It can't be him.
Can it?
"Al."
She pushed branches aside as she went forward through the marsh.
She was aware of the water creeping into her shoes, but still she continued.
People could come back. She knew that.
But it hadn't worked.
Could it have taken this long?
She had to see.
"Al."

Did it sound like him? After all this time, would he even sound the same?

"Al."

It was so close now. Louder and clearer. She could hear a rasp in the voice, like it was holding back a cough.

"Al."

She was upon him, she was sure.

She peered into the reeds. And she saw him. He was hunched and thin, but it was him.

"Mark."

It was Mark.

But only for a moment.

When it moved, she knew she had heard and seen only what she had wanted.

It was not Mark.

It was something else.

The thing unfurled itself before her. Many long, thick limbs reached out on either side of its stunted, bulbous torso. Bunches of eyes bulged black.

"Al."

A sick dread crept over her to hear her name spoken by such a creature.

She began to back away.

She had so wanted to believe.

It dragged itself forward through the reeds like half a man. She saw its face in the fading light.

It looked to be smiling. Its inhuman grin spread wide with rows and rows of glistening teeth like long, black fingernails.

"Al."

She remembered now. Manmerra. Swampsinger. The Voice Thief. They listened and learned and called out to the unwary to lure them to their deaths.

And she bloody fell for it.

Maybe she'd be seeing Mark soon after all.

She knew she could not escape. The thing knew the swamp, knew the water, knew her name.

She would know only death.

It heaved itself ever closer.

Hadn't she wanted this? Hadn't she known all along that Mark was not out here? Or had she wanted so badly to be with him that she was prepared to let this monstrosity take her?

Maybe it was time?

The thing leered at her and leaned forward, gurgling. No, it rolled forward, slumping to the wet ground.

It had six arrows in its back.

Long, thin shafts topped with green-feathered flights fluttered in the dusk air.

It was hurt.

It hadn't called her here to die, it had called her here to help.

It wasn't the first time an animal had recognised her as a Witch. It was said many creatures can sense friend from foe better than most people can. Or maybe they just liked her scent.

It couldn't have got far with those wounds. She peered around into the mist and gloom. The hunter would be close.

"Al."

The thing peered up at her with its many eyes and she felt its pain.

There was always somebody needed help.

She stepped forward and the thing let out a sigh, heaving its glistening, rubbery torso.

She looked at the long limbs spidering out from its body - Eight? Ten? - and wondered how far they could reach. She hoped she didn't hurt it.

She waded closer and the thing shifted uneasily, still watching her.

"Don't worry," she said.

"Al."

So close now, she could see the pulsing veins branching over its back. She saw the viscous white liquid bubbling from where the arrows pierced the flesh and knew they were tipped with Baelicberry. The poison would stop the wounds closing and would spread soon to the blood.

There wasn't long.

She gently reached for the nearest arrow and the Manmerra stirred beneath her.

If it lashed out now, it could snap her legs like twigs. She took a deep breath and closed her fist around the arrow.

"You don't wanna be at that, my love."

Althea stopped dead. The voice from behind her was young, female and strange. The beast before her cowered at its sound and began to drag itself away. Althea turned to see the speaker.

It was a monster.

It was all huge, round, glassy eyes and wooden pipes and leather.

Wait -

It was a woman.

She stepped forward. The huge, glassy eyes were the bottoms of beer bottles, strapped to her face. There was a cylinder of wood - like a long, thick reed - attached to the side of her head, running up from her mouth to a good foot above her bizarre leather headpiece.

She wore leather armour, covering her from boot to chin. Althea noticed the bow and quiver slung over her back.

"What business have you with my quarry?" the woman asked, lifting the bottle-bottoms from her face and peering intently at Althea. She had green eyes. She noticed Althea's at the same time.

Her pale face broke into a smile. "Sister!"

Althea nodded. "Sister."

A Witch. A Witch in the swamp. A Hunter. She hadn't set eyes on another of her order since she left the Galdorschol in Etheldrealm as a girl.

The wounded creature skulked behind Althea, whimpering.

The strange Witch scrutinised her. "A grengim falling for a Manmerra song? Perhaps you're green elsewhere than the eye?"

Althea frowned. "A grengim hunting for sport? Perhaps our laws mean nothing out here in the swamp?"

The new Witch smiled. "This isn't sport, this is pest control."

Althea could now see an angular, pointed face, younger than hers. The Witch was a girl not much older than Katherine.

Little upstart.

"This is their land," said Althea. "In the swamp, we are the pests."

The strange Witch said nothing.

"We only kill what we eat," Althea continued. "I doubt you'd be eating this." She pointed to the wallowing monstrosity behind her.

"Doesn't mean they won't eat us, given half a chance." The Witch drew her bow and nocked an arrow.

"You should've thought of that before you set up home in a marsh. Now are you going to stand there trying to threaten me like a warrior, or are you going to be a Witch and help me heal this poor thing?" Althea turned back to the Manmerra. It looked up at her with pleading black eyes.

Behind her, the Witch stepped closer. "I could end it," she said. Althea heard the bowstring tighten. "Sometimes death is easier."

Death is easier?

Maybe this Witch was right. Once you have faced Death so completely, can you ever face life again? Was it better to never come back?

"No," she said. She yanked the first arrow out of the creature's hide. It yelped and writhed, but didn't make to strike. She could feel the Witch closing behind her. "I'd appreciate if you'd give me a few drams of Aedrench for the poison."

She heard the bow slacken. "How did you know..?"

The girl wasn't too bright. "First rule of poisoncraft is to always carry the antidote." She turned to look at the younger Witch. "I assumed that was a law you would be following."

The girl lowered the bow.

With both Witches working, they soon had the arrows removed. The Manmerra was wary of the hunter, but Althea placed a hand on its head and urged calm upon it. They poured Aedrench over the bubbling holes in the creatures back and they began to seal almost immediately.

Like magic.

When they were done, the creature looked up at her, grinning its nightmarish grin. "Al," it said.

"You can go now," she whispered.

The creature cast a look at its hunter and dragged itself away into the reeds.

"Al," it cried as it ploughed into the black water.

Althea watched it go, that nightmarish head lowering to the surface until only the black eyes were visible. Then they too were gone.

"You lost someone?"

Althea turned to the girl.

"What?" She couldn't know, could she?

"Out here. You must've had a fierce yearning to find them, wandering this far from your camp."

There were no words for what she had lost. No way to make someone else understand. Especially this stranger, Witch or no.

"I did lose someone," she said. "But I think maybe I found someone too."

"What, that big boga?" said the young Witch. "That wasn't who you were looking for, was it?"

"What's your name?" Althea asked.

The girl drew herself up. "I am Tabitha Greenteeth, Daughter of the Hardwater and Warden of the Marsh."

"Tabitha? What happened to Jinny?"

Tabitha looked proud. "The mother of our chapter of the order. She took to the swamp and started a Galdorschol of her own. She made it our duty to protect the marsh and all that lived within it."

Althea's eyes widened. "There's a school here? In the swamp?"

"Well, yes." The Witch looked at the wet ground. "I mean, it's seen better days, but we're still taking students."

"And Jinny?"

Tabitha shook her head. "That was a long time ago."

Althea thought about it: A woman was driven into the marsh with hate at her heels, but she could not abandon her duty. She was a Witch, and the world needed Witches.

There was always hope.

"You haven't given me your name, Sister."

Althea looked in the girl's green eyes.

She had been called so many things. Maybe it was time to bring some of them back?

"I am Lady Althea of Elderhaime. White Witch of Crossford. The Queen's Blessing. The Salve of the Green Shadows."

"My lady!" Tabitha looked suitably impressed. "They said you were burned! It is true you can confound Death himself, then?"

If only. "Don't believe everything you hear, Sister." She looked back in the direction of the camp, where her friends and her duty lay. "Maybe the only way to really beat death is simply by living?"

She looked back at Tabitha. "I have to go," she said. She placed a hand on the younger Witch's shoulder. "Stop killing things, Sister. We're Witches. Life is our business." The girl nodded. "My regards to your chapter." Althea turned to leave.

"Can I… …come with you?"

Althea looked back to see the girl looking sheepish.

Althea smiled. "Your duty is here. Mine is out there." She jabbed a thumb in the direction of her friends.

"The Daughters will never believe me," said Tabitha.
"There's truth in every tale," said Althea.

I know she's there.
In the water.
Lost.
The children watch.
I shiver in the cold air.
I shouldn't be out here.
The ripples lap the edge of the swamp.
She's coming.
There's a Knight.
His sword is in the ground.
He's praying.
Making oaths.
She rises from the murk.
Dripping.
Covered in weeds.
Rotten.
Rotting.
There's crabs in her eyes.
She climbs the bank towards me.
I can't move.
She reaches for me and I know her hand will be cold.
We're not supposed to be here.
Her wet fingers enclose my wrist.
It burns.
Oh, it burns and burns.
She says she's sorry.
She says she loves me.
And my skin rots off.

The Princess

She watched the sun come up.

When Althea had got back from her little hike into the swamp, they had started a fire and settled in to camp.

Through the night, they had taken two hour shifts and hers was the last before dawn.

A Queen standing guard over her guards. She wondered if she could've ordered the Fool to take her shift instead. As if she could've slept after the dream.

It was different again. She hadn't been in her bed, she had been here, in the swamp.

And her mother…

It was that stupid old man and his tales of Water-Witches and Angshrikes. Putting terrible images in her head.

This wasn't the only reason she couldn't sleep.

They were almost home.

Nearly safe, back in Elderhaime Castle with nothing to fear but the towardness of her own loneliness. A lifetime alone with her fate and her choices.

Something to look forward to, then.

The rest of the camp slept. The Fool out in the open air, wrapped in a blanket with his head on his pack, Warwick and Althea covered by canvas raised in makeshift tents.

The sun peeped over the distant Eastrod mountains, casting its tentative gaze over the misty swampland they had stumbled through the previous day.

She knew they wouldn't approve of her wandering from the camp, but they weren't awake to chide her.

She climbed a limestone rise through the trees, into the whispering breeze of the morning.

From a small peak on the edge of the Hardwater, she looked south. The sun hauled itself over the mountains and the new day crept silently upon the Siblands.

She couldn't help thinking this was it.

This was her last free day. Her last sunrise.

All they had to do was climb the Lip and she was home. A simple matter of scaling a few hundred feet of stone, and they would be safe in the Reeceland.

They would reach Elderhaime by tonight, and then she wouldn't be able to run any more. She would have to be a Queen. Everyone would be looking to her to do right by them. Everyone.

She thought about her plan to call the army of Elderhaime to her and march on Fairford.

This seemed less of an option now she was returning with the enemy King in tow.

He wasn't the enemy.

He could've let the Finder take her eyes if he wanted.

He could've cut her throat and left her in the swamp if he wanted.

She was beginning to think he was serious. About the wedding. About peace.

About everything.

It wasn't fair.

There was a sound behind her.

Someone was there. Someone moving quietly toward her.

She spun -

It was Warwick.

His hands were raised in surrender. "Good Morning, Highness."

Some sentry she turned out to be.

"Sorry to startle you," he said. He was so terribly polite. "May I join you?"

She wondered if an arranged marriage to a rude man would be worse.

She turned back to the sunrise. "Of course."

He stood beside her, looking out on the swamp.

Silent. At first the silence was peaceful, welcome. But thoughts began to race to her with silence as their conduit. Why wasn't he saying anything? Why wasn't she? Why was he beside her? What did it mean? What did she want it to mean?

She had to say something - anything - just to break the silence.

"I couldn't sleep," she said.

"I never can. But the mornings are beautiful out here…"

She looked at the mist and trees and streams, all golden. "Yet another thing that is not as it seems."

She knew she had something to say to him. That was why the silence wouldn't shut up.

She looked at him, which was difficult for some reason. He smiled a little smile at her, and she saw a warmth in him that almost made her despise him. How dare he? How dare he turn up out of the blue and be all likable and… pleasant? This was much easier when he was the villain. He had tricked the nobles of Elderhaime out into the wilderness and killed them all on the road. He was a cur and a bounder.

Only he wasn't.

Her Father was dead. His dying wish had been for her to marry this man. This kind, handsome man. Warwick was, more or less, the very Prince she had read about in childhood tales. Dashing, honest, honourable, and entirely wrong. Your love was supposed to sweep you off your feet and fly away with you, not proposition you with politics.

Still, without him, she would likely be blind or captured by the brigands by now.

"I didn't say thank you," she said, "for saving me."

"Please, think nothing of it." He seemed to find it equally difficult to meet her eye.

They both looked out at the swamp again.

More silence.

She became aware that now it was his turn to struggle with words he felt he must say.

"My lady, about my proposal…"

Here we go.

She went to speak, but Warwick raised his hands.

"No. You have been through an arduous time. To expect you to make such a decision under these circumstances would be wrong, but know that my offer still stands."

He took her hand in his. He felt warm in the cold air, but something within her was drawing away from him even as he spoke.

"Alone, we have power, but together we could become legends." He spoke as if to hundreds, but this was not some studied speech, written and rehearsed; Warwick genuinely believed what he was telling her. "A story of light, whispered in the dark, bringing warmth and hope to the coldest of hearts. Marry me, your Majesty…" He finally floundered. "It'll be nice. I promise."

She saw in his eyes all the hope and need a man could contain. Warwick had to believe that he could atone for the sins of his father, and the only way he saw was by marrying her. She held the fate of Warwick's dreams and the peace of the land in her hand.

But what of her dreams?

Could she give herself to a man she didn't love?

She felt as if she were at a crossroad, and her hope and everyone else's lay down different paths.

She couldn't do it.

"I cannot. Would that I could…" There was no excuse. "I'm sorry."

"No, your Highness, it is I who should apologise." Warwick hung his head. "I could never ask you to give up so much with so little offered in return."

She felt a weight lifting. A cloud that had hung over her since her father died was parting. The decision was finally made.

It was her turn to squeeze his hand now, consoling. "I see the good in your heart, the hopes you nurture…" How to explain? "But…"

There's someone else.

There was, wasn't there? The possibility of true love had taken precedence in her mind.

Marrying you would be giving up all hope for myself.

She couldn't explain, but he knew.

He nodded. "'But'..."

She was aware of a presence, and looked to see Althea and the Fool watching from the trees.

The Fool looked so angry.

Warwick followed her gaze, straight to the Fool.

"I understand." Warwick said. Without another word, he turned away from them and disappeared into the trees.

Katherine looked at the others. The Fool turned away with a shake of his head. His bells jingled.

Althea shook her head, looking unsurprised.

"What?" Katherine shrugged at her.

The Fool

So that was that.

She had her chance to change her mind, and she just kept the old one.

He wasn't glad, was he? Why would he be? The Princess had just chucked aside the hope of unity for all because of a naive dream.

But who was she dreaming of?

He began packing his bag. They might as well get a shimmy on. They could be at Elderhaime by sundown.

And then what?

What?

He shouldn't hope for that.

He shouldn't.

He promised.

"What are you doing, Fool?" She was behind him.

He hated it when she called him that. And he loved it. He wanted to tell her his real name. And he wanted to bury it deep inside him, never to be spoken again. He wondered how it would feel to hear his name, his true name, spoken in her voice.

But he couldn't. Could he?

He shouldn't.

He didn't look at her. "I'm going home," he said.

"You're leaving me?"

"Well, I assumed you'd be coming too, seeing as you've concluded all your business out here in the wild."

"What business?"

He couldn't look at her. He didn't know what might happen if he did. "How about casting aside any chance of peace on a selfish whim? At least that's all taken care of now."

There was a pause and he knew she was hurt. He wanted to turn around and take her in his arms and tell her he was glad. Glad she was not to marry Warwick.

But that wasn't true, was it? They had a responsibility.

"I cannot marry a man I do not love," she said. Her voice wavered.

He steeled himself. It was what Duncan wanted. He wanted his daughter to assume responsibility for the lands they lived in. He wanted the Fool to watch over her.

He did not want his daughter to run away with a court Jester.

He promised to protect her.

Six years back.

Duncan had saved his life, dressed him as a Fool and made him his daughter's bodyguard. He had pledged to protect her. Even if that meant protecting her from himself.

"Warwick would give anything for a chance of peace. You will give up everything because Warwick might be the 'wrong man'!" His voice was not his own now. He felt himself shrinking away inside.

"Not 'might be'…" she said.

If not "might"?

She had to be sure.

He finally turned to face her.

And she was gone.

He could see her disappearing through the trees.

He dropped his bag and followed her.

He was chasing her through the woods again.

He'd been doing that for so long.

He finally caught up to her.

"I want you to be sure, Princess." She stopped when she heard him. "Don't throw away this possibility on a whim."

She turned on him then, in a rage. "Why should I listen to a word you say? What right do you have to dictate my actions? "Go here, Princess, do as you're told Princess"…

You seem to have complete control over me, yet I don't even know who you are…"

Change the subject. "You don't even know who you are, Your Majesty. You're Queen Katherine of Elderhaime. It's about time you stopped acting like a child."

"Growing up is not the same as giving up." Her anger seemed to fade to sadness. "Do not ask me to enter a loveless marriage. I have seen that end and it is not a good one."

So that was it.

It all came back to that one night.

Her Father's heartbreak had only led to hers.

You stay where your parents leave you.

"That's the root of all this?" he said. "You think she didn't love him? Or you?"

"She left, didn't she?"

"You fool." He regretted that as soon as he said it. She was ignorant of the truth only because nobody ever told her.

The King would not speak of his wife once she was gone, so nobody ever did. None of the courtiers wanted to upset the King or the Princess, so they never mentioned her, and pretty soon it must have been like the Queen never existed. Through negligence and misguided sympathy, they had unintentionally conspired to delude Katherine for most of her life.

Maybe it was time for the truth?

Or some of it, at least.

The whole truth would be a mite too much truth.

"She left because she loved you both," he said. She didn't look convinced. "Your Father never spoke of her, did he?"

Katherine shook her head. "I read about it. He won her when he killed a Wyrm, and they lived happily ever after. Except there are no Wyrms, and there is no happily ever after! She was a trophy! He didn't love her, he owned her."

Her rage was quiet now. Controlled.

"Truth in every tale, Princess. Your mother was a trophy, right enough, but your father treated her like any noble woman. When she arrived at Elderhaime, she was given her own chambers as a guest of the Crown. King Duncan courted her, they fell in love, they married."

Her shoulders were heaving with every breath.

She scowled at the ground.

"Then why did she leave?" she said.

He was surprised at how difficult the story came. It was not just something he didn't talk about, it was something he tried not to think about. After six years of beating back the memories every time they approached, he finally let them come.

He sighed. "She became Afflicted, but it was different. Her skin was as pure as yours, yet her touch burned. It was as if the illness lived in her. To look at her, you would think her in great health, but…"

The pain on Katherine's face made it impossible to tell. He was breaking his promise. He was hurting her.

"But what?" she said. Her blue eyes fixed on his. She wasn't skriking.

"Not even Althea could help her," he said. "Your Mother wanted nothing more than to reach out and hold you and your Father both…"

He began to unbuckle the glove on his right hand. Some things it was easier to show than tell.

"She knew she had to leave or she would destroy everything she loved." He looked in Kathy's eyes, making sure she understood. "I found her one night standing over your bed while you slept. She reached out for you. To brush your cheek or something. She was half asleep herself, I think. I stopped her."

He held up his gloveless right hand, revealing the scarred and blistered palm. Her eyes widened at the sight of the perfect hand-print scar around his wrist.

He had only touched Queen Amanda for a second. Held her arm to stop her touching Katherine. His hand had welded to her flesh as if it were a griddle.

He remembered only pain beyond that, but she must've wrenched his hand free with her own, hence the eternal bracelet scorched on his wrist.

He'd dined with Death every night for three moons following, but Althea stopped him going home with him every time. And nobody had seen Queen Amanda since.

He didn't need to tell Katherine every detail. The scars spoke for themselves.

"You're looking at the only person ever to be cured of the Affliction." He wasn't proud.

Katherine seemed torn between reaching out to touch the mottled skin of his hand, and turning tail to run.

"How?" she whispered.

Magic.

"I was chancy. And Al was the best. She might not be able to raise the dead, but close enough." He pulled his glove back on. "The Afflicted hold no danger for me now. Reckon the sickness knows I've bested it before, so it gives me a wide berth."

Katherine was stunned to silence.

So now she knows.

"Even a loving marriage can end badly, Highness. You look for love as some kind of guarantee, but nothing is certain. There is only hope."

He realised that perhaps only now could she make a truly informed decision. She had been through so much, and laboured under a misunderstanding for so long, maybe now she could see clearly.

But what would she see?

She looked so alone. Lost in the woods.

He stepped towards her. "I may be a fool, but I've nous enough to know that sometimes I have to use my head instead of my heart, no matter how much I wish it could be different."

She said nothing.

They could just run.

Run away into the woods.

Build a tree house.

Live together alone.

They could be happy ever after.

While the rest of the lands burned and fell into chaos and her kingdom collapsed and her name was dishonoured and lots and lots and lots of people died.

Romantic.

He couldn't do it.

He couldn't take her away, could he?

The rest of the world deserved her more than he did.

He stepped closer, reaching out his gloved hand.

He lifted her chin, raising her eyes to his. He tried to recall if she had the eyes of her Mother or Father, but all he could think of was her. They were just hers.

"You're gonna change lives," he said. "But you have the chance to do it on a grand scale, rather than just one to one…"

They were so close now.

He felt her breath.

"But if you must say no to him," he said, softly, "I want you to be sure, Princess."

"I'm not a Princess anymore."

He smiled.

She smiled back. Just a little. A slight upturn at the left side of her mouth.

He wanted to -

She looked down for a moment. "I would have accepted Warwick's offer this morning, but…"

She brought her eyes back to his.

And he knew.

There, in that moment, it all became clear.

He understood. This is what they would have to give up. Both of them.

All he had to do was kiss her.

So close.

There was a whistle and a thud.

And pain.

Katherine saw his expression change. "Fool?"

This was just bloody typical.

"You should probably run away now, Highness," he said.

"What? Why?"

"'Cos I've just been shot in the back."

The Monster

This couldn't be better.

This would be worth the wait. Worth the traipsing through the wilderness on their trail.

The two of them. Alone in the woods.

Perfect.

He watched them bickering, waiting for his moment.

His men surrounded them, but they were too engrossed in one another to notice. Typical. So self-absorbed.

When they looked like they were about to kiss, he'd had enough.

He raised his hand.

From the trees opposite him, Bowman loosed his arrow.

From this angle, he could see the look on the Idiot's face change from earnest to pained.

He couldn't help but laugh, covering his mouth.

He didn't want to spoil the game.

The Idiot staggered forward into the Princess' arms. Or wait, she was a Queen now, wasn't she? After he killed her father, she ascended. He marvelled for a moment at his own power, the power to take lives and irrevocably alter them in the process. The Bane of Kings and the Raiser of Queens. He should write those titles down and have the men refer to him with them in hushed tones as he passed.

Better than the alternative.

Bowman called out his find, as if the rest of the men weren't already here. "THEY'RE HERE! I HAVE THEM!"

The Idiot was slumped over the Bitch as an overzealous brigand, maybe his name was Jon or Jor or something ran towards them, drawing a sword.

Fury hoped this man knew not to kill either of them.

He needn't have worried.

The Idiot pulled the arrow out of his own back and rammed it into Jon or Jor's throat mid-stride.

That idiot thinks he's so clever, with his fighting and jesting and stupid puppet and clothes. Killing my men? We'll see about that.

The brigand whose name he couldn't remember spluttered and died.

The Idiot picked up his sword.

This wasn't going quite according to plan.

Part of him wanted to run down there now and stab that idiot in the back, slice his guts out and throw them at his Princess harlot, but more of him wanted to wait. The perfect moment was coming.

Still another part of him wanted to run away. Run away and hide because the Idiot was capable of terrible things and he would be so, so angry when Fury killed the Queen.

More brigands were approaching.

The Idiot pushed his wench away. "Go, Princess! Find Al."

So the Witch was out here somewhere. He should probably hurry this up.

His men were running to the Idiot, hurtling through the trees.

"What about you?" she begged of her idiot guardian.

"Some things are worth the sacrifice."

The way the Idiot looked at her when he said that. A look loaded with meaning, with love. It nearly made Fury puke.

This was going to be so much fun.

"No!" she knew she wouldn't see him again if she left him. Fury could see her little heart breaking. It put him in mind of how tiny birds felt in the palm of your hand as you screwed up their bodies, their bones disintegrating like brittle clay.

"Katherine, Your Father ordered me to protect you! I will not let you die out here!"

Such a bloody hero.

The first Brigands were upon them.

Katherine stepped backwards as the Idiot knocked two of them down with barely a glance, his blade flashing left and right.

Chains, he thought. *Where are the chains?*

The Idiot turned one last time to his Queen. "Kathy, RUN!"

Come to me, Your Majesty.

It was perfect.

She seemed to wake from a dream. Suddenly seeing the hopelessness of the situation, she turned to run. Straight into Fury's arms.

She felt warm against him.

Her eyes were wide as they looked on his bandaged face, on her Father's crown atop his head.

"So nice to meet you finally," he said in his politest tones.

She struggled, but his arms were around her now. She called out to him, to her guardian, and Fury relished again the look on the Idiot's face as, just for a moment, he knew he was beaten.

A moment, and then he just looked very angry.

"Let her go, Ken!" The Idiot cut down the brigand he fought with, and turned to him. "It's me you want. You don't care about her."

The chains.

He called to the brigands gathering in a semi-circle around the Idiot.

"Take him!"

Four of them swung the chains. Long links of black metal, ending in terrible meat-hooks.

They tore into the idiot's flesh and pulled him to his knees.

The Princess screamed and struggled as the Idiot roared in agony.

It was like a symphony. Music made just to please his ears. This was true beauty, the exquisite poetry of pain.

It just needed a climax.

"But you do care." He ran a hand through the wench's hair as he spoke to the Idiot. "You would rather die than see her harmed. How poetic, sacrificing yourself for the one you love. Everyone enjoys a good romance."

He turned Katherine to face the Idiot, holding her close to him, one hand around her throat. He saw the moment their eyes met, the Idiot's eyes full of regret. An apology.

He felt his hand on the knife.

"But, being a cynic, I always found a terrible tragedy -" he raised the knife, just long enough for them to recognise it - "much more compelling."

He plunged it into her belly.

He held her tighter as she gasped, her whole body heaving against him.

It felt nice.

He could hear the Idiot bellowing in rage and pain as he whispered in her pretty little ear. "Do you feel that, Highness? That is your Father's blade. It ended his life, and now it ends yours."

He yanked the blade out of her and watched the blood surge forth. She slumped in his arms, still gasping. He was again filled with an awareness of his own power.

Look what I did. And look what HE couldn't do.

He spoke to the Idiot, whose face was clenched in rage. "Now that's poetic, idiot." He held Katherine up, her soft face against the bandages of his. "Your Jester failed your father, Highness, and now he has failed you. His world is built on broken promises."

He stabbed her again.

"Good night, Princess."

She was a pretty little thing. Now more than ever. He felt a warmth inside him at the thought that he had made her feel the way no one else ever could.

He could do her again.

He pulled the dagger from her gut once more.

Only he didn't. He couldn't.

The bitch had got her hands around the hilt. She was actually holding the knife in her. Clutching it to her like a babe.

He tried again.

Her dying body would not release her Father's blade.

Bitch. How can she..?

She was smiling at him.

Why was she smiling?

He punched her in the face and dropped her to the ground, still clutching the knife in her belly. "Keep it then! I don't need it anymore."

It had served its purpose. Let her have it. It wasn't like she'd defeated him by holding on to a knife. Who was alive and who was dead here anyway?

He kicked her, just to make sure she knew she hadn't won.

When he turned to the Idiot, he thought he had never seen such brilliant pain and rage and sorrow and frustration on a human face.

It was going so well.

"You'd better kill me now, or you'll live to regret it," said the Idiot through clenched teeth.

He leaned over his prisoner, enjoying the feeling of talking to a pet. A dog on a chain.

"On the contrary, I think I will regret it if I don't keep you alive for as long as I possibly can. 'Til you have paid in kind for what you did to me."

He felt all the pain. The humiliation, the name-calling, the ridicule, the blows, the cuts, the burning, all the rage and all the wrongs done to him by this man, this man who was less, so much less than he, it all boiled down to one physical act.

He punched the Idiot in the face, the weight of years behind his fist.

The Idiot's hat fell off.

The Idiot leaned forward, drooling blood. "Your quarrel was with me…"

"Now, Idiot, you cannot always be centre-stage." He knelt down next to his quarry. "If that harlot had married Warwick, it would've banjaxed everything for us. Suspicion and fear keep the weapon trade healthy. A union would just be too costly, I'm afraid."

"So you kill Duncan and Katherine and everyone thinks it's an assassin from Fairford."

"And then when I kill Warwick, everyone will think it's Elderhaime retaliating. Genius."

It was a great plan.

"That's why I doubt you thought of it," said the Idiot.

What did he mean by that?

Never mind.

"But now my work here in the wild is done, finally," he pinched the Idiot's cheek. "So it's play-time for you and me."

The Idiot fixed such a gaze on him then that, just for a moment, he believed what was said next.

"You know I'm going to kill you, Ken."

There was a world of darkness in those eyes. He knew the Idiot capable of things many would wonder at, but he was just a man. An animal. In a cage.

He laughed in the Idiot's face and stood up.

"Muster the troops," he called to the men. "We're going home."

Bowman was by his side "What about the other he spoke of? The Witch..?"

He would love to see Althea back on the rack, but every moment spent in the wild was another moment the Idiot might spring some improbable escape. He needed to get him within walls as quickly as possible.

"Leave a brace of Finders behind. She'll be close." He pointed to the Idiot, hunched and bloodied. "Bring him."

As the men dragged the Idiot away, he looked at the bodies on the ground.

Four of his men and a Queen had fallen. There was blood on the bracken leaves. Katherine lay on her front, her body curled around the dagger that killed her like a child with a doll.

He was beginning to get a taste for politics.

He'd killed a Queen, set a war in motion and captured his nemesis.

And, best of all, his burns hadn't itched the whole time.

The Princess

It wasn't supposed to end like this.
I was supposed to die in some far away castle, buried deep in soft sheets and pillows, surrounded by adoring family. Bathed in love.
And yet, here I lie, numb and broken, bleeding on a forest floor. I was supposed to be so important, a symbol of peace, and all it took was the prick of a blade to put an end to that.
It hurt at first.
The blade was cold and my blood was warm.
I could smell his breath, feel him against me. You're supposed to die in the arms of your love, not some monster.
He wore my Dad's crown.
He used my Dad's knife.
Took a King's knife to end a Queen's life.
I wasn't going to let him take it again. We held on to the hilt. We might need it.
I didn't feel the blows. I was already leaving.
Leaving. Like her.
Only not like her.
Had I thought she was dead? Maybe she is.
She was beautiful.
I think.
It's hard to tell. I can never really see her face. As if she were veiled or in shadow. Perhaps the beauty I remember is the way she made me feel. Safe. Warm. Loved.
There was only cold when she was gone.
I remember she would read to me. Stories of Princes and heroes. Glory and love. Maybe I believed that was what the life of a Princess was all about, back then.
Didn't last.
Nobody talked about it. Perhaps they thought I would forget in time.
And I did.

I forgot, though the dream kept returning. I lost count of the nights I saw her again, shrinking away from my touch as if the very thought of me repulsed her.

He might as well have left too, for he was no more present than she was. He would hide away in study or in government, leaving me to the care of handmaids and the Fool.

Over time I began to hear the rumours.

Even a Princess can't be locked away all the time.

I heard two messengers in the courtyard say she had run away. "What do you expect from a trophy wife?" they laughed. I didn't want to believe it. Others said she was taken, abducted by Brittle the Banwarch or Gargrin the Blood-Bather or some other boggart. Many claimed she was dead, murdered or diseased and the King was driven mad with grief.

All I knew was she was gone.

I thought I found the answer in my own studies one day. I found record of how my father came to marry my Mother. A tale of derring-do and budding romance and dragon-slaying.

I thought I knew the truth then.

There are no such things as dragons.

My mother left because she was betrothed to a man she didn't love. There was probably a stable boy back in her village with a claim to her heart.

I comforted myself that wherever she was, she must be happy. Still, whenever I tried to talk to my father, there yawned an unfathomable chasm between us. A chasm which grew with every passing day.

So I stopped trying.

And then he was gone too.

And I was alone.

And the Fool tells me I have it all wrong.

He's always been there.

Trying to protect me.

She shied away from my touch to spare me.

She would've burned the skin from my bones.

*And after all I've seen.
All that's happened.
Heroes and monsters and witches and knights.
Maybe dragons are real.
Maybe.
Maybe there is hope.
So here I lie, watching ants hurry past my dying eyes. I wonder if they'll eat me. I could keep them going for a long time. Is it comforting to know that your body is useful in death? Does it make your sacrifice worthwhile? The ants would probably say so. But they'd say it with their mouths full.
Everything is so bright.
They're talking. Not the ants, the people.
They seem so far away. And growing further all the time.
I need to close my eyes.
He says he needs war.
He is fear and rage and I am hope. Hope and...
And...
Something so far away now.
I was hope.
I failed.
I failed everyone.
My Father. What happens now we're both dead? Our line is lost.
My People. Who will they turn to now I am gone?
My self. All the things I could have been. Or should have been.
My Fool.
Oh, Fool. What are they going to do to you? Will I see you soon?
I watch the grass turn red. And everything else turn white.
And I die.*

Part Six:
The Dead and the Living.

The Wanderer and the Wyrm

Extract from
"The Adventures of Duncan the Wanderer"
by Freemung Lerner.

Prince Duncan rode on until, one day, he happened upon a maiden, weeping by the road.

"Whatever is the matter, fair maid?" he asked.

"Oh, woe! Woe is me!" cried the maid. "My village is terrorised by a mighty Wyrm, and the elders say I am to be offered as sacrifice, for I am the fairest maid in all the land."

She was indeed fair, and Duncan was filled with remorse to see one so pretty weep for her life.

"Fear not, fair maid, for I am Duncan the Wanderer, Prince of Elderhaime, and I shall slay the beast and free your people!"

The maid's heart was filled with joy and she rode with Duncan back to her village.

The maid's Father was glad that he would not have to feed his daughter to the beast, and the village Elders told Duncan the way to the Wyrm's cave.

The Prince rode up a narrow mountain path littered with the dead, but his heart was sure. He saw the bones of many who had gone before him, yet his courage did not waver.

When he reached the mouth of the cave, he called out to the beast to come forth, for all creatures are subject to the command of royalty. And lo, the Wyrm slithered out of the cave. A hundred feet long with teeth the size of the Prince's sword, but Duncan was not cowed.

"Wyrm!" he cried. "Ye pestilent, Baelic-spawn. You have terrorised these good people for the last time. Prepare to die!"

"I'm going to gobble you up and spit out your armour!" hissed the serpent, and he lunged at the prince.

They fought for three days and three nights, without food or water or rest and in the end it was the Wyrm who faltered first.

Duncan stood over the creature, his sword raised, and the Wyrm began to beg.

It offered him riches, the hoard it had amassed lay waiting in its cave, but Duncan was unmoved.

It offered him power, for a Wyrm's magic is strong, but Duncan's heart was stronger.

It offered him anything his heart desired, but Duncan desired only one thing and it was not the Wyrm's to offer.

Duncan sliced off the creature's terrible head with one swing of his blade, and carried it back to the village.

The villagers rejoiced to see the serpent dead, and hoisted the head high above their gates.

"How can we ever repay you?" they asked.

"I ask only one thing," replied Duncan. "For the hand of the fairest maid in the land".

And so it was that Duncan married the fair maid and she rode with him on many adventures, until they finally returned to Elderhaime to sit in happiness as King and Queen until the end of their days.

Extract from Lord Felix Tyrantson's Diary:
Thirteen Years of Age

Fourth Rynesday, First Moon of Summer, 209
He's dead.
    The Tyrant is no more and only now do I feel I can write about it.
    He lay on his death bed and looked at me with pleading eyes as the rot covered him.
    So I told him. I told him that I saw him push Mother from the tower, I told him that I spent the last couple of months searching for an afflicted girl of sufficient beauty and vigour for her disease to go unnoticed by a drunken King. I told him I had paid her to go to his chamber.
    I told him he did this to himself.
    He tried to get up, but he was already too weak.
    Before I put the pillow to his face, I reminded him of Belinda. He asked if I had killed him because of the cat. I said I was doing it because I could.
    I have built my snare for the world and it is time to spring it.
    Aren't you happy, father?
    Aren't you proud?

The Witch

Whatever happens, they should probably be alone.

That's what she had thought as the Jester followed Katherine into the trees.

Now she wasn't so sure. They weren't out of the woods yet.

She had gone to try and find Warwick, but had no luck, so she returned to the campsite and had started a small fire. Might as well get some breakfast going. Nothing works up an appetite like emotional confessions in the morning.

She put a pot of weak stew on the flames to heat.

She poked the fire and pondered. What next? The Princess had made her mind up. Would the Jester follow her lead? She wouldn't blame them. Not everyone gets a real chance at what they could have.

A terrible thought occurred to her.

The Jester as King.

She couldn't help laughing out loud at that.

Her laugh startled something behind her.

It hissed.

Finders.

She grabbed the pot out of the fire and spun around, swinging the boiling stew into the face of the first.

It dropped and scrabbled away from her, shrieking.

She smashed the pot over the head of the other and it fell, stunned.

"FINDERS!" she screamed.

There were only two of them. They scuttled back together and approached her again, warier now.

They found us.
That's what they do.
She hoped the others were safe.

They weren't going to take her without a fight this time. Witches were only supposed to kill what they ate, unless it was a matter of life or death for the Witch in question.

Even if the Finders took her alive, death was sure to follow.

She'd had enough of death.

She snatched a burning stick from the fire and waved the flame in front of her, backing away from the beasts.

They leered and hooted as they crept forward, long, wet fingers reaching for her, those slimy tongues unfurling.

She didn't want to die.

A sword was drawn.

Althea and the Finders looked across the clearing to see Warwick.

The Finders split up, one sloping toward her, the other turning to the King.

"Are you well, my lady?" he asked.

The Finders crouched low.

"I'm alive." she said.

They surged forward.

She had to fight.

Every day, she had to fight. Every day, she woke up on the brink of an abyss, and every day she had to think of a reason to step away from the edge instead of leaping headlong into despair.

She was damned if some grotty Baelic-spawn was going to make the choice for her.

Althea brought her torch down on the head of the beast as it raced towards her.

It stopped.

She was screaming.

It was screaming.

She felt the shock in her elbow as she drove the stick into the animals skull again and again. She felt the long, damp fingers trying to push her away.

It screamed for its life.

She fought for hers.

She may not have been able to master Death, but he would master her no longer.

She hit it again.

And again.

It looked up at her.

She screamed. "I am alive."

She screamed every ounce of her hatred for these oily, reptilian abhorrences as her arms shook and the creature's head caved in in a bloody flaming mass.

She caught her breath.

She turned away from what she had done to see Warwick match his attacker.

The Finder didn't stand a chance.

She thought it cruel that some were able to make death seem beautiful, like some macabre ballet. A terrible gift.

She had always heard that Finders had black blood, but she could see now it was merely a very dark red. She wondered how far removed from humans they really were.

When his bloody dance was done, Warwick's eyes met hers. "We must find Lady Katherine."

He set off through the trees.

As they ran, she was still fighting. Fighting against despair. The Queen would be fine, surely? She had the Jester with her.

And all they would see was each other.

Had she failed in her duty so soon after accepting it?

She hoped she was wrong and they wouldn't be blind to all around them. Or maybe it would be better to find them in some lovers' nook, oblivious to the horrors outside. Or maybe the Jester had talked some sense into her and they would be discussing royal wedding plans and unification strategies.

Katherine was dead when they found her. Pale and bloodied.

Althea knew just by looking.

She was gone.

Warwick knew too, she thought. He was searching the scene, checking dead brigands and looking for tracks. "They have taken the Jester," he called.

She knelt by her dead Queen and gently rolled her onto her back.

She was clutching the knife into her gut, as if she did it to her self.

So it was over.

"She's gone," she said.

Warwick was standing over them, looking at the knife Katherine clasped to her belly. "Did she…?"

"No."

She looked down at Katherine's sightless eyes, staring up through the trees to the clear blue sky.

She felt blood soaking into her robe where she knelt. She thought of Amanda and Duncan smiling and cooing over their newborn child all those years ago. It was the first time Althea had seen a new life. She had helped the Midwife, an old nanny named Carla, with the delivery. Carla had hauled the tiny Princess from her mother's womb, bellowing "Come on now, little one, don't be shy!"

She was there at the beginning and now here at the end.

She looked at Katherine's pale, empty face, so far from the tiny, red, crumpled one she had met eighteen years before.

"Will we bury her?" she asked.

"Is there nothing can be done?"

She knew where this was going.

"No." She took a deep breath.

He walked to her side, looking down at Katherine. "I have heard so many stories," he said. "Tales of great healers…"

She'd heard them all. "Not of me."

"Yes, of you," he said. "'Althea could wake the dead if she wished'."

It was impossible. "Warwick, she's away by now. It's too late."

"So it can be done?" his hand was on her shoulder, pulling her to face him.

She shook her head and shrugged him off. Not again. "Even if there was time, I have not the skill."

"You're a healer. The best."

If she was so good, why had she failed? Why had she failed him? "Maybe I was…"

"You know the ritual?"

"Nobody's performed a successful awakening in years…" Her voice was raised, shrill and unfamiliar in her own ears. "I cannot wake the dead!"

"You can but try!"

"I've tried before!"

She wept then. She wept for Katherine and she wept for the Fool and she wept for Duncan and she wept for her Mark. How she had failed him. She remembered him, lying in the mud and rain outside the house. The house that burned down around her. She wanted to wake him. She performed the ritual. She bled and she begged and she pleaded.

But no one was listening.

She lay next to Mark's body for a whole night and the following day.

She waited and she waited.

At dusk, she dragged him up the hill and buried him under the Bluefire tree.

And here she was again. Kneeling in the mud and blood.

Warwick was looking at her sadly. "Your man Mark." He remembered.

She looked back at Katherine. She seemed almost peaceful. Clutching the dagger to her like a wreath. Or a wedding bouquet.

"He was not long gone when I found him." She looked back to Warwick, wiping tears from her eyes. "I couldn't save my husband, how could I heal anyone else?"

Warwick gingerly placed a hand on her shoulder once more.

"If all that we hope for Katherine is truly possible," said Warwick. "Then we are not merely saving one life…"

She couldn't save her husband with just her hope. Her love was not enough to secure his release. Could all their hopes, all their love, succeed where she had failed?

"We have nothing to lose by trying," said Warwick.

Would the hope of the land hold sway in the bargain?

Warwick squeezed Althea's shoulder. "You will not labour alone this time. You have my faith."

The faith of a King. That had to count for something. Especially one so noble as Warwick.

She put her hand on his.

It could work.

Althea smiled weakly. "Our business is life."

Faith, hope and love. A King, a Queen and a Witch, with the fate of a kingdom in the balance.

If any plea could be heard, it was this one.

"We'd better get to work," she said.

The King

She was dead.
You don't come back from that, do you?
Do you?
Althea's reputation was deserved he was sure, but could she heal death itself?
If anyone could, it was her.
He had to believe.
He thought about stories of necromancers, Witches and Warlocks who could raise corpse armies as puppets for their evil will.
He didn't think Althea's will was evil. His father would've burned her alive all the same, just for suggesting she could resurrect a person.
And she would've deserved it.
Shut up.
Warwick peeled the bark off a silver birch.
What else did she need?
Althea had sent him out into the woods to collect various ingredients, presumably for a potion or tincture of some kind. She wanted flowers. Gnomes' Thimbles and Noonsuns. Small flowers with purple bells and fluffy yellow flowers. He was no florist, but he'd spent enough time in the Holtlands to be able to recognise them.
He hurried through the trees, eyes roaming for his colourful quarry.
Could someone come back from the dead?
He had to hope.
When he returned to the camp, Althea was waiting. Katherine lay by the fire. He was relieved to see that the knife had been removed from her belly and her grasp. He was glad he didn't have to see that come out.
He gave Althea her collection of flowers, mushrooms and tree bark and she thanked him.

A pot boiled on the fire, and the Witch began sprinkling herbs into it, flaking the flower petals with her fingers.

It looked like soup.

She cleaned Katherine's wounds. Two inch-wide slits in her abdomen were all it took to kill her. She had a black eye, too.

She looked so pale.

When the wounds were clean and the pot was bubbling away, Althea raised the knife she had pulled from Katherine's body, still coated in her blood. She placed the blade flat in her hand, closed her fist around it and, with a muttered word, sliced her palm.

Warwick winced as Althea held her fist over the pot, squeezing it tight as blood trickled over her knuckles, into the mixture.

"We must give of ourselves so that she might live." Althea presented the knife to Warwick. She saw his uncertainty and smiled reassuringly. "Just a gesture, really."

He'd never deliberately hurt himself before, but he knew the feel of a blade on his flesh. It was not something he enjoyed. He steeled himself.

It was a small price to pay.

He carved his hand and held it out to join hers. Two fists trickling life and hope and promise into a cauldron.

When they had bled sufficiently, Althea waved Warwick away and continued assembling her supplies.

He watched the bizarre routine with increasing incredulity.

She poured the weird mixture onto Katherine's wounds and into her mouth.

She plucked a hair from her own head and threaded it through the eye of a needle made from a long, curved thorn.

She held the thread before her and allowed the needle to swing back and forth over Katherine's body. She closed her eyes and muttered under her breath.

She sewed up Katherine's wounds with the makeshift needle and thread, as easy as if she were darning some worn-but-well-loved item of clothing.

She snapped off the thread after the last stitch, placed one hand on Katherine's forehead and took her hand in the other.

She spoke quietly, but this time Warwick heard. "Time to wake up, Princess. Come on back to us."

Althea walked over to where Warwick sat, leaving Katherine lying alone by the fire. She sat down on the ground with a sigh. "It's out of our hands now. We can only wait and see if our plea is heard."

Warwick looked at the still form of his former betrothed. *Heard by whom?*

The Fool

He was sore.

There were holes in his skin where the hooks caught him. Deep holes. Holes his fleas could go exploring and find the hidden cave systems of his veins.

His hands were rubbed raw by the manacles. He wondered if he could break his thumbs and squeeze out of them, but he was too fond of his thumbs. They were good for holding tankards and nocking arrows and wielding blades. Who's got two thumbs and would like it to stay that way?

This Fool.

His legs were killing him.

The Brigands had been dragging him behind a cart for what seemed like days now. There was no time without mealtimes, bed time, home time. They just kept moving and occasionally someone would toss water over him or throw him a strip of beef. If he was lucky.

If he was unlucky they'd stand on the back of the cart and piss on him. After a while he started catching it in his mouth and spitting it back at them.

That showed them.

They knew who they were bungling with then. A slash-spewing madman. A mouth-micturating maniac.

At least they stopped pissing on him.

It got in his wounds.

It stung.

As bad as it seemed, there was one thing that he kept reminding himself.

You deserve worse.

You let them all die.

The girl under the cart, Ivor and Edmund, Addlish, Saro and Blenheim, Lorna, Mark, even old Jolias Arch the craven traitor was no more.

Poor Jolias.

But that was all so long ago.
And now Duncan was dead.
And his daughter.
Two more people he'd sworn to protect.
Two people he loved.
He hadn't really noticed Katherine becoming the most important thing in his life until it was too late. His job was to keep her amused whilst keeping her safe, and he had grown to yearn for her laughter and even just her smile, ever more as they became rarer and rarer.
And now she was gone.
And it was his stupid fault.
He fell in love.
He let his guard down.
He broke his promise.
She died.
And he deserved so much worse.
It was his fault.
Wait.
A hooded figure approached on horseback, riding back from the main column of the caravan as the Fool shambled along behind the cart.
Actually, it was *his* fault.
Ken was looking his smug-bastard self, even through a layer of bandages. The whole journey, he had worn the face of the cat that got the cream. Well, a hideously disfigured cat that got the cream.
"There, Jester," he announced jovially, pointing ahead. "There is no sweeter sight than home."
Up ahead was a dark, stone keep. A high wall around a courtyard and, in the centre of the yard, a single tower. It huddled at the base of a low mountain, called the Greyberg, a long, dull, white-capped slope which lived up to its name. Behind that, the Eastrod mountains rose.
No sweeter sight.
"I can think of a few."

My foot down your throat.

He knew where they were. This was the Otenward Spire. An ancient outpost at the south edge of the Stonefold. Supposedly built by Arnhult the Mason for the Siblings as a watchtower to warn of Eastrod Oten raids. Long abandoned when those giant terrors slipped into legend.

"Come, you are my guest!" said Ken, still enjoying the warm host routine. "This will be your home also, for the rest of what life I deign to allow you."

"If this is to be my home, can I have a set of keys? And you could think about brightening the place up a bit; few murals, bit of landscaping—"

He was cut off by Ken's boot in his face.

He felt blood in his mouth again.

Never got used to the taste. Metallic. Like chewing gobbets. Or had a tooth come loose?

"Sorry, do go on! I obviously have nothing better to do than listen to your bleatings." Ken had given up his amusing pleasantries.

The Fool spat blood.

He was going to kill him.

Or maybe just annoy him into forgetting he wanted to keep me alive.

"Finished?" asked Ken.

For now.

"Good. Save your breath, Fool. Before long you will treasure each one I allow you to take."

Ken spurred his horse forward and the Fool called after him in his best, simpering Ken impression. "'Save your breath, Fool'. I have to hold it when you're around. Stinkin' Smeggy—"

He sighed. He could barely muster an insult any more. What was the use?

She was gone.

And he deserved whatever Ken had planned.

It's so bright.

My eyes hurt. Only for a moment, before darkness settles over me once again.

What was I doing?

Have I been asleep?

I am in bed. A big, soft, warm bed.

Moonlight leans into the room, stretching across the floor from a thin window and I know where I am.

I'm home. The moonlight must've woken me.

Why do I feel relieved? Was I dreaming? If I was, the vision is lost to me now. Only a misty memory of regret remains.

And even that is fading.

I remember I was happy here.

In bed.

Do I remember?

I am happy here.

I am.

Someone's coming.

Footsteps in the hallway.

No torchlight flickering under the door. Someone is sneaking.

Pretend to be asleep. Hope they pass by the door.

They don't.

The footsteps stop.

Hold your breath.

Maybe I imagined it.
Maybe there's nobody there after all.
The door creaks open.
Don't look.
Don't look.
Don't look.
Whoever it is, they walk slowly and quietly to the bed.
My eyes are squeezed tight.
Go away. Please go away.
They've stopped again. Right by me.
I have to look.
I have to.
Through my squinting eyes, I can see.
It's so tall.
It looms above me, crooked over like a long hook. Leaning its head towards mine.
Framed in the moonlight, I see it is hooded. Cloaked. A black shape filling the room from floor to ceiling.
It makes a sound. A soft, whispering sigh.
Is it crying?
A hand reaches from the folds of the cloak. A pale, slender, naked arm.
Reaches for me.
For my face.
Somebody says "No."
And he's there. Like he always has been.
And I know where I am.
I'm back then. Back when it all went wrong.
I can't see their faces.
His hand is on her pale wrist and then he is screaming.
I sit bolt-upright in bed. I've seen this before. This is my dream.
Of course it wasn't a dream.
I never want to hear anybody scream like that again.
It's as if he can't let go. His body writhes and spasms and he can't let go.

She throws her shrouded form against him and heaves. His flesh comes away in her hands like a seething, bloody onion-skin.

He hits the stone floor.
She looks at him.
Looks at me.
I still can't see her face under the hood.
She runs.
"Wait," I say.
This is different. This never happened.
She stops.
"Please don't go." I never said that. I do now.
She has her back to me. Just a black shape in the doorway.
She runs again.
But I'm not a child anymore.

Did I even know it was her, the last time? It has always been a dream to me. Is this a memory? If so, how can I change it?

It's my memory, I can do what I want with it.
I'm running after her.

The corridors seem so long. She's a patch of shadow running through blades of light as she passes windows and skylights.

This is my home, but it's not.
The corridors are too long and my feet are too heavy.
I need to see her face.
She's getting away from me.
My feet are sticking to the floor.
So this is a bloody dream after all.
Well.
My dream. My rules.

I will tear this castle down with my bare hands. It's not really Elderhaime castle. And these aren't even really my hands. My hands are off somewhere else with the rest of my body -

My body.

My body.
Lying on the forest floor.
This isn't a dream.
Or a memory.
This is something else.
The castle tips, like a pouring jug. I fall, like the water, and the castle falls with me. Stone by stone it tumbles around me, as if it remained together only because I expected it to.
There are trees and daylight and -
I'm on the road now and I know where this is going.
I'd rather not.
They line up on either side of the road.
I'm so sorry.
They tell me not to worry. Wasn't my fault. But I know it was.
Afol, Egesung, Langmon, all brave men. All warriors. I didn't know them very well in life, but they smile at me in death.
Lord Gregory's Son waves at me. He wasn't much older than me. He smiles too.
The smiles are warm. Their eyes bear no malice.
There amongst the wreckage of their carriages, amongst the corpses of their horses, and standing over their own lifeless bodies, my father's bannermen and nobles forgive me.
They kneel.
I stand alone in an avenue of the dead kneeling at the feet of their Queen.
And there's my father.
Dad.
I run to him.
He holds me and tells me where we are. I already knew.
I try to tell him I'm sorry. Sorry I sent them all here for nothing.
He tells me not to be daft.
He says he's the one who's sorry. So many things he never said.

I ask him why he didn't tell me about her. About what happened.

He says he did. He tried to tell me about it so many times, but I insisted it was a nightmare. I would scream and cry and pull my hair if he tried to mention the night Mum left.

He hated hurting me, so he let me believe what I wanted.

I was a liesayer, but I only fooled myself.

I suppose I just didn't want her to be gone.

And now I'm gone too.

I tell him she was here, in my room.

He says she wasn't. She's not here. And neither is the Jester. Only my memories of them.

I feel like someone's calling me from a long way away.

He says it's time.

Time for what?

You're going back. You don't belong here. Yet.

But I need more time.

There'll be plenty of that. Eventually. I love you Katherine. I'm so very proud of you. Of everything you are and everything you're going to be.

But...

Send him to us.

There are others now. Strangers.

Your life for his.

Send him to us.

I know who they mean.

He sent so many of them here.

My dad holds me close and just for a moment he is really there.

We didn't die for nothing. We died for you. Now you must live for us.

The light is fading. My father stands before me, along with throngs of strange and half-forgotten faces already drifting away.

He smiles at me. "Kick his arse, Kathy".

Air fills my lungs as the darkness of day hits my eyes.

I will.

"Time to wake up, Princess. Come on back to us."

The Witch

She heard a cough.
Almost a retching sound.
She thought Jet must be passing a hairball.
Scratch-happy, mangy old thing he was. Grumpiest cat alive. He hadn't taken the move from the castle very well. He'd been spoiled by the serving girls and lazy kitchen rats, and wasn't enjoying having to actually hunt for food or wait for scraps.
She heard him cough again.
Silly cat.
He'd been dead for years.
She was sitting in the woods.
She'd fallen asleep leaning on Warwick's shoulder.
She rubbed her eyes awake.
The coughing.
King Warwick was already awake. Had he even slept? He was getting to his feet, his eyes fixed on Katherine's body.
No. Not a body anymore.
Katherine was sitting up. She had her back to them and was hunched over in front of the fire.
Did it work?
Althea thought for a moment of all the warning stories, of people being brought back without blood sacrifice, of people bringing things back from beyond, and of others coming back in their stead.
Warwick was moving towards Katherine. Althea leaned forward to hold his arm.
"Wait," she said.
Katherine coughed again, shuddering slightly.
Warwick looked at Althea and she saw his eyes were wide with wonder. Or fear.
"What's wrong?" he asked.
"She needs time. To collect her thoughts."

She thought of the tales of madness brought on by the shock of awakening. Catatonia, shrieking mania and murderous rage. It was said to be difficult to rediscover ones' self upon returning to the mortal plane. She thought it must be like waking a sleep-walker.

"A small part of her self may already have been lost for ever," she said. "So we needed to replace it with a part of ourselves."

Warwick looked at his hand. At the bloody rag tied tight around the palm. Althea bore a matching dressing. Small sacrifice, but hopefully enough. As far as she remembered there were no measurements dictated in the blood sacrifice ritual, just blood given willingly.

"Right now, she's trying to work out exactly who, where and what she is. Disturbing her during that process could cause irrevocable damage."

But perhaps the damage was already done. Would the Princess ever be the same again? What knowledge would she return with from the other side? Following the experience of death, how does one readjust to life? And how does it feel to have aspects of yourself replaced by aspects of others?

"And... she may inherit certain characteristics of ours for a short time. Personality traits, stuff like that." Althea picked at her bandage.

Katherine coughed again.

"A short time?" Warwick's face inquired as to the length of a "Short Time".

She had to be honest. "Maybe the rest of her life." Althea shrugged. "I never brought anybody back from the dead before."

The Queen

She felt the air in her lungs once more.
She felt the surge of life as her heart began to beat.
She felt as if the light that had dazzled her somehow receded into her, warming her very soul.
Her first breath caught in her throat and she coughed.
That hurt.
She looked down at herself. Sitting on rocks. Was she in the woods? She was, wasn't she?
She saw the hole in her dress. Someone had cut away a square of the fabric, revealing her stomach. She ran a finger over the two small rows of rough stitching on her skin.
There was a knife.
A man wearing her Daddy's crown had stabbed her with her Daddy's knife.
That was why she was back. That was what she had to do.
Send him to us.
She had to do other things too, but first things first.
She thought she should probably take another breath. Didn't she used to do that without thinking?
She was aware of them. Somewhere behind her. They were waiting. Waiting for a sign of life. Waiting for any indication she'd been replaced by a wight of some sort so they could bash her back to oblivion.
She should probably put them out of their misery.
How did she used to do it?
Talking, they called it. Pushing that troublesome air out of your lungs whilst vibrating your throat to make noise and shaping your mouth to make words.
Simple as that.
She reached down inside herself.
Come on. You used to do this literally all the time.
Don't think about it, just do it.
What do you want to know?

How long have I been away?
How long have I been away?
How long...
Wait, did I say that?
Try again.
"How long..?" was all she could manage.
A voice from behind her. Close by. "Highness?"
It was a man. She heard blood and sorrow and hope - above all, hope - in his voice. She knew him, though she had not known him long.
"How long was I gone?" she managed the full sentence this time.
She watched the embers of the dying fire before her, wondering how much wood it would take to rekindle. So much sacrifice.
"A day. Maybe less." Another voice from behind her. A woman. A noble, frail woman. She heard regret and love and bitterness and again that echo of hope. She knew this one too.
Only a day? It seemed so much longer.
The sunlight was hurting her. The world that had seemed so dull upon her return was now a sharp throb behind her eyes.
Like a hangover.
She remembered her first hangover and the dancing and drinking and living that preceded it.
"My head hurts," she said.
Only a day. That was already too long.
Things to do.
She stood up.
Althea and Warwick were at her side, reaching out to support her. She waved them away. "I'm fine."
"You're not fine, Princess," said Althea. "You're still half-dead."
Half dead. Half alive. Neither one thing nor the other.
She laughed. "Yeah, but which half?"

Laughing made her head hurt even more. She pressed her palm to her forehead, trying to push the pain in to the back of her mind. She could feel Althea and Warwick looking at each other, trying to decide if they'd broken her.

This world was pain. For a moment, she heard them calling. Beckoning her back to where she would be free of pain for ever. She saw that dazzling light. She felt the warmth.

She pushed harder.

"I have to come back now," she whispered to them. "I have things to do."

And then they were gone. And she was alone again, in the cold.

She sat down on the rocks.

She felt Althea's hand on her shoulder and she realised.

She wasn't alone.

She was clinging to Althea's knees like a child. A voice in her mind said "Well, this is embarrassing."

Althea's arm was around her now, and she buried her face in the witch's neck.

She clung onto her for her own dear life. So much was taken away. Not just from her, from everyone. Pains upon pains are heaped on men and women from the moment they crawl into the light. So many fall to darkness and darkness falls upon so many. She wanted to cry for them all.

But she didn't have time.

It wasn't over yet.

"There, there." It was Althea's voice, soothing in her ear. "There, there."

She marvelled at the nonsensical simplicity of the phrase. There, there. So abstract and yet so grounding.

You are there.

"Where?" She smiled at Althea.

She closed her eyes and realised she was breathing. She could taste the air.

"They don't have this…" she didn't finish the thought. Her friends wouldn't understand.

And she had work to do.

She stood up. "Well. We'd better get a shimmy on."

"Princess?" Althea still looked wary.

She felt a new energy scatter through her body.

A purpose.

"It's not Princess any more, Al."

Althea looked afraid, Warwick just looked confused.

What was next? She glanced around. "We're going to need horses," she said.

She looked at Warwick. King Warwick the Patient. She smiled at him. "My Lord, I want to thank you for your patience with me. You are a good man."

"Thank you..?" He was even more nervous than Althea.

"But you have been away from your kingdom long enough on my behalf." She placed a hand on his arm and looked into his eyes. "You and Althea must ride to Fairford Castle. To prepare for the wedding."

"What?"

"I will marry you at dawn tomorrow and we will drag these forsaken lands into an age of peace if it be the last thing we do."

"What?" said Althea.

She was busy now. A hundred thoughts bouncing round her head. So much to do, so little time.

She turned to Al. "Fury is torturing our Jester as we speak. He will have reached the Brigand's Keep by now…"

"The Brigands have made the Otenward Spire their home. I know the road." said Warwick. He was as loyal as the Fool.

She thought for a moment. Somewhere in the back of her mind, she could see the thin finger of the Spire, alone in fields of stone, mountains crowding behind. She could see the path, though she had never walked it. That was odd. "So do I."

She shook her head at Warwick. "No. You must return to your people. Let them know that a change is coming. Tomorrow at sunrise, we unite the lands."

Althea was still concerned. "Princess, you are not yourself…"

Al was right. But wrong.

Would there always be a ghost of her, wandering these woods?

You are not yourself.

Then who in the four corners was she?

For the first time, she felt like she knew.

No, she didn't feel it, she just knew it.

"I am Queen Katherine of Elderhaime. The Princess is dead."

A tentative smile crept onto Warwick's face. "Long live the Queen."

Althea still protested. "This is absurd. You can't make this decision in your state."

"The choice is made, Al." Katherine shrugged. "Suppose I just had to die to realise the value of my life."

She thought again of all the clamouring voices calling to her in the light. All the sadness. All the regret. The frustrations of lives unlived.

Well, not her.

Not any more.

"What are you talking about?" said Althea.

Katherine placed a gentle arm around the Witch's shoulder. "Stop fretting, Al. All we need to do is follow the Fenbrim north to Solsted town, beg, borrow or steal a few nags and then you just need to get to Fairford." She looked to Warwick. "Make the preparations for tomorrow, and we'll see you there for the wedding. Yay!" She waved her fist in faux enthusiasm.

"You're serious," said Warwick.

"Dead serious."

She noticed something on the ground. A rucksack. A wooden handle protruding from the top flap.

She picked it up and spoke to Althea. "I'm going after the Fool. But I'm going to need help."

Althea frowned at her. "What are you planning?"

She wrenched Mister Punch out of the sack and studied the rictus grin on his scarred, wooden face.

"Something very Foolish."

The King

So it seems you can come back from that.
Althea was a necromancer.
Was that the correct term? He wasn't sure. He didn't want to ask for fear of causing offence. He would continue to call her a healer, though he thought that hardly did her justice.
How do you heal death?
With gramword magic and Rynish pacts, that's how.
Stop it.
Burn her.
Don't be ridiculous.
You're ridiculous.
He had seen incredible things in his days: A swarm of red Bloodspinners scrambling out of their cave to carry a grown man away. Massive Jim, the self-proclaimed Half-Oten who stood eight feet tall at least. He'd once seen a potato that looked like it had a human face.
He'd never seen someone come back from the dead.
He had so many questions, but he thought it would be rude to ask.
Where did she go?
What did she see?
Was his mother there?
He doubted Katherine and his father would've gone to the same place.
And anyway, there wasn't really time for questions.
They were running.
It had been decided that he and Katherine would run north along the bank of the Fenbrim until they reached Solsted. They were to acquire horses and return to Althea.
He wasn't keen on leaving Althea alone, but she had assured him she would be invisible the whole time they were gone.

You can't really argue with someone who just performed a resurrection.

It was a beautiful morning, and if they weren't running flat out in a race against time to save the life of a friend and perhaps restore peace to the lands as he had always dreamed, he might have stopped to admire the verdant greenery they were passing through. The further they got from the fens, the less twisted and gnarled the trees became.

He looked at Katherine.

She was an actual miracle.

She had been a corpse an hour ago, and now he was struggling to keep up with her.

She ran barefoot, where his feet were bound in flannel, but she never flinched once as they ploughed through the tall bremels and patches of rynelich. It was as if she felt nothing but her purpose.

He drew alongside her. "How are you feeling?" he said between gasps.

She seemed confused for a minute, as if she was really having to think about her answer. Then she smiled. "Really well, I think. I feel... rested. Come on-"

She was suddenly ahead of him again.

He had marvelled at her before, he supposed, but now...

When he lost his footing on a rotten log, she was at his elbow, bringing him back to balance with a "Careful there, your highness." Her momentary proximity was exhilarating, but she was gone again as soon as he found his footing.

He could only follow.

His muscles burned and his bones screamed.

His heart rattled his ribcage.

And still they ran.

Ahead of them, the sheer white cliff-face of the Lip stretched up into the sky.

After what, an hour? - two? - they could see Solsted. A small settlement of wooden buildings at the base of the Lip, at the point where the Underfarway crossed the Fenbrim.

A couple of miles outside the town was a small farm.

"Stables!" said Katherine, pointing at the farmhouse. The stables were alongside. No horses to be seen, but they could well be indoors.

As they approached, they saw a large, red faced man seated at a table in the yard in front of the farm house. He was eating breakfast in the sun, and didn't look to be long out of bed. He was chewing a wedge of white cheese and supping from a flagon.

Warwick quite fancied a pint himself.

The man looked up as they ran up the path. A scowl appeared on his face.

"Lord Hortha!" Katherine called.

The large man's eyes went wide. He stood up, scattering crumbs of cheese. "Florence!" he shouted towards the house.

They ran up to the table and Warwick flopped forward, hands on knees. Katherine leaned on the table.

There was a pause as they tried to catch their breath.

"Princess Katherine!" said the man, agog.

"Yes," Katherine gasped. "Well… It's Queen… now."

"I'm sorry?"

"Dad's… dead."

Warwick didn't think this chap's eyes could go any wider. "FLORENCE!" he shouted again.

"Brigands…" said Katherine. "Explain later… We need horses…" She straightened up. "Oh, by the way, this is King Warwick of Fairford." She pointed at Warwick.

The man looked at Warwick in terror. He waved.

"FLORENCE, GET OUT HERE THIS INSTANT!" shrieked Lord Hortha.

"We're getting married tomorrow morning… and we need to get to Fairford." Katherine pointed to the stables. "Can you spare horses?"

"What are you shouting about, Alo?" A woman about a third the size of Lord Hortha emerged from the farmhouse, wiping her hands on a cloth.

"Lady Hortha! Nice to see you again!" Katherine gave her a wave.

"Who's that?" the woman shielded her eyes from the sun.

"It's Queen Katherine of Elderhaime, my Lady. And this is King Warwick of Fairford."

Warwick also gave her a wave. He was just about able to stand up straight now.

"We met at my birthday party?" Katherine said.

"Oh, hello dear!" the woman peered at them, squinting in the sunlight.

"My father was killed by Brigands on the road, along with all the nobles and his guards, I've been lost in the wilderness ever since and now I need to borrow some horses to get to Fairford in time for the wedding tomorrow morning. Could you spare any?"

Lord Hortha was just staring at them.

"Of course dear," said Lady Hortha. "We only have the two cart horses as our plough horse lamed himself the other week, would they be any use?"

"They would be wonderful."

"Wonderful," agreed Warwick.

Two horses would be enough, wouldn't it?

"Right enough, then," said Lady Hortha. "I'll have the stable boy get them ready for you and I suppose you're hungry too, so I'll put some food together for you to take with you."

"You're too kind," said Katherine. "That would be much appreciated."

"Not at all dear," Lady Hortha waved the thanks away. "Not every day we get royalty popping by. Close your mouth Alo, before a bird nests in it." She gently tapped Lord Hortha's chin and he seemed to snap awake. She went back into the house.

"Sorry for your loss!" he blurted out. "King Duncan was a good man."

"He was that," said Katherine. "And I think he would appreciate your sentiments. And entrust you with one final duty to your King…"

Lord Hortha seemed to swell with pride.

"My Lord, the Kingdom of Elderhaime must know that my father is dead. His body lies on the Elderfarway near The Longing Cliff…"

"He is buried under stone but many more are not," said Warwick.

"Would you do me the honour of arranging their safe passage back to Elderhaime?" said Katherine.

The Lord puffed up even more and his face went even redder. "I shall see to it personally, Your Highness."

"My father would be grateful."

"And so are we," added Warwick.

When the horses were saddled and ready, and he and Katherine were astride them, Katherine turned again to Lord Hortha and his Lady.

"My friends, you don't know the service you have done us today. Spread the word, all are welcome at the wedding tomorrow."

"And at Fairford henceforth," said Warwick.

"What love did hew shall same renew!" roared Lord Hortha.

Katherine smiled at Warwick. "Something like that."

He felt a lightness flutter in his chest, as if his heart was become a butterfly.

You're pathetic.

Don't start.

He kicked his horse forward.

Extract from Lord Felix Tyrantson's Diary:
Thirteen Years of Age

Second Dracaday, Third Moon of Summer, 209
There has been a slight setback. Since my father's death, my brother has been making some changes. He thinks he can make right all the wrongs of the past few years. Including Dad making Bronwenson Chief Enforcer. Warwick says he's just an animal and had him arrested. He doesn't seem to realise that sometimes it's good to have an animal on your side.

Second Dorenday, Third Moon of Summer, 209
It is done. I went to Bronwenson in his cell and made the arrangements. I told him I would implore my brother to be lenient and merely banish him if he pledged his allegiance to me and my cause. He will go into the wilderness and cause havoc, much like the Green Shadows did against my father. I will send him men and provisions and he will build an army. We will own every forge from here to Elderhaime. We will run the weapon trade. He will pay sixty percent back to me and wait for my summoning when the time is right.

I can't kill Warwick yet. His trust is the most valuable weapon at my disposal.

The Queen

Althea opened the cage and the tiny yellow ball of feathers hopped out.

The little bird - a merecandle, Katherine somehow knew - fluttered up into the trees and perched on a branch.

She watched as it cocked its head to peer at her.

"What's he doing?" she asked Al.

"Preparing."

The bird was preening itself. The message capsule strapped to its leg.

"You have emphasised the urgency of this mission to him?" she said.

"Oh, yes. He understands the message is of the utmost importance."

She watched the yellow bundle of feathers puff up and shake out, smoothing itself down like a maid in an ill-fitting dress.

"When's he gonna crack on then?"

Al raised a finger. "Wait."

The bird gathered itself, hopped twice and disappeared.

It was off so quick she had to squint into the sky to see the tiny shape bounding away on the wind.

"Nippy little beggar," she said. "How long will it take?"

"With any luck, you'll be ready by midnight."

She reckoned up in her head. They would have to move fast.

"Better get moving."

Althea placed the cage on the ground and picked up her pack. "It won't be easy. The walls of that keep are high and strong."

Katherine smiled to herself. "Walls matter not to an army of ghosts."

Althea didn't look convinced. She slung her pack over her back and swung up into the saddle she was to share with Warwick.

"Be careful." Katherine kept her voice low as she helped her up. "There may yet be danger in Fairford."

Althea glanced at the King, collecting his belongings a short way away.

"You don't think…"

She smiled. "No. I have seen his heart, and it is…" She shrugged. "…nice. Look elsewhere once you reach the castle, I fear some there may yet have reason to resist peace."

That's why I doubt you thought of it. She remembered the Fool's words as if heard in a dream. A petty jibe at the Bandaged Brigand's vanity, or a glimpse of the truth?

"I have something for you," said Althea. "A parting gift."

Althea held out the knife, hilt first.

She stared at it. Gleaming steel and crimson handle, golden crown on the pommel.

The thing that killed her father.

The thing that killed her.

"I think maybe this blade has a tale of its own to tell," said Althea.

Katherine reached out a hand to her bane.

It felt cold.

"A tale soon to end," she said. She looked Althea in the eye and felt a new warmth and light in the green irises, as if something had awakened within the Witch. "Thank you, Al. They were right about you."

"How's that?"

"You're the best. Althea the Deadwaker."

Althea grimaced. "That makes me sound like some Ryneslave necromancer. It's hard enough being a Witch."

"We cannot be defined by our titles."

"No, but we must bear them like a burden. Be careful what name you make for yourself," Althea smiled down at her. "Your Majesty."

"I will, Althea."

"Good luck, Queen Katherine."

Katherine stepped back and bowed low to her subject. Warwick approached and placed a hand on the horse's flank.

"It won't be easy on him carrying two of us," he said.

He cared about the horse. She could've embraced him like a child right then, but she thought better of it. "He'll be fine," she said. "Just make sure he is treated like a King when he gets you home."

He smiled. "He shall receive a royal welcome."

He hoisted himself up into the saddle in front of Althea. "Pardon, my Lady," he said to the Witch.

"Not at all, my liege," she said. "I've always wanted to be carried off by a handsome Prince. Suppose a King will have to do."

She winked at Katherine.

Warwick looked flustered and concentrated on securing his boots in the stirrups.

Katherine thought everyone was coming to life today.

"Until tomorrow, then?" he raised an eyebrow to Katherine.

She smiled and bowed. "'til our wedding, my King, and the rest of all our lives."

"Farewell, my Queen."

And they were gone.

Part Seven:
The End and the Beginning.

The Witch

Was this actually going to work?

There'd already been one miracle today, was it too much to ask for another? Or were the floodgates open now, allowing all manner of wondrous improbability to flood through into the mundane world?

She wondered about the man sitting in front of her. Her arms were locked around his waist and her cheek pressed against his shoulder blade. He felt... sturdy. Reliable. It occurred to her that, apart from Ken, this was the closest she'd been to a man since Mark.

Mark. All her love couldn't bring him back, but maybe Katherine returned for something greater. Perhaps there was a difference between the love and hope of an individual and that of nations.

She had needed Mark and been denied him. The lands needed Katherine and had been granted her.

Hardly seemed fair.

She thought of her years since Mark left: lost, lonely, haunted, a prisoner of despair.

She thought about the Siblands going through that.

She wouldn't wish it on anyone.

Warwick kicked their steed ever-faster, leaping ditches and fallen trees, racing between trunks and bushes, barrelling into their uncertain future.

What was this feeling she had swelling in her stomach? Like a knot untying. A knot that had pulled taut when Mark died, now loosening.

It was hope.

She hoped it would work.

She hoped the Princess - nay - The Queen would marry King Warwick in the morning. She hoped that a marriage contract would mean more to the people of both lands than a faltering peace treaty. She hoped the Queen could get to the Jester in time. And she hoped that wouldn't change her mind.

Was it all too much to ask? What were the chances of the fates staying in a good mood for the rest of the day?

Slim. But slim hope is some hope.

They raced out of the woods and into the wide meadow of the Fairfold. Flowers spread over the ground as far as the eye could see. A knee-deep, speckled ocean of all colours rolled before her to the foot of the Eastrod Mountains and Fairford itself.

She heard Warwick's voice blowing back to her on the breeze. "Almost there!"

The towers of Fairford Castle reached over the meadow, looming like a pale beckoning hand in the gathering shadow of the mountains.

In the old days, this was a place of death and danger, the seat of the Tyrant King. Now it was to be a beacon of hope for all the land. Fairford would be fair again. Here, under a darkening sky, racing through so much beauty, she still couldn't help the cold dread that tickled at her as she looked on that place. Memories of friends lost and evil deeds done are hard to shake off.

And what of Katherine's warning? Could there yet be an evil presence in King Warwick's house? She would have to remain vigilant.

As they passed under the portcullis, she couldn't escape the sensation of being swallowed by some vast, lazy beast waiting for the unwary to stumble into its maw.

Once in the courtyard, people were rushing to meet Warwick as he swung down from his horse like the returning hero he was.

He hopped out of the saddle and reached up to assist her. A true gent. Katherine could've done a lot worse. She refused his help all the same and slid out of the saddle.

"Make sure he is well fed," he told the stable hands as they took the horse. "It's been a rough ride."

She peered around in the twilight, taking in the high battlements, the wide marble staircase that led up to the main door, the guardhouse above the gate they just passed through.

Know the exits.

"Brother!"

She turned to see a young, handsome man, or perhaps a boy, hurrying down the steps. He was dressed in the royal purple of Fairford. She had never met Warwick's brother, but she knew him immediately. Felix Tyrantson.

"You are safe!" Prince Felix grabbed Warwick in a fierce embrace.

Warwick laughed. "That I am!"

Felix held his brother at arm's length, eyeing him earnestly. "Well? What news? Did you find her? Was she…?"

Warwick tilted his head. "She was alive. Then not. Then again."

"Pardon?"

Althea thought she saw something there.

"She was wounded by Brigands," Warwick said. He pointed to Althea. "Lady Althea healed her."

Felix turned to her for the first time and she knew for certain. His face smiled warmly but he couldn't staunch the poison in his eyes. Katherine's survival was terrible news to his ears.

"Our saviour, eh?" He bowed to her, but she felt he'd much rather put a blade to her. She felt rage and frustration humming around him. This boy was as wild as anything in the Holtlands.

She was reminded of the vicious children back in the village, all smiles and politeness when their parents were present, all hurling rocks and abuse when they were unsupervised. She imagined those kids born into Princedom.

He was his father's son.

"The Princess and I will be married at dawn tomorrow, all being well," said Warwick.

Warwick didn't know. Felix was on his best behaviour, but the show wasn't for Althea, it was for his brother. He needed Warwick's trust.

And he had it.

"Where is she now?" Felix asked the King.

Althea answered. "Tying up some loose ends."

Extract from Lord Felix Tyrantson's Diary:

Sixteen Years of Age

Second Dracaday, Second Moon of summer, 212
The time has come.

This wedding is the last straw. I have sent word to Bronwenson (or Mister Fury, as he's calling himself since his "accident") that he is to intercept Duncan's caravan and leave none alive, especially the Princess. Then I'll kill Warwick and blame it on an assassin from Elderhaime, take the throne and invade Elderhaime while they're still reeling from the death of their royals.

They'll probably welcome me with open arms. Peasants need rulers.

I'll bring peace to these lands, not Warwick. He thinks he can trick the people into unity with an illusion of love.

My power will be no illusion.

The Fool

This was interesting.

Well, not so much interesting as unusual.

He'd been tortured before, but in the past it'd always been with a purpose. "Where are the others hiding?", "What is your mission?", "Who sent you?" and all that. This time it was just for laughs. The pain was the purpose.

Ken was enjoying himself.

It was hard to say how much time had passed, or how many times he'd passed out. Conscious and unconscious were bleeding together.

Lots of bleeding.

The rack held him fast, chains digging into his wrists and ankles, and suspended him vertically so he couldn't slump to the floor.

Which was a shame, cos he really fancied a lie down.

He was fairly sure he remembered being dragged down narrow stone stairs and narrow stone corridors, into this narrow stone cell which had the unfortunate design-flaw of being entirely under the ground, so really struggled to catch any daylight.

He could only measure time in violence.

It was three punches past crotch-kick.

He could feel the swelling on his face from blow after blow, but the pain was almost constant enough to be numbness now.

There's only so much agony a body can endure before it starts to disregard it. If the pain is constant, there's no need to alert against it anymore. It becomes a dull murmur in the back of your head.

And he'd spent so long ignoring pain anyway.

Run away. Hide from the pain.

Go home.

Way back to the beginning.

Not his beginning, but theirs.

She was a child. But then so was he, really.

He could see her sad little face. A girl still young enough to smile at Mister Punch's bungling. To laugh at the Fool's rolypolys and giggle at his terrible jokes.

He could see her legging it away from him in the gardens. Hear her shrieks of laughter.

He could see her dancing on her birthday. He tried not to notice how beautiful she was.

He could feel her in his arms at the top of a cliff. Clinging to him as they rode on the wind.

He felt her hand in his as she lifted him on to a cart.

He saw her blue eyes.

He saw her bleeding out on the ground. His name on her lips.

His false name.

He was still a traitor.

Maybe he could apologise to her soon.

He could hear someone shouting.

He couldn't get any peace.

The voice made him angry.

Someone was hitting him in the head. It was like knocking on a distant oaken door. Impatient, half-heard thuds.

"Oi! Wake up!"

He didn't want to.

"Idiot!"

A slap in the face. He opened the eye that wasn't swollen shut. His right, he thought. At least he could still do directions. Up, down, left, right. He hadn't had that knocked out of him yet.

Ken's bandaged face loomed before him.

"What is the meaning of this?" Ken was waving a thin roll of paper in the Fool's face.

He tried to focus on it, couldn't make out the writing and looked back at the bandaged bastard. "Just 'cos I'm your prisoner doesn't mean I'm gonna read to you."

"A pigeon just brought this from Fairford." Ken was spitting. "It says that the wedding is going ahead. The Witch! Is she a necromancer?"

Ken's bandages were blurring and twisting into one another. The Fool felt his lips split as he tightened his face into a grin. "Well, she is in love with a dead bloke. Is that what that means?"

His plan to annoy Ken into killing him wasn't working out. Ken was surprisingly calm and deliberate in his sadism. As if he'd been planning this for a long time.

Ken was thinking. "And she never brought her dead husband back…" He made up his mind. "This is a falsehood. They try to panic us with stories of magic and wonder."

Ken screwed up the paper and forced it into the Fool's mouth. "I will not be distracted!" he bellowed.

He could just swallow it, he thought. Swallow the paper and choke and this would all be over. If the wedding was going ahead… then he was no longer needed. Kathy was still kicking. She was alive and she was marrying Warwick. Everything was going to be okay and his small, nameless role in the unification would be forgotten.

He hoped she would be happy. He hoped she was really alive.

Al was the best.

His lips cracked again as he started laughing.

Ken heaved on the rack handle.

The Fool screamed the ball of red, spitty paper onto the bloody stone floor.

The Guard

"Those are the kind of screams that linger."

It's bloody freezing up there. Me and Cutter are on watch, right, and I can't be bothered with Cutter's stupid babbling.

"You what?" I say.

He's got his "ghost story" face on, like when we sit around the camp fire and he tries to shit everyone up by talking about Gargrin the Bloodbather or the Fearies.

"Screams that echo long after the lungs that cast them have breathed their last."

Mister Fury must have been doing a rotten job on that Jester for the screams to carry all the way up there. Hell of a long journey for a scream, bouncing up through the corridors and grates and out into the dark and fog to our ears on the battlements.

I'm not squeamish, though. I've made enough men squeal in my time.

"Broken spirits find no rest. Fury will bring a curse upon himself. And us." He goes on.

I'm just about to tell him to shut it when I hear it.

I tell him to shut it for a different reason.

I tilt an ear to the wind. "Listen."

For a moment, there's nowt but the wind and the echoing screams. The screams stop and we hear it again.

Someone's crying.

A child. What in the four corners would a child be doing out there, eh? The hairs on my neck are crawling by now and I curse Cutter and his horror tales.

It's close.

Very close.

"You hear that?" I ask.

He nods.

Peering through the fog, we see it. A small dark shape, curled up in the shadows of the parapet, just a little way along the wall.

I look to Cutter and he nods.

We begin our approach, perhaps a little more cautiously than a crying child would normally warrant. But this was no ordinary child, was it? Out here on the battlements of a brigand keep in the middle of a curiously foggy night? Summat not right about this. I try not to think of the legends of the Demon Children that live on the moors.

As we get closer, its shape becomes clear. It's a young girl dressed head to toe in black, hooded. She's crying with her face in her hands.

"It's a little girl!" says Cutter. "We could put her to work in the Kitchen."

I'm not so sure. We're about six feet away from her now, and I draw my sword. "Are you lost, petal?"

She stops crying and looks up.

We both shrink back. Her face is deathly white and her eyes sunken and black.

The illusion lasts for a moment before I realise it's warpaint.

A moment is all they need.

Cutter is already over the wall by the time I know what's happening.

There's a noose around my neck and someone's yanking me towards the parapet.

It all happens so fast, my sword is on the ground and I'm off my feet before I can land a blow.

I'm hanging.

They've only bloody hanged me.

I can see Cutter kicking his last, dangling from the wall beside me, and I'm tearing at the rope at my throat.

I've been hanged by children.

There are so many of them. That must be how they lifted me off my feet so easily. They're crawling up the walls like black spiders. There's more on the ground.

The rope will not give. Something warm and wet runs through my fingers as I try to get hold.

I hear the portcullis raising.

Maybe Fury did bring a curse down on us.

I hope he gets worse than this.

I just work here.

And now I'm dead.

The Fool

Maybe he had been in worse than this, but Ken was using all the lowest tricks in the torturers handbook. He would not have been surprised if he'd started squeezing lemon juice into his open wounds.

The Fool felt as a pet at the mercy of a cruel child. A dreng just trying to see how much damage he can do to a living thing before it pops its clogs.

He wondered how long it would take.

He should just give up.

He could feel how near he was, but the closer he leaned towards the release of death, the more he felt his suspicion confirmed:

Death was a door with nothing on the other side.

No matter how intently he listened at the threshold, he heard nowt.

Just the end.

And he was afraid.

There was no light at the end of the tunnel for him. And even if there was such a tunnel, he was fairly sure the life he had led had earned him a seat at Ryneweard's table, where he could sit in eternal darkness and torment at the hands of everyone he'd wronged while beautiful innocent Princesses got to go and spend eternity in the company of their loved and cherished.

But if she truly was alive, wasn't that something to live for?

He was vaguely aware of someone else entering the room, probably the one called Bowman.

Their voices were distant noise, drowned out by the dull racket of agony.

He strained to hear their words.

"What?"

"A scream! I heard a scream!"

Concentrate.

The Fool squinted his one good eye, and saw Ken pointing at him. Dangling from the rack, dribbling blood down himself, the Fool wondered if Ken was better looking than him now.

"Yes, I heard one too," said Ken.

"No! It was something else. Somewhere in the keep!" Bowman was afraid.

This perked the Fool up no end.

Something was coming.

Before Ken had the chance to dismiss his lackey, another scream echoed down the corridor, accompanied by a clatter of steel.

The Fool was suddenly wide awake. "Someone's coming," he said.

Ken glared at him for a second. He said "Watch him," to Bowman, and he was out of the door.

Bowman looked at the Fool. The Fool smiled. A wide, bloody smile. He wondered if any of his teeth were broken.

In the corridor, sounds of chaos. Screams and cries and crashes and bangs.

Sweet music.

Bowman pulled the dungeon door closed, pressing his ear to the inside.

"The Prince is abroad." Bowman jumped at the Fool's words.

Bowman shushed him, but he was just getting started.

"He's gonna drag you back into the pit with him."

"Shut up!"

"He's come to punish you all."

Bowman yanked his head back as something hit the door hard.

A moment of silence -

Something banged the door again.

Somebody was performing.

"They're knocking," said the Fool. "You should let them in."

More banging. Louder, more insistent.
Bowman backed away from the door.
"They're here for you, Bowman. They know all about you."
Someone or something was now pounding heavily on the door.
Bowman was transfixed.
The Fool could only imagine what horrific boga Bowman's imagination would have stationed on the other side of the door.
He wondered what was really out there.
Whoever it was, he admired their dramatic flair. Hell of an entrance.
The pounding on the door reached a crescendo, and Bowman screamed.
"GO AWAY!"
Silence.
The knocking had stopped.
A moment passed like an age.
Bowman sighed -
"Maybe they listened?" said the Fool.
More silence.
Bowman crept slowly to the door, listening intently.
Still nothing.
He drew his sword.
Nothing.
He placed his ear back against the door.
Nothing.
Fool watched a cowardly man gather all his courage.
Bowman turned the door handle and pushed.
The heavy oak door creaked outward, opening into the corridor.
Bowman peered across the threshold.
A noose fell around his neck -
He was hoisted out of the doorway and into the corridor as a dark, hooded figure swung nimbly into the room. Landing

lightly, it turned, pulled on the rope and tied the end to the door handle. Bowman's legs kicked and struggled in the air in the corridor.

The figure gasped when it saw the Fool.

It pulled back its hood.

The Fool felt he recognised her, but the girl he was thinking of had much longer hair.

And was dead.

Couldn't be her.

You don't come back from that.

Unless -

Truth in every tale.

She hurried towards him. "What did he do to you?"

It was definitely her. She was definitely alive.

Or maybe he was dead too?

Maybe they were both dead and now they were together finally and nothing else mattered. No duty. No loyalty.

Just him and her.

She was cutting his bonds with a familiar knife.

"You look terrible," she said.

She smiled at him then, and he knew he was alive. He lived because she lived. His heart started beating again. It made everything hurt more, but made the pain worthwhile.

It was Kathy.

She was alive.

"I look terrible?" He looked at her cropped locks. "So does your hair."

That smile.

"We needed a lot of bow-strings," she said.

The Monster

Wretched. Cowardly. Craven.

He'd been called them all and he didn't care. Not one bit. He wasn't afraid.

The keep was dark and the torches were out and nobody was at their post, but he wasn't scared. He was the bane of Kings, the slayer of Queens and the horror of The Holtlands, whatever was out there in the dark should fear him.

Fearful. Awesome. Terrible.

These were what they would call him now.

But where was everyone?

Three posts he had passed on the corridors. No sentries. Just an upturned stool and a spilled jug of wine.

Drunk. That was it, they were probably all drunk and got to fighting.

And putting out torches.

He rounded another corner and there was someone there.

Only for a moment, there was a torch lit at the far end of the corridor. Then all was dark.

In that moment of light, a black figure was visible. Hooded. Cloaked. Like the image of Death.

He had seen Death. Made a friend of Death. He was Death's master. Death was no dead face behind a black hood. Death was nothing. The change from something to the absence of that something.

He drew his sword.

Whatever was in that corridor was no agent of death, so it would meet him just the same.

"I'm not afraid of you!" he called into the dark.

"You should be."

The voice whispered in his ear. Cold breath on his bandages.

He swung blindly, cutting only air.

And he was running.

Running away. Cursing himself for proving them right. He was a coward.

He bounced off a wall and sprawled to the floor.

There was light.

A flickering light.

Three brigands stood above him, one held a torch.

"Are you well, Mister Fury? We heard some noises."

He scrabbled to his feet.

Idiots.

He looked at the empty corridor behind him.

"Outside," he said.

"Sir?"

"Outside, get them outside so we can get a look at them. Draw them into the open."

They hurried towards the door to the courtyard.

He would show them. He wouldn't fight on their terms. They were using the darkness, so let them step into the moonlight where their true forms would be revealed.

They ran into the night air and the arrows rained upon them.

He grabbed the nearest man and hid behind him as best he could. The archers were all around the battlements, however, so there was no way to hide from them all.

He felt a punch in his thigh, and pain.

Maybe he was a coward, but he was no stranger to pain.

Black hooded figures loosed more arrows from their vantage points. He dragged his human shield with him, limping back through the door to the keep as bolt after bolt thudded into the now dead man.

He couldn't remember the man's name. Not that it mattered.

When he was out of sight of the archers, he dropped his shield and fell to the floor. He was only hit once.

He grabbed the shaft of the arrow and pulled. It slid slowly out of his thigh, leaving minimal damage. It was little more than a sharpened stick. It would take more than that to stop him.

He hauled himself to his feet, already running. He bounded through the corridors of his castle. His stronghold, now darkened and strange to his eyes. He needed more men. Perhaps the barracks would be undisturbed.

He reached the door unmolested and pushed it open. Inside, rows of bunk beds held still-sleeping brigands. He was simultaneously thrilled and enraged.

"Wake up, you fools! We're under attack!"

They began to stir, just as somebody kicked Fury into the room and slammed the door shut behind him.

He was in the dark. Trapped. He was being defeated. They were spoiling everything. He needed to get out.

He heard the door lock.

He needed to get out.

He was punching his knuckles to a pulp on the door.

An axe. By one of the bunks.

He grabbed it up as the men began to rise.

He could feel the air escaping from his lungs.

Why couldn't he breathe?

He needed to get out.

He didn't like being locked in places.

He hauled the axe into the planks of the door.

He had to get out.

The Queen

He was heavy.

Heavier than he looked, anyway.

He slumped into her, his arm around her shoulder, and she tried not to look at his bruised, swollen face.

She couldn't weep for him. Not now. There was work to be done.

The sounds of battle rang down from the corridors above.

She led him along the dungeon tunnel, as fast as his limping legs would allow.

"So…" his voice slurred like a sot's. "What's it like being dead?"

Someone was there. A brigand rushing from the shadows.

Movement. A thud and a grunt and their attacker was out cold on the stone floor.

She realised she was holding Mister Punch in her left hand. The blow had been instinctive and instantaneous. As if some ancient lesson had been brought into violent practice.

"Carry on, Your Majesty," said Punch.

That voice was not slurred.

She looked at The Fool in amazement.

He shrugged.

She brandished the puppet and heaved the Fool once more on their way.

"Well?" The Fool continued. "What's death like?"

"You look like you should know."

They hobbled up a stone staircase.

"Did it hurt?"

She thought about it. Did it hurt? Hadn't there been a feeling of calm? Of peace at the realisation she didn't have to worry any more?

"Living hurts. Dying hurts. Being dead… doesn't." She smiled at him. "And nobody expects you when you're already dead."

They made it onto the ground floor, hobbling along the darkened corridor. She could see the courtyard up ahead.

"Where is he?" she said to herself.

Someone screamed behind them. A high-pitched exclamation of disbelief and dismay.

She glanced over her shoulder.

The Bandaged Bastard looked her right in the eye. The tattered holes in his bandages might have filled with tears of rage right there and then.

He was holding an axe.

There was a good deal of floor between them, so she flicked him two fingers and turned back towards the courtyard.

And there he was. The Wolf pulled a horse-drawn cart to a standstill, right at the door. They were mere yards away from freedom.

"That dead bitch is stealing my Fool!" That shrieking voice again. Ken had obviously got over his shock. "Get her!"

She heard their feet. Their blades unsheathing.

She ran. As fast as she could, burdened with Fool as she was.

Ken ranted and raged, the brigands shouted, and she ran.

She wasn't afraid. She was amazed. Amazed at the beating of her heart and the blood in her veins. She was aware of every sound, every sensation, from the cold rock surrounding her to the misty morning about to dawn outside. She felt it all.

She was alive.

And she aimed to stay that way.

Bursting into the open air, she threw the Fool into the back of the cart.

"Go!" she cried, leaping aboard.

Wolf cracked the reins and the cart jolted forward.

Wolf called out a single word: "Disappear."

She saw movement on the battlements, in the courtyard, all around. Tiny black figures huddling out of sight, vanishing like the ghosts they were. They had played their part well.

But we're on our own now.

Looking behind, she saw the brigands spilling out of the doorway, into the courtyard. Some made straight for the stables, others just watched the cart barrelling out of the main gate.

Just before they were out of earshot, she heard Ken screaming. "She's still alive! They're ruining my beautiful vengeance!"

She smiled at that.

Wolf urged the horses on towards the woods, and she knelt beside the Fool.

"You're bleeding all over this nice cart," she said.

"Sorry." He could barely lift his head.

"Successful rescue and escape, I think."

"Yeah, we'll see."

She took his hand, and something came to her. She could help him. Couldn't she?

She placed her other hand on his forehead and closed her eyes.

Unfamiliar words came to her then, unbidden muttering in some forgotten language.

"What you doing?" said the Fool.

"Not sure." She kept her eyes closed. She felt something. As if something was moving from her into him, a part of her becoming a shared aspect of them both.

Or she might have imagined it.

"Are you a healer now?" he asked. "'Cos I don't feel any better."

She opened her eyes to give him a look.

"Delusions of grandeur." He grinned at her.

She wanted to kiss him.

An arrow slammed into the wooden siding of the cart and, in an instant, she yanked it free, nocked it and loosed it back from whence it came. A brigand fell from his horse as it hit home.

Again, she was uncertain as to what had happened. Her bow had been on her back, but now it was in her hand and a man was dead.

The brigands were approaching. A couple of dozen, all on horseback.

She tried again, nocked and loosed another arrow and another man died.

The Fool had dragged himself into a sitting position, peering over the side of the rattling cart.

"What happened to you?" he said. "You can't shoot like that!"

She nocked another arrow. "The Princess who couldn't shoot straight is dead." She loosed it and it pinged off into the woods to her right.

That was more like it.

She sucked her finger and shrugged at the Fool.

"She is risen again!" he said.

Wolf tossed the Fool his bow and a quiver of arrows. "Make yourself useful."

The Fool pulled himself further up, taking aim at the approaching Brigands.

"Where are we running to anyway?" he said.

"We're going to a wedding," she said.

They both loosed arrows simultaneously and two men fell. He looked at her. "You changed your mind?"

"Not really. I always knew it was the right thing to do, I just… didn't want to do it."

She caught an arrow.

She was talking and then she just… knew it was there. As if she was reaching up to pick an apple, she plucked it out of the air beside her.

She looked in amazement at the arrow, trying to figure out where it came from.

"Braw!" The Fool cried. "That's one of Warwick's tricks."

Katherine shrugged. "Looks like it's one of mine now."

She twirled the arrow between her fingers, as she somehow knew she could, and loosed it back at the brigands.

"I knew you'd see for yourself in the end. About the wedding." The Fool was beginning to seem more lucid.

"I think I understand now," she said.

A Brigand was on the cart.

He must've come alongside them in the trees and broken through, leaping aboard.

The Fool was on his feet in an instant.

She'd already knocked the villain into the dirt with Mister Punch. He rolled under the hooves of his friends' horses.

She was killing a lot of people today, and somehow it felt familiar.

And easy.

The Fool wasn't ready for standing up and he fell forward into her arms. She knelt down, easing him back to the floor, cradling him still.

"I swore to protect you," he said.

"You're doing a great job." She ruffled his hair. "I've only been killed once."

"Don't patronise me."

She saw it in his bloody grin. In the one eye he could open. She saw what they could have.

She hoped the world was worth it.

"I want you to know," she said, "that I would cast it all aside: the marriage, the throne, any hope of peace…"

She gazed into his good eye and she knew the sacrifice was not hers alone.

He smiled. "We've got a wedding to get to, your Majesty."

She nodded and redrew her bow without thinking, loosing two arrows before she realised she'd dropped the Fool on his head.

"Don't worry about me," he said. "I'm protecting you."

He lay on the bed of the cart as they raced on.

The Witch

She knew it.

As soon as she laid eyes on him, she knew.

At first she wondered how Warwick could not see, but it soon become apparent.

King Warwick loved his brother, and his love rendered him blind. Blind to the truth about Felix.

Felix was an evil little shit.

Katherine had told her to be wary at Fairford, but this kid was so accustomed to wandering freely, unquestioned by anyone, that his misdeeds were hidden by only the thinnest veneer.

His eyes had told her so when he first looked on her in the courtyard. Poisonous little pustules, filled with contempt. A smile masking a sneer.

He had his father's eyes.

But she had been wrong before.

So she waited.

Since her arrival the night before, Fairford Castle had been abuzz with news of the wedding and alive with activity as the preparations were made. The Great Hall, with its immense stained-glass window, was to be the setting, and was being decorated accordingly.

Everyone was busy but Felix.

After greeting them in the courtyard, he had hurried away. She had followed, after Warwick bid her get some rest, and found him hurrying from his chambers with a thin strip of paper. She followed him to the aviary in the gardens, and shortly a single pigeon was launching skyward into the dark.

He maintained his composure quite well, only a sly kick at a cat on his way out of the gardens betrayed any kind of disquiet.

She reckoned she knew where the pigeon was heading.

Felix had retired to his chambers for the rest of the night, but she waited. And watched.

She needed to be sure. She needed proof.

She hid in the shadows of the corridor outside his room, wrapping her cloak around her.

Just before dawn, as grey light began to creep through the high windows, there was an exclamation from inside Felix's room.

Althea had barely raised her head before Felix's door was thrown open and he was racing past her, naked under a flowing gown.

He was running from something or to something. Either way, he'd left his door open.

She tiptoed across the hall and stepped into the Prince's chamber.

Inside was opulence, velvet drapes and elaborate carvings. A window in one wall looked out onto the Fairfold and the coming dawn. Althea saw then what had startled Felix.

Out on the fold, a single cart was racing towards the castle. Some way behind it was a column of riders, evidently giving chase. They would reach the castle gate in a matter of minutes.

It was her. She had rescued him and now they were coming here.

This was bad news for Felix. His reaction proved it.

She looked down and saw a book open on the desk.

A heavy tome, but only half-written.

She read a few lines.

She closed the book and read the engraving on the cover. She smiled.

Lord Felix Tyrantson's Diary: Final Entry

Third Sunday, Second Moon of summer, 212
No word from Fury. If she's alive I'll kill him. Warwick came back with that witch bitch. The one they say can raise the dead. Remember to kill her too. They cannot be allowed to ruin my plan. I will be king. I've spent too long planning this. I will not fail. I will show you, father. You'll see when your beloved first born is dead at my hands how you only had one true son and heir. I am the rightful King of Fairford. I am

Bollocks

The Gatekeep

This is the life.
Everyone else running around the castle, putting up banners and chucking flowers around. Me, I'm sat up here looking out onto the fold, barrel of ale at me side, drinking the sun up.
It'll be rising in a minute.
A new day for us all, apparently. Queen Katherine on her way and the wedding to unite the Sundered Siblands once and for all.
Should be good.
Many would mock the idea of a marriage solving all our problems, but I get it. People need their icons. It's all about what the wedding represents, innit? It's not a "happily ever after" sort of thing, really, it just shows willing from both sides to try and mend what once seemed irreparable.
What love did hew and all that.
Anyway, it'll be a good do. I saw them rolling barrels up the great hall for the feast. The good stuff.
If she ever shows up, that is.
When my shift ends at dawn I'll go and sleep the day away in the barracks, ready for the party tonight. I don't mind missing the ceremony as long as I'm there for the night do.
The food and the booze.
Hang on -
There's something out there. On the fold.
Must be her, I suppose. Maybe we'll get a dawn wedding after all.
It's a cart, for certain. I can make it out if I squint. Damn these fading eyes of mine. What use is a watchman who can't watch?
There's more behind. They're being chased. It must be her!

Sound the alarm. The King can send out riders to chase off the Brigands.

Who's this? The Prince?

"Lower the portcullis!" he shouts.

I tell him it's her. The Queen. She's come to save us, but we have to save her.

I'm looking out of the window when he smashes my own tankard over my head and pushes me forward.

It's a long drop.

I'm going to miss the party.

The Fool

The portcullis cut the cart clean in two.

He thought they were home free, but someone in the guard tower obviously didn't know they were all friends now.

He pulled himself to his feet. The horses were trying to drag the front of the cart around the courtyard. Wolf and Katherine were sprawled nearby.

He looked behind. Through the enormous gate, he could see the brigands reining their horses to a stop by the rear half of the shattered cart. He could see Ken's bandaged head and feel his glare.

He gave Ken two fingers as Katherine appeared by his side, sliding under his arm in a way that felt altogether too natural.

She was only propping him up, but still.

"Where's the bloody wedding?" she shouted to Wolf.

"Main hall."

She guided him away, toward the stone steps up to the hall. Serfs and stableboys had begun to appear, wide-eyed at the peculiar visitors.

They must have looked a sight, him in his tattered and bloodied green-and-reds, her in her black tunic and boyishly short hair and the old feller, striding ahead of them up the stairs.

The Fool looked back to the gate, but Ken was gone. They both knew there were other ways into the castle. Whoever dropped the portcullis had only bought them a few minutes. He doubted that was deliberate.

She hauled him up the steps, and with each one he felt his strength returning. They needed only reach the main hall and all would be well.

Wolf pushed the atrium door open as they caught up with him at the top of the stair.

"Quickly, now! Almost…" The Master stopped. As the Fool followed him through the door, he saw why.

The entrance hall was full of guards. Armed and drawn and filling the other end of the hall.

The door to the main hall was beyond them.

"…There?" said Wolf.

"Knackers," said the Fool.

Someone the Fool thought he recognised leaned his head out of the main hall.

"These brigands must not be allowed to enter the hall! Kill them all!"

The strangely familiar face retreated through the door and it slammed shut behind him.

The guards stepped forward with swords drawn.

They had about forty-nine more steps before they were on them.

"Why doesn't anybody like us?" said Katherine.

There was a staircase around half way down the entrance hall. The Fool pointed it out to Katherine. "Upstairs, Highness! There may be a way into the hall."

They hurried to the bottom of the stairs as a couple of overzealous guards came forward. Wolf put them down without a fuss and the others were suddenly wary. This apparently frail old man moved with the speed of one half his age.

Appearances could be deceiving.

Katherine tried to heave the Fool up the steps, but he resisted.

"We'll hold them off," he said.

Wolf looked at him. "We? You can barely stand!"

The Guards stalked closer.

"I'm a lot better." He turned back to Katherine. "Maybe you do have something of the healer in you."

He noticed then that she was brandishing Mister Punch, her eyes fixed on the craven group gingerly approaching them.

She was ready to take them all on.

She would fight to the death and beyond.

She'd always been stubborn.

"Besides," he said, easing Mister Punch from her grasp. "War is the province of Fools and puppets..."

He smiled at her and her face softened for a moment.

"I won't lose you again." she said.

"Nor I you."

"No, I mean I can't be arsed comin' to rescue you again."

In the next few minutes he was going to lose this woman for ever. Either he'd be killed, or she would, or they both would. If the impossible happened and they both survived, he was going to have to watch her marry another man, something which he had a hand in convincing her was the right course of action.

Maybe he was a fool after all.

"Get gone!" he shouted and, with one last look, she got.

She cast off her black cloak and ran up the stairs.

The Fool and Wolf backed up to each other as the guards slowly began to encircle them.

"When did she get so annoying?" he asked Wolf.

The old man looked over his shoulder at him. "She's had some bad influences in her life."

"Haven't we all?"

Why was this so hard? He couldn't let her see.

The Guards had them in a semi-circle around the foot of the stairs.

"You up to this, old man?" he said.

"Are you?"

"Is she gone?"

"Yes."

Good.

The Fool collapsed face-first on the wooden floor just as the guards attacked.

He was aware of a flurry of movement around him, light feet and heavy armour hitting the ground. He wasn't being stabbed, so he presumed Wolf was protecting him.

All the energy he'd felt returning had left him when he realised that whatever happened, he was lost. Whatever the outcome of this battle, his heart would be broken.

It was bitter ale to swill.

"I thought you were better!" he heard Wolf shout between clattering steel and screams.

"I am," he told the floor.

There was another voice, a voice that woke something up in him. "Kill them!" cried the voice.

He sat up.

If you can't be fuelled by love, there's only one other thing as potent.

Hate.

Never let rage be your fuel.

Unless it's all you've got left.

Ken and his brigands had entered the hall and were running to where Wolf was single-handedly laying a squad of guards low.

Ken.

He could still get one thing he wanted this day.

"Ken!" he shouted, leaping to his feet and ploughing Punch into a couple of guards.

"Welcome back," said Wolf.

The brigands were on them, but the Fool was ready. Rage coursed through his veins.

Fury.

That man took everything from him, and now it was time to return the favour.

He brought the puppet down in a brigand's face, savouring the tuning-fork vibrations as Punch hit skull. There were four brigands between him and Ken, the guards and the brigands were now fighting each other, so Wolf had it a little easier. It was only a matter of time.

Ken saw something. The Fool watched him hurry away from the skirmish, heading up the stairs.

Coward.

He picked up Katherine's cloak.

"Ken!" the Fool shouted again.

The bandaged head turned towards him.

"I'm gonna kill you!"

This time, Ken gave him two fingers, and ran up the stairs.

Bastard.

He had to beat him to Katherine. He couldn't let him take her again.

He looked around, ducking another couple of clumsy blows from brigand blades.

High above him was an enormous chandelier. Looked wrought iron. Suspended by a rope. He knocked down a brigand, took up his sword and ran to the wall cleats where the ropes were tied.

Holding on for dear life, he cut the rope.

And then he was in the rafters.

The Monster

This isn't how it was supposed to be.

It was going so well. So well. Everything had turned out wonderfully. She was dead, he was his prisoner. He was having fun.

Now it had all gone wrong.

It was her fault.

Back from the dead.

Who ever heard of that? Nobody. You can't come back from the dead.

Bitch.

He couldn't even kill a girl properly. He was pathetic.

No. She was cheating. It was that other bitch, the necromancer. She was next. He'd find her. He'd teach her.

After he got the Queen.

He ran up the stairs.

The staircase opened onto a long corridor which ran parallel to the main hall and, just as he rounded the corner, he caught sight of her ducking into the lens room. With the rest of the junk.

"Ready to die again, wench?" he cried.

Did she think she could hide from him? This palace used to be his home, he would run rings round this idiot girl.

He ran down the corridor.

Pushing the door open, he stepped into the darkened room.

Peering into the gloom, he could make out the shapes of cases and piles of books and the various trinkets that couldn't find a place anywhere else in the castle.

Fitting that she should die amongst so much useless bricabrac.

He was going to kill her, wasn't he? He wasn't going to be defeated by a little girl?

Of course not.

He couldn't see her in the darkness.

"I know you're in here, Princess." That's right, scare her. "Come out so I can kill you properly!"

Not too loud. The west wall of the room was a stained window looking down on the main hall. He didn't need the congregation to know they were up here.

"You will not kill me, Ken."

Where in the four corners did that come from? She spoke as if from everywhere. Like she was in his head.

She wasn't in his head, was she? He had really seen her, hadn't he? Hadn't he? She *was* back from the dead?

He shook his head clear. "Why not, pray tell?"

There was a moment of silence.

"Because I came back for you."

She came back for him? What did that mean?

"Your name carries some heft on the other side," she said. "They're all waiting for you."

They were waiting for him? Who? Where were they waiting?

Don't be such an idiot. You know who and you know where. The place you sent her is the same place you sent so many others. And none of them went willingly.

It couldn't be true. Could it?

"Shut up! You can't scare me!" he was surprised at how shrill his voice sounded in the silence.

"You made your choice, Ken. To devote your life to the misery of others…"

"Show yourself!" He wanted that voice out of his head for good.

"You wanted all to share in the hopelessness you abandoned yourself to," she went on. "You spread pain and fear like a fever throughout this land, but now…"

What was that? Something on the glass wall.

A light. A tiny spot of light.

He turned to see the lens, a circular window high in the wall, as the first rays of sunrise shone through it.

"Now comes the time of healing."

The lens spread the light to illuminate the window behind him. It was blinding.

The sky turns white and I am gone.

He staggered back. He couldn't see.

He couldn't see.

She was upon him and there was a dagger in his heart.

It wasn't just a dagger. It was a king's dagger. He hadn't needed it, but she had.

It didn't hurt. He just needed to catch his breath.

He dropped his sword.

His eyes became accustomed to the light.

He wasn't blind.

She held him, gently, but tightly.

He thought it was the tenderest touch he had ever felt.

She whispered to him. "I miss my Dad, Ken. Can you tell him for me?"

He felt something warm rising in his throat as she stepped away from him.

There was the Fool.

And his puppet.

The puppet arced towards him, and he was falling. Shards of rainbow glass fell with him as he turned over and over and over.

The King

His days had been strange lately.

This day was no different.

Making arrangements for his wedding to a woman he didn't even know was only the start of it.

He oversaw the decoration of the great hall, flowers were scattered, banners raised and a feast laid out on a long table. The High Priest was summoned and briefed, and seemed optimistic about the possibilities of the joining of the two Royal families.

The hall was full of last-minute guests - every Lord within an hour's pigeon flight had been invited - and the band was tuning up in the corner while Warwick sat on the steps in front of the throne and realised he'd done all he could.

Katherine was out there in the wild, fighting for the life of their friend, with possibly the fate of entire nations at risk, and he had been sent home to organise a party.

It was an important party, though, wasn't it?

You're pathetic.

Shut up.

She's not even going to show up. She just said that to make you go away. She's going to rescue the Jester and ride away with him into the wild forever, leaving you to sit in humiliation amongst the decorations and cakes, avoiding the eyes of all the lords and ladies.

I said shut up.

Try explaining that one to your people. Your King can't even control a woman.

No. She was not to be controlled.

People were not to be controlled as his Father had always believed. His royal blood made him no better than a farmer or a beggar, but it gave him a duty. Responsibility was his birthright. The people looked to him for guidance, and today he would lead by example. He would show them that they could love their neighbour.

She'd be here. She would come.

Together, they would bring freedom to all.

Your ways die today, father.

There is only my voice now.

And hers.

When he heard the commotion outside, he drew his sword, fearing the worst, but Felix entered the hall and blocked his way.

"What goes on, Fil? News of the Princess?"

"Brigands, brother," Felix seemed breathless. "They would sabotage our joyous day. My men will take care of them."

There was a gasp and muttering from the congregation.

Warwick was tired of waiting. He would show them he was willing to fight for the future.

He strode forward, but Felix grabbed his shoulder.

"I would not have our King risk his royal neck on his wedding day."

He looked at his little brother. Poor little Felix, always so afraid. He was about to shrug him off, but he saw the plea in his eyes and knew that Felix wanted the wedding as much as he did.

He sighed. He sheathed his sword. "As you wish, brother."

He listened as the sounds of a battle rattled through the great wooden door under Gunnar's Window.

"How many were there?" he asked Felix.

"Oh, not many. Just a couple of miscreants. The guards will make short work of them, I'm sure."

Felix was nervous. It was understandable, of course. The possibility of their hope being snatched away from them at such a late hour was a galling one indeed. And Felix loved his brother so that the thought of any threat to him would be almost unbearable.

Ah, Felix. He was still the scared little boy clinging on to Warwick's leg when their father flew into one of his rages.

The heartbroken kitling weeping for his murdered cat. The new world would be kinder to him, of that he was certain.

He squeezed his brother's shoulder and someone fell through the window.

Gunnar's window.

Centuries old, years in the making.

Shattered.

Shards of coloured glass rained down on the marble floor and the gathered courtiers, and the falling someone hit the ground with a wet crack.

Warwick's sword was drawn again.

Screams and more gasps from the crowd.

The fallen person seemed to have left a trail of cloth stretching from his head, all the way back up to the hole in the window, where it was snagged on a jagged blade of glass.

It was an unravelled bandage.

The man - if that's what it was - lay on his back, dead eyes staring at the ceiling, bulging out of his red, blistered face.

In his hand he held a crown.

The crown of Elderhaime.

So this was Mister Fury.

Warwick knelt by the body and picked up the crown. He looked back up to the hole in the window and there she was.

She looked tired, and her hair was cut short like a pageboy's, but at that moment he thought her the most beautiful thing he'd ever seen.

"Lady Katherine!" he said.

The room was deathly silent.

"We're here for the wedding," she called down with a shrug.

The Fool was up there with her. He didn't look well, and Warwick was surprised to find that made him happy for a tiny moment.

The Fool took hold of the end of the length of bandage still snagged on the window, and Katherine swung on it, out over Warwick's head.

The band played the Bridal March as she slid down to the ground.

He caught her arm as she landed, steadying her.

"What happened?" He pointed at Mister Fury. "Who was he?"

"I think Lord Felix should answer that question."

It was not Katherine who answered, but a voice from across the hall.

All heads turned to see Althea standing in the doorway. She was holding a weighty leather book.

Warwick looked at Felix, and saw a look on his face he couldn't place. Was he angry?

"Fil?" he said.

Althea stepped forward into the hall.

To Warwick's amazement, his brother tried to run. He started sidling away as if no one could see him.

Warwick grabbed his arm. "What's going on Fil?"

Did he know? Had he always known? Maybe he just didn't want to believe.

Althea spoke to the room. "The medium rare on the floor over there is none other than Kenneth Bronwenson, former leader of the Tyrant King's secret Police."

The crowd gasped.

"He has been marauding the Holtlands since King Warwick banished him…"

Kenneth? Warwick remembered him. His father called him his Mad Dog. He had been a stable boy, but the Tyrant King had placed him in charge of the secret police after witnessing him stab an impolite Knight in the back. Warwick would've had him executed for his war crimes if not for…

He looked in his brother's eyes.

Felix had advised Warwick to have mercy. To banish Bronwenson.

Althea continued: "'Mister Fury' performed the bidding of The Tyrant King many long years, but the order to kill King

Duncan of Elderhaime and his daughter," she pointed to Katherine, "came from Felix Tyrantson!"

The crowd was doing a lot of gasping.

Warwick thought his heart had broken before. When his father killed his mother, when his father kicked his brother down the stairs, everything his Father ever did, really, but it all paled next to this.

It couldn't be true.

"You can prove this?" he glared into Felix's eyes.

Althea held up the book she carried. It bore the legend 'FELIX'S DIARY' embossed in large letters on its cover.

He sneered at his brother, "You kept a diary?"

Althea hefted the book to him. "It's all in there, your Highness, in your brother's own fair hand. He gave your father the Affliction, and he even had plans for you."

Could it be? Had Felix been working his way towards the throne? Was he nothing more than an obstacle for his brother to overcome?

"Is this true, Fil?"

A nearby guard - Warwick thought his name might be Garrett - answered first. "Yeah... It's all true."

Another guard piped up. "Yeah, he's been doin' stuff like that for a while now."

A mutter of confirmation rippled through the guards, and Warwick had never felt so stupid in his life. He thought Felix was just shy and lonely, but he was leading some sort of double life. And it seemed that he was the only one who couldn't see.

"You all knew?"

The Guards shuffled their feet, nodding and muttering agreement.

"Why didn't anybody tell me?"

They all looked at each other or at the floor, some shrugged.

"Dunno," said Garrett.

His blood was boiling.

He turned back to Felix, every fibre of his being raging at this betrayal.

"You…" After everything he had done, all the times he had distracted Father from beating the little weakling by infuriating him himself, all the times he had nursed his brother because the Chamber maids were all pregnant, all the times he had thought his brother loved him.

"You."

Felix shrank away from him. "Don't look at me like that, Brother."

"You." There was no word.

Felix's face began to crumple in an all too familiar way. He had seen his brother cry too many times to be moved again.

"If you paid attention to what was happening around you," Felix sobbed, "instead of dreaming of some impossible future-"

"Don't you dare try to blame me. Don't you dare…"

Felix let out a single, heaving sob. "You were always his favourite…"

Warwick hit his brother in the face with his own diary. "Oh, piss off, you worthless oik!"

Felix must've known he was defeated then, his plans and ambitions destroyed, for he screamed.

He screamed like a madman and launched himself at Warwick.

He didn't see the blade, only the light glinting from it.

He was only off guard for a second.

But that was long enough.

The Queen

She was sick of it.

Everyone.

People either telling her what to do, or trying to kill people she cared about.

Enough was enough.

She saw the Prince's move before Warwick did.

She saw the knife.

And she took it off him.

As he lunged for his brother, she ducked between them and caught the younger man's wrist.

She twisted his arm and bent his elbow the wrong way.

She heard a crack.

The boy screamed and dropped the knife.

He fell to the floor again, clutching his arm.

He scrabbled backwards, away from her. He was afraid.

Before that day, nobody had looked at her like that.

Warwick picked up the knife.

Felix's eyes fixed on the blade.

"Murderer," said Warwick.

He stepped forward and raised the knife.

Felix cowered back.

Warwick faltered.

And she put her hand on the fist clenched around the knifehilt.

Their eyes met.

They understood.

Enough was enough.

She nodded.

And together they lowered the weapon.

She was fairly certain it was bad luck to kill a close family member at your wedding.

Warwick dropped the knife.

He looked down on his bloodied and broken brother. "Get him out of my sight."

Two of the guards picked Felix up. He began to weep in earnest as they dragged him away, and Katherine's heart tore a little. What hope did such an angry, lost boy have in such a world. Born above everyone but his own family, they were all that stood between him and absolute power. What choices had led him here? Choices of his and others.

Then Felix starting screaming.

"You think this is over?" he cried through his tears. "I'll get you for this, brother! You and your bitch queen! I am the one true King! I am—"

One of the guards knocked Felix's broken arm against the stone doorway and he wasn't screaming words anymore.

The door slammed on the Prince's wailing, but she suspected Felix's cries were silenced for everyone but Warwick.

Katherine took the King's hand.

"You can't blame yourself," she said. "Nobody forced him to do what he did."

She knew the loneliness of the royal orphan. She wondered if circumstances were different, would she be the one being dragged away in bloody tears?

She felt something.

Tears, behind her eyes again.

And was there any reason to hold them back?

Had there ever been?

So she cried.

She cried to be so lucky, in birth and in friendship. She cried to be alive.

But most of all, she cried because it had been so long since anyone had let her.

Including herself.

She cried for the girl who couldn't touch her mother, and the father who couldn't talk to his daughter. She cried for the girl forced to marry against her will, she cried for the father dead in the dirt and the legend's bitter end. She cried for the suitor marrying for love of his people. She cried for the lonely Witch living a life haunted by the spirit of love. She cried for the old Master devoting his life to an unreachable dream. She cried for the King betrayed by his brother, and for the brother who was his father's son.

She cried for all the people dead because two royal families couldn't solve their petty differences.

And she cried for him.

She cried for a Fool, loyal to the end.

She folded against Warwick, her body wracked with sobs.

He put a tentative arm around her.

"Why do you cry, Highness?" said Warwick. His grey eyes. A sad smile. "Is today not a joyous day?"

She laughed through the tears. "The day is yet young."

"Do not cry for Felix," he said. "He is not worth your tears."

"It's not for him." And she realised. "It's for me."

It was for her. She had to cry for herself now, because it wasn't going to happen again. She had to say goodbye. Goodbye to the little girl chasing through the gardens, goodbye to the sad child watching her Mother disappear in the night, goodbye to the angry young woman perched on a cliff, and the lost Princess who died in the woods.

Their time was gone now, but maybe she would see them around some time.

She dried her eyes.

"I've learned something in the past few days." She straightened up as she turned to address the congregation. Trying to recall posture and public speaking from etiquette classes.

Hold your head up.

Speak from your gut.

"There comes a time when we all must face our choice…"

She couldn't see a familiar face, in the gathered Lords and Ladies, but she made a point of looking at as many of them in turn as she could. She was talking to them, after all.

And she didn't want to look up and see the Fool.

"There is always a choice, but it's not always an easy one. I hope that this union will show you that we have made our choice."

She needed them to believe her.

She could feel every eye in the room on her as she took Warwick's hand and led him to the dais where the thrones and the High Priest stood. She looked to Warwick and he gave her an almost imperceptible nod, as if to say "go on".

When they reached the thrones, Katherine turned again to address the room.

Big finish.

What would the Fool do? He'd end on a bawdy song or a saucy joke.

She wasn't a fool.

"We have chosen to believe in peace. To believe that together we can heal the rift between our lands. We walk a hard road, but together I think we can make it. What love did hew, let *hope* renew!"

The room was silent. Wide-eyed faces. Open mouths.

She could feel Warwick staring at her. He seemed to be having the same experience as everyone else in the room.

Why were they so quiet?

Maybe she should have done a joke.

Suddenly a boisterous cheer split the silent room. She looked up to see the Fool bellowing from the hole in the shattered window. The Wolf stood beside him, applauding, and soon the entire room was following suit.

She breathed deep.

That was a start.

She looked back over the cheering audience to see the Fool wiping away a mock tear and flicking it at her.

The Fool. He was anything but.

In the midst of the uproar, she turned back to Warwick. She leaned close and whispered. "Do you really think this is gonna work?"

He shrugged. "We'll find out." He took her hand. "Together?"

Katherine nodded. "Together."

He held out a crown.

It was her Dad's.

Fury had had it on his head when he came through the window.

The crown of Elderhaime.

She maintained her newly discovered Queenly poise, but inside, she quailed at the weight of years that crown bore. How many of her forefathers had it belonged to?

And now it was hers.

Warwick buffed a bit of blood off it with his sleeve.

He slowly raised the crown, and placed it on her head.

They applauded more.

It didn't fit. It slid down in front of her face.

She held it up out of her eyes and smiled at her King.

She took his hand and they turned to the High Priest.

The Fool

His head hurt.

The ale and song weren't helping.

Most of the guests were giving him a wide berth, and he couldn't blame them. Dressed in his tattered garb with his face all puffed up, he was hardly an appealing dinner guest.

This was usually his favourite part of a wedding. The ball. He should be out there cartwheeling amongst the nobles, flirting with the wives and patronising the husbands.

He wasn't really up to it tonight.

It wasn't just that he felt like he'd been kicked down the stairs from the tallest tower, either. He was nursing a hollow feeling somewhere inside.

It was as if he had discovered a secret room of riches, only to have to seal it again un-plundered.

This was how it had to be.

She could do so much at Warwick's side.

He sat alone at a table at the edge of the hall, watching the people dance. There was a carefree joy in the air of the room, and he hoped it would last.

Hope. Sometimes that's all we have. Would it all be worth it? Could this be the start of something better?

Hope.

The Children of the High Moors had made an appearance shortly after the ceremony, and now the hall was dotted with nippy little black-cloaked figures running under people's legs, stealing food, playing chase and dancing.

They deserved a better world, and maybe they would even help shape it. But for now, let them play.

He watched Wolf approach Althea and hold out an open palm. She sighed and placed some coins in his hand. He nodded in thanks, bowed to her, and dragged her onto the dance floor.

Hope.

Maybe Althea's had been restored. And maybe Wolf's had been proven right. The Master had spent his life trying to build a better tomorrow, to make people see the greater good they were capable of, and here they were at the dawn of a new age.

Their work was just beginning, but he couldn't help thinking his was done. The Princess - no, The Queen - would be safe with Warwick, wouldn't she?

Wandering the Holtlands had reminded him of the world outside castle walls. Who knew how many more brigand groups there were in the woods? How many more marauding boga? And how many innocents in need of a helping hand?

He watched her and Warwick dance, watched them both working the crowd. She was a natural, and they complemented each other perfectly. He would only get in the way.

All it would take was a few wagging tongues to tarnish the new Queen's reputation. She needed to be pure, not sullied by some mysterious Jester hanging around. Who in the four corners was he anyway? Where did he come from? Did anybody know his name?

No, there would be too many questions.

Better for the Fool to disappear. Let her memory of him go untarnished by the truth.

He told himself it was for her own good.

His time as a Fool was over. He had been many things over the years: orphan, vagabond, squire, soldier, assassin, murderer, traitor, liar…

What would he be next?

He told himself she didn't need him. But maybe somebody else out there did.

He would be whatever they needed him to be.

Punch spoke up from the under the table. "Time to go, boss?"

He snorted a laugh. Nothing got past that puppet.

He necked his ale and slammed his tankard down.

He grabbed Mister Punch and was gone.

The Queen

He wasn't going to get away that easily.

"Fool!" she called.

He stopped limping at the top of the steps and turned back to her. She hurried to him.

Many of the guests were enjoying the night air in the courtyard and they gave a small cheer for her. She gave them a wave and a smile.

Must maintain decorum.

They stood together at the top of the stairs, looking out over the Fairfold, she fancied she could just make out the rise of the lip and the Magen crag on the horizon in the gathering gloom. Somewhere up there, on the Reece, lay Elderhaime castle.

She wondered if she could ever really go home.

Did she even have one anymore?

She looked at the Fool.

Recently, every time they parted felt like it must be the last.

This was no different.

He was looking at her. She held his gaze in hers and smiled.

"I have something for you." She told him. "I found it when I… woke up."

She handed him his hat. It was even more battered than usual, but his bruised face still lit up at the sight of it.

She knew he'd missed it.

"Thank you."

He looked at her then and she was lost again for a moment. She would spend the rest of her life craving that look, she knew.

She felt that overwhelming urge to just run course through her again - run away with him to wherever they ended up. She shook it off.

It wasn't going to be easy.

"So, where do you think you're sneaking off to?" she said.

"Bed."

"Sure you're not going to disappear?"

He laughed as though she had rumbled him. "I won't go far, Princess."

"Queen."

He smiled down at her, taking her hand. "My Queen. A long time ago I made a promise to your Father that I would protect you for as long as you needed me."

"You might as well clear off, then." All was well as long as they could still make japes. Bunglery distracted from the pain of reality.

His smile widened and he gently pushed a short lock of hair away from her face.

There was that urge again.

Run away and live happily ever after.

Or stay and try to make everyone else happy.

She looked away, attempting to break the spell. Not ten yards from them, Garrick and the girl called Tia were sitting on the steps, kissing vigorously. At least somebody was doing it right.

She had to laugh. "Do you think we'll ever truly be at peace?" she asked the Fool.

"We can only hope."

She looked back at him, remembering a question that used to seem so important.

"Who are you? Really?"

He pulled on his battered, three-pronged hat.

He kissed her hand.

He bowed low.

He straightened up.

"Just a Fool," he said.

He turned gracefully away from her and fell face-first down the staircase.

He rolled and tumbled all the way down the steps, before landing on his feet in a acrobatic flip at the bottom.

He bowed to the crowd in the courtyard as they applauded and cheered, then he turned back to her.

She clapped politely. At least some things would never change.

He smiled a sad little smile at her.

She watched him turn and limp away.

The End.

The Acknowledgements

Thanks to Jess for nudging me when I nodded off and for supporting me emotionally, motivationally and financially while I intermittently pretended to be a writer. Without you I would be nothing. You know what I don't say.

Thanks to me Mam and Dad for putting up with me always being a disappointment without ever calling me one. I can't ever express the infinite thanks I owe you. So I'll just send you a cheque if this makes any money. Also thanks for reading us Lord of the Rings when we were kids, Dad. That was probably where this all started.

Thanks to my brother and sister for talking to me about films and books and comics and music and telly for years on end. Everything I know about me, I learned from you two.

Thanks to Bails for tech support and for reading several different versions of this story over the years and always suggesting I put in a gay dragon or Richard Pryor or something.

Thanks to Dr Chapman for reading a couple of versions about ten years apart and being a killer editor/proof-reader (if there are still mistakes, I'm blaming you).

Thanks to Ed for knocking up a super sweet cover, and for telling me you weren't going to read the book.

Thanks to Sushan for excellent feedback. And thanks to Khyan and Chelsea for assistance and encouragement. I promise I'll get round to reading your books soon.

Thanks to Roz, Gav and Jules and anyone else I sent it to. Whether you read it or not, you all helped.

Thanks to you, whoever you are, because a book isn't a book until it's read. Thanks for making it to the end.

And finally thanks to me. I wrote a book. That's good going, even if nobody did want to publish it. Go me.

The Princess and The Fool will return.

Take care.

Neafcy. 19/02/2015